Prai

"Jones's story is an eye-open[...]
paced thrillers."

—*Booklist* on *The Trade Off*

"Jones unapologetically stares down the ugliness of the modern media and its coldblooded exploitation of celebrities to benefit those truly in power, as well as the rampages of fake news."

—*Kirkus Reviews* on *The Trade Off*

"Jones devises a thrill ride filled with an abundance of twists."

—*The Free Lance-Star* on *The Trade Off*

"The perfect summer (or anytime) read."

—*Bookreporter* on *The Trade Off*

"Explosive . . . Filled with twists and turns, the story will keep you guessing until the end."

—*National Examiner* on *The Guilt Trip*

"Riveting . . . The twisty plot builds to a shocking conclusion. This puzzler reinforces Jones's status as a rising suspense star."

—*Publishers Weekly* on *The First Mistake*

"One of the most twisted and entertaining plots."

—Reese Witherspoon on *The Other Woman*

"Whiplash-inducing final pages."

—*The New York Times Book Review* on *The Other Woman*

ALSO BY SANDIE JONES

The Other Woman
The First Mistake
The Half Sister
The Guilt Trip
The Blame Game

THE TRADE OFF

SANDIE JONES

MINOTAUR BOOKS
NEW YORK

For every woman within these pages

Published in the United States by Minotaur Books, an imprint of
St. Martin's Publishing Group

THE TRADE OFF. Copyright © 2023 by Sandie Jones Ltd. All rights reserved. Printed in the United States of America. For information, address St. Martin's Publishing Group, 120 Broadway, New York, NY 10271.

www.minotaurbooks.com

The Library of Congress has cataloged the hardcover edition as follows:

Names: Jones, Sandie, author.
Title: The trade off / Sandie Jones.
Description: First U.S. Edition. | New York : Minotaur Books, 2023.
Identifiers: LCCN 2023015939 | ISBN 9781250836939 (hardcover) |
     ISBN 9781250836946 (ebook)
Subjects: LCSH: Women journalists—Fiction. | LCGFT: Thrillers (Fiction) |
     Novels.
Classification: LCC PR6110.O6387 T73 2023 | DDC 823/.92—dc23/eng/
     20230403
LC record available at https://lccn.loc.gov/2023015939

ISBN 978-1-250-83695-3 (trade paperback)

Our books may be purchased in bulk for promotional, educational, or business use. Please contact your local bookseller or the Macmillan Corporate and Premium Sales Department at 1-800-221-7945, extension 5442, or by email at MacmillanSpecialMarkets@macmillan.com.

Originally published in Great Britain by Pan Books, an imprint of Pan Macmillan

First Minotaur Books Trade Paperback Edition: 2024

1   3   5   7   9   10   8   6   4   2

PROLOGUE

"You've got a nerve showing up here," he hisses, coming to an abrupt halt beside me as he leads the mourners back up the aisle. Every sinew in his body looks to be on full alert, twitching against the fabric of his black suit. Even the stiff white collar of his starched shirt is flexing with the rhythm of the involuntary throbbing of his neck muscles.

My pulse quickens as I look at him. Tiny pinpricks of sweat instantly jump to the surface of my already tingling skin. I'd naively believed I could attend and leave unnoticed; pay my respects and go. Or, at the very least, get out of the church before he realized there was a traitor in their midst.

But I should have known I wouldn't get away with it. I don't deserve to.

My eyes smart as I look at the laughing photo atop the coffin, my ears unable to drown out the poignant words of Bette Midler as she sings about the wind beneath her wings.

"I . . . I'm so sorry," I stutter, as he stands there, unmoving, his eyes seemingly burrowing into my soul, as if wishing it were me in that wooden box.

"Get out," he barks. "If I ever see you again, I swear I'll . . ."

He launches himself toward me and I flinch, instinctively holding my plastered arm across my broken ribs protectively.

But just before he reaches me, someone pulls him back. "Leave it," says the woman. "You'll get your chance. But now is not the time or place."

He sucks in the raging spittle from his lips, but his eyes stay focused. It's only when I follow his manic glare that I realize he's talking to the person standing right behind me.

1

Jess

"So, what would you bring to *The Globe*?" The revered editor of the country's top-selling newspaper is perched on the edge of his desk, making himself at least two feet taller than me as I sit before him.

"Er, I've got lots of ideas," I say, desperate for saliva to moisten my mouth. "I'm a team player, my research skills are exemplary and I'm eager to learn."

He exaggerates a yawn. "Bor-ing."

I shift in my chair, fearing I've blown the only chance I'll ever get to learn from the best.

He looks at me with even less interest than ten seconds ago. "That's what every kid who comes through that door says, and it's why they all leave the same way—without a job."

My throat clenches and my head throbs as I search desperately for something more exciting to offer.

"You're going to have to sell yourself," my boss at the local newspaper that I work on had advised. "Max Forsythe is a man of great means, but he has exceptionally high standards. That's why I've recommended you for the position, as much as it will pain me to lose you."

"Well, I must be exactly what you want, otherwise I wouldn't have got this far," I say to Mr. Forsythe, squirming in my seat.

He looks at me with an amused expression, his interest piqued.

"And what is it I want?" he asks.

"Me," I say resolutely, while trying to quash the color that I can feel flooding my cheeks. "You must have approached the *Essex Gazette* for a reason. A million junior reporters would kill for this opportunity if you'd advertised it, but you didn't. Why not?"

My ears grow hot as I pretend to be the person I think he wants: assertive, driven, hungry, not afraid to step out of my comfort zone.

"I need someone I can trust," he says, getting up and walking round to his side of the desk. "And your editor seems to think I can trust *you*." He narrows his eyes as he sits down and looks at me.

I nod and swallow, conscious not to break eye contact, because I imagine he's someone who can tell a lot from the way you look at him.

"It's a whole different ball game to working on a local rag," he says. "There's no such thing as office hours; you work until the paper's put to bed, until I'm happy with every single word and picture in it."

I nod fervently before pulling back, not wishing to come across like an overexcited puppy.

"And then you'll go straight out and get me stories for the next edition."

"OK," I say, unable to stop myself smiling at the thought of me and my notepad venturing out onto the streets of London in search of the next big exclusive. "I can do that."

"Do you have a boyfriend?" he asks, changing tack abruptly.

"Erm, well . . ." I stutter, taken aback, unable to see why that's relevant.

Mr. Forsythe's eyes are wide with anticipation, making me feel as if my answer's the difference between me getting this job and not. But something in the way he's looking at me makes me think it's not just the job at stake here.

"Well, yes, actually I do," I lie.

For some reason it makes me feel safer; gives me a false sense of security.

He can't hide his disappointment in my answer. "Shame, it would be a whole lot easier if you were single."

My hackles stand on end in sudden indignation. Is he suggesting what I think he is?

"Do you live together?" he asks, seemingly oblivious to my discomfort.

"Well, yes . . . we . . ."

"Are you faithful to him?" He asks the question without even looking at me.

I instinctively pull the coat on my lap tighter to me and reach for my handbag, from where it sits on the floor. I want to turn around to check that the almost deserted open-plan newsroom I'd walked through, to get to this office, still has a few people milling about. But I don't want to show my nerves and make him think he's got the upper hand. Though I almost laugh at my own naive thoughts. Of course he's got the upper hand; he always has—he's one of the most powerful men in media.

"I don't think that's a question I need to—"

"It gives me an insight into who you really are," he says, cutting me off.

I straighten myself up, hoping it will strengthen my resolve.

"My personal relationships have no bearing on my suitability for employment," I say, desperately trying to keep my voice steady.

"Well, they do if it stops the man employing you from getting what he wants," he replies, looking at me suggestively; daring me to ask him to quantify what his statement actually means. Though I know he'll only deny what we both realize he's implying, if I challenge him.

The phone on his desk buzzes and I'm grateful that the tension is broken, but as soon as the tightness in my shoulders begins to dissipate, his assistant sends me into free fall again.

"I'm about to leave," she says through the intercom. "Is there anything you need before I go?"

He raises his eyebrows at me in question, and I want to scream at her, "Yes, take me with you," but my lips feel as if they've been glued shut.

"Is anyone else still here?" asks Max, looking out through the glass walls of his office.

I follow his gaze to the fifty or so desks that stretch out across the floor, desperately wanting to see activity, but even the harsh strip lighting that had shone so brightly when I arrived has been reduced to a low-level night light.

"Only Bill on the back bench," says the voice through the intercom. "But I think he's packing up as we speak."

"Thanks, Gail," says Max, smiling and widening his eyes. "I'll see you in the morning."

I go to stand up. "Thank you for your time," I say. "I really should be going as well."

He looks at his watch. "Why? Do you turn into a pumpkin at nine thirty?"

I force a smile, but alarm bells are going off inside my head. When Gail told me it was a 9 p.m. interview or nothing at all, I'd not even questioned it. Max Forsythe had a daily newspaper to run, a nightly deadline to meet; I was just ridiculously grateful for the opportunity. But now that tomorrow's edition has been put to bed and I'm sitting here, alone with the man whose reputation precedes him, I wonder whether he has me down as being *too* eager to please.

"Sit down, relax," he says, walking over to the drinks trolley, which I'd assumed was merely for show. "I only mention it because not many relationships survive this newsroom. You need to be sure that yours is strong enough."

"Women can work hard *and* hold down a relationship," I say.

"Good to hear," he says, lifting a cut-glass decanter in midair. "Now, what can I get you?"

"I'm fine," I say tartly, still standing with my coat over my arm and wondering if I have time to catch the same lift as Max's assistant. "I'm not much of a drinker."

He smirks. "Not even when we've got something to celebrate?"

If that's his way of telling me I've got the job, I'm no longer sure I want it.

I shake my head. "Not even then."

"A word to the wise," he says, taking a sip of his drink. "You'll be nobody's friend if you abstain. People won't feel like you're one of them. They'll have their guard up. And that'll get you nowhere. *But* if you can perfect the art of making them believe you're drunk when you're actually stone-cold sober, it could put you at quite the advantage."

He smiles, more to himself than to me as he warms to his theme. "In fact, if you're able to pull that off, it could set you head and shoulders above the rest. While all my other journalists are matching their marks shot for shot, line for line, *you* could be getting the story."

"I'm not sure that sounds like me," I offer, still unsure what he's suggesting.

"Do you *want* to be a journalist or not?" he asks, moving toward me, invading my personal space.

I force myself to stand firm, not to allow my feelings of intimidation to show.

"Well, yes, but . . ."

"Then you *have* to get used to being in uncomfortable situations, because no story worth having will come your way without you being backed up against the wall, having your loyalty questioned and your ethics challenged. If you're not prepared to be put under that kind of pressure, then you either get out now or you find a way to fake it, because I don't need a rookie-shaped liability around my neck."

"Are you offering me the job?" I ask.

"Only if your moral compass is pointing as far north as it appears to be," he says with a smile, moving back to his desk.

It's then that the penny drops. "Was . . . was that some kind of *test?*" I ask, feeling relieved and foolish at the same time.

"I need to know that your core values are gold-standard," he replies. "That your sense of what is right and wrong is imbued in your very being."

I nod enthusiastically.

"Because it's time that tabloid journalism cleaned up its act."

"I won't be trading my morals for a byline," I say, a coil of excitement swirling in the pit of my stomach.

"Then I think we're going to get along just fine," he says, finishing off his drink in one. "Now, as much as I'd like to sit here and discuss the merits of your morality all night, I have a prior engagement with the prime minister."

2

Stella

"Is everything ready?" asks Stella as she walks into the Belgravia suite at the Dorchester hotel.

"Almost," says Rob, the go-to man for all things technical. "We've got to install one more camera, as I'm worried that there's a blind spot in the lobby."

Stella nods. "Yes, make sure we've got one hundred percent coverage, as it will be just our luck if the action starts as soon as they close the front door."

"And we don't wanna miss a thing," sings Rob, in Steven Tyler style, as he reaches into a vase adorned with lilies on the console table.

"Exactly!" Stella laughs, taking out her phone.

OK, so we've got half an hour to go, she types into the group WhatsApp. I want everyone in position.

Her phone pings with four affirmatives and she feels a familiar tug in her chest as she waits for the fifth and final person to check in.

"Come on, Tom," she says under her breath. "Where are you?"

"Here," comes his typed reply to her silent question, after an agonizing beat.

She types fast.

So, you all know the score. Marianne Kapinsky is aiming to
arrive at the back door at exactly the same time as our target.
She's going to attempt to kiss him before entering the hotel—so,
Tom, be ready to get that shot. There's every chance that he's
not going to play ball; he won't be expecting to see her there,
since they'd agreed to meet in the room. But if she manages to
catch him off-guard, I want it on film.

Her phone pings with five thumbs-up emojis.

"OK, so that's the hallway covered," says Rob, almost to himself,
before unclipping a walkie-talkie from his belt. "Boj, can you confirm
that you've got a clear picture of us on camera six?"

There's a momentary pause as Rob and Stella look at each other.
"Affirmative," comes the reply. "Though if you two could perhaps play
out what we're hoping to see, I'd feel much happier." Stella rolls her
eyes. "Just so I can make sure I've got every angle covered!" He chuckles.

Stella's phone rings and her chest tightens as she sees Marianne's
number on the screen. There's still so much that can go wrong, and
it's never a good sign for her contact to call so close to the sting.

"Hey," says Stella, picking up on the third ring. "We're all good to
go."

She's learned not to ask if everything is OK. It gives them the opportunity to pull out or move the goalposts, and saying everything's
ready puts them under pressure to follow through.

"There's a problem," says Marianne.

Stella draws in a deep breath. They're too far in for there to be a
problem now.

"What is it?" she asks, mentally calling up all the possibilities and
ticking them off one by one. No stone has been left unturned in this
operation. The only deal-breaker is if the target doesn't turn up, but
Marianne has promised that he will.

"*The Post* has been in touch," says Marianne. "They've offered me
ten thousand more."

Stella's heart sinks into her stomach. She's spent weeks on this story, meeting Marianne in clandestine places so as not to attract any unwanted attention, from either the public or other newspapers, which aren't averse to following her to sniff out what stories she's working on, so inept are they at finding their own.

At their last meeting, over a coffee on the concourse of King's Cross station, Marianne had left with a £5,000 down payment, and Stella had walked away with the promise of her loyalty—whatever that was worth.

"How did they find out?" she asks wearily. "You said there was no way anyone else could possibly get wind of this story."

Marianne offers a sly laugh. "Darling, I've been walking through the Houses of Parliament in nothing but a fur coat. Do you honestly believe no one will have wondered what someone like me was doing there?"

Stella pictures the flamboyant call-girl prancing around the corridors of Westminster, daring anyone to question her. With her lanyard and security clearance, reserved only for MPs and their esteemed guests, Marianne would have revelled in them trying to thwart her lover's indecent intentions.

"We're about to go on this," sighs Stella. "I've got a whole team ready and waiting."

"I understand," purrs Marianne. "But as you know, I have expensive tastes and I have to be kept in the style to which I have become accustomed." She lets out a high-pitched laugh and Stella can't help but picture Cruella de Vil at the other end of the line.

"We haven't got time for this," she says brusquely. "You're supposed to be here in fifteen minutes."

"And I will be," says Marianne. "*If* you match *The Post's* offer."

"Who have you been speaking to there?" asks Stella, her mind working at eighty miles an hour, desperate to claw back this story. Not least for the kudos it will bring her, but also to escape the wrath of Max if she doesn't.

"Oh, I forget his name," says Marianne. "He just phoned and, as I'm nervous about all this, I don't remember."

"I'm going to need to make a few calls," says Stella. "Where are you now?"

"I'm parked up around the corner in the car you sent for me."

"And where's Ned Jacobs?" asks Stella.

"He's on schedule, but I can tell him I'm running late?"

"No!" exclaims Stella, knowing that the chance of them meeting outside the hotel is getting slimmer by the second. It's not the be-all and end-all, but if they don't get the footage they're expecting from inside the suite, then she'd feel better if they had it as a fall-back.

She taps her phone, deciding whether to call her informant at *The Post* or Max, back at the office, unsure which is the lesser of the two evils. No, it's too much of a risk. She doesn't want to give any more away to her rival than she needs to, and there's no way of finding out what she wants to know without having to divulge information she doesn't wish to share.

Max picks up on the first ring. "I'm in a meeting," he barks. "Is it urgent?"

"Marianne wants more money," she sighs down the line.

"For fuck's sake," he bellows. "I thought this was in the can."

"It was," says Stella. "Until *The Post* came along."

"That's bollocks—she's calling your bluff."

"Possibly," says Stella. "But is it a chance we want to take?"

"How much are we paying for this?"

"Seventy-five thousand," says Stella.

"The greedy bitch!" hisses Max.

Stella can hear him thinking; feel his temper emanating from deep inside him. There's nothing he loathes more than grasping kiss-and-tells. They may well be a tabloid's bread and butter, but he hates them with a vengeance for their questionable morals.

"So offer her the trade-off," he says simply, knowing that Stella will realize what he means.

"But no more money?" she says, double-checking.

"Not a penny more." The phone goes dead before she's even had a chance to acknowledge his instruction.

She immediately calls Marianne back to deliver the bad news.

"Hi, I've spoken to my editor and I'm afraid he's not prepared to budge."

"Ah, that's a real pity," says Marianne. "I was really hoping we could strike a deal."

"We already have," Stella reminds her. "And not only are you under contract to us, but if you decide to renege on what we've agreed, I'm afraid it won't be easy for you."

Marianne laughs uneasily. "Are you threatening me?"

"No, not at all," says Stella, aware that the conversation might be being recorded. "It's just that this story is perfectly pitched to present you in the best possible light. Even though you're a sex worker who entertains at least ten high-profile punters who *all* believe they're paying for your exclusive services, I was happy for you to remain anonymous as long as you exposed the shadow home secretary to be the deceitful, devious love-cheat that he is. *But* if you're going to accept a higher offer, I can no longer promise that same anonymity."

"You wouldn't," seethes Marianne. "We had an agreement."

"Indeed we did," says Stella. "Except you've just ripped up the pages. So we either do this my way—the way we both talked about and agreed upon—or you can take the extra ten thousand, in the knowledge that the whole country will know who you are and what you do."

She can hear Marianne's breath quickening down the line.

"We have five minutes and the clock's ticking," says Stella. "So, what's it going to be?"

"Fine," hisses Marianne.

"OK, let's do this," says Stella, before ending the call and typing the same message into the WhatsApp group.

3

Jess

The newsroom seems a whole lot different than it did the last time I was here, and a new sense of embarrassment washes over me as I remember how I'd mistaken Max Forsythe's integrity test for something else entirely.

I was still cringing when I'd got home to my flatmate, Flic, that evening, but she'd had the grace to pretend she would have jumped to exactly the same conclusion if she'd been in my position.

"I mean, he could just have pounced on you, there and then," she'd said thoughtfully, as she spooned out the last of the cookie-dough ice cream from the tub. *My* cookie-dough ice cream.

I'd swallowed my consternation—you have to with Flic, otherwise we'd be falling out every day.

"Well, if that *had* been his intention, I'm not sure that telling him I had a boyfriend would have stopped him in his tracks."

"Yeah, but I get why you thought it might," Flic had said, though her vexed expression suggested otherwise. "In the heat of the moment and all that."

I'd shaken my head. "I mean, I don't know what I was thinking.

What happens if, by some small miracle, I get offered the job? I'm going to have to invent a boyfriend I don't even want."

Flic's eyes had widened as she'd lifted herself up on the sofa, tucking her legs beneath her. "It's more the problem that you're going to have to get rid of him again pretty quickly, because of all the hot celebs you're going to meet."

I'd rolled my eyes, tutting. "Meeting celebrities is not my sole reason for wanting this job."

"Yes, but if you're sent to LA to interview Josh Matthews about his new blockbuster film, you better be ready to dump that phantom boyfriend's ass, 'cause there's no way I'm letting you pass up *that* opportunity."

"*What* opportunity?" I'd scoffed. "If I were ever to find myself in that position, I'd be the epitome of professionalism. I'd go, get the job done and take the first flight out of there."

"But what if he asked you out? What if he saw you and said he couldn't live without you, and that you had to let him take you out for dinner, otherwise . . . ?"

I couldn't help but smile, but much as I'd have liked to participate in Flic's fantasy for a little while longer, I only had to catch a reflection of myself in the living room mirror to know that it was pushing even the realms of fiction. I'd seen the kind of women Josh Matthews hooked up with: the type that didn't need to use a filter on their Instagram posts; successful women who have totally got their shit together. At least that's what they'd have us all believe.

"I'd say *no!*" I had offered in mock indignation. "Just because he's a Hollywood superstar doesn't mean he can click his fingers and have whoever he wants."

Flic had looked at me as if I was deluded. "Well, if *you're* not going to go for it, do you mind if I come along and try *my* luck?"

She'd ducked from view as I sent a cushion flying across the room and we'd both laughed at the insanity of it all, though a little frisson had been set alight at the possibilities that lay in wait, if I were to get the job.

"This is going to be the making of you," she'd said optimistically, if not a little prematurely. "I only hope it's going to be everything you imagined it would be."

Seeing the newsroom now, buzzing with energy and excitement, I can sense it's all that, and more.

"OK, so this is the Sports desk," says Max's assistant, Gail, as she walks me quickly across the floor. I smile, getting ready with a wave, but awkwardly put my hand back down when none of the eight-strong team even look up. "This is Politics," continues Gail, moving swiftly on. "Over there in the corner is the World desk, and behind us is the back bench."

There's not a single smile on offer and I can't help but wonder if I'm cut out for this. Maybe I need to be wrapped in the warm, genial atmosphere of the *Essex Gazette*, where Brian wheels the tea trolley out twice a day and "Confused of Southend" sends in the same letter every week.

"And this is where *you'll* be sitting," says Gail, rolling out a chair from underneath a sign reading "News" that hangs from the ceiling. "That's Rich, Zoe, Marcus and Lottie," she goes on, pointing to the top of several heads.

I notice that Rich's hairline is thinning a little.

"You'll be reporting directly to Stella, our deputy editor, who sits at the end there."

I look at the desk of my immediate boss and can't help but feel instantly inadequate. There are at least fifty Post-it notes stuck to the whiteboard on the wall to her left, each color-coded, though for what reason I don't yet know.

"Is Stella around?" asks Gail to no one in particular.

"She's out on a job and due in around midday," pipes up one of the women, I forget who, from behind her half-height divider.

Gail shrugs her shoulders. "Well, I'll leave you to get acquainted," she says, instilling the same fear I felt when my mother left me in the playground on my first day in infant school.

"Thanks," I say, dry-mouthed as I watch her walk away.

"We've just had this tip come in," says the man with the balding head from behind the screen separating our desks. He reaches toward me with a yellow Post-it note in his hand. "Can you check it out? See if it's kosher."

He disappears from view again, leaving me with a phone number and a scrawled message: *Tina Mowbray seen with bruises on her face. Could it be her boyfriend?*

"So-sorry, do you want me to ring this number?" I stutter, half hoping he won't hear me.

"Well, that would be a good start," he replies brusquely.

"Oh right, then," I say, looking around furtively, as if hoping someone is going to magically appear, take the note from my hand and make the call *for* me.

I finger the piece of paper and pick up the phone on the desk, not knowing who or what to expect at the other end. I know exactly who Tina Mowbray is—she's the queen of reality TV, the surgically enhanced model who was coupled with a former cage fighter called Rex Macy on last season's *Fake It Till You Make It*. They'd waltzed off the show with £100,000 and had biweekly shoots in *Welcome!* magazine, proclaiming their love for each other ever since.

I'm shaking as I dial the number and I don't know if I'm relieved or even more nervous when I hear Tina's unmistakable Scouse accent.

"Hello."

"Oh, hello, Tina, is that you?"

"Yeah, who's this?"

"My name's Jess and I'm calling from *The Globe*."

"What do you want?" she asks accusingly.

I'm instantly on the back foot, and the man opposite me sticks his hand up and turns it in a rolling motion—as if encouraging me to press on. He must know how these conversations go.

"Erm, I understand you've been involved in some kind of . . . incident . . ."

"I don't know what you're talking about," she sneers before putting the phone down, leaving me staring at the receiver in my hand with a thumping chest.

"Let me guess," says the girl next to me, with a pencil haphazardly skewering a mass of mousy-brown curls on top of her head. "She denied it."

"Er, yes—yes, she did."

She rolls her eyes heavenwards. "She's most likely with the fella and can't talk. It means that our theory is probably correct then, otherwise she'd just tell the truth."

"Oh, right," I say, trying desperately hard not to take the brutal rejection personally.

"Don't take it to heart," she says as if reading my mind. "I'm Lottie by the way." She offers a smile and I instantly feel as if Mum has come back, even though the girl doesn't look that much older than me.

"Here's today's titles," she says, handing me four women's monthly magazines. "Check out the celebrity interviews and highlight any angles that might be worth exploring."

I thumb through the glossy pages; the quality of what they produce is at odds with the cheap fish-and-chip paper of today's edition of *The Globe* that lies beside them.

Inside *Better Living* there's a four-page spread on Yasmin Chopra, recent winner of the BBC's flagship cookery show *On the Ranch*, in which twelve contestants had battled it out to be the best barbecue connoisseur. Yasmin had delighted the nation with her Guinness-coated chicken wings and chocolate-flavored spareribs, though there was still the odd keyboard warrior who had protested that she didn't deserve to be in the final because she was of Indian descent.

The headline You Just Can't Win! alludes to Yasmin answering her critics. "If I'd hailed from Texas, people would say that I shouldn't have been allowed to enter a barbecue competition as I would have had an unfair advantage," she's quoted as saying, alongside a picture of her tucking into a double-decker burger.

Momentarily distracted by the need to see how easy the recipe is, I continue to scour the article, reading between the lines for anything that the friendly publication fails to follow up on.

"Who are *you*?" comes a woman's voice from right behind me.

I spin round in my chair to be faced with a messy blonde bob, perfectly coiffured to look like she'd woken up like this. Maybe she had.

"Oh, hi, I'm Jess," I say, offering my hand. She's standing so close that it seems rude not to.

"What are you doing here?" she asks, her hands remaining on her hips. I throw a brief look to Lottie, who I'd envisaged being my best friend just moments ago. But her eyes stay firmly focused on the computer screen in front of her.

"I'm the new reporter."

"Since when?" snaps the woman, taking a step back to remove her Burberry scarf and camel coat. Everything about her screams power and class. She even smells expensive.

"Erm, I . . . I was hired by Max," I flounder, falling over my words and hating myself. "Mr. Forsythe."

She looks over to his corner office, as if weighing up whether the meeting he's in can be interrupted.

"He's with Peter," says the man opposite me, which appears to be all the answer she needs.

"So what are you doing?" she asks, turning her attention back to me and brushing a curl from her eyes.

"I'm going through these," I say, hoping that answers the question she's asking. "Looking for any possible leads that we might be able to follow up on."

She reaches out to thumb through the pages of the magazine on my desk.

"Does *she* say anything of interest?" she asks, cocking her head toward Yasmin, smiling out from the pages.

"It's all pretty innocuous stuff," I reply with a trembling voice. "I don't think anyone's going to get any dirt on the barbecue queen."

"Well, it's your job to find it," she says. "Why are her children all facing away from the cameras? Are there any shots showing their faces?"

I hadn't even noticed. "I . . . I don't think so," I say, feverishly flicking back and forward through the pages.

"God, I hate this bullshit," she says. "Why put yourself in the public eye if you're then going to spend the rest of your life hiding your children from the world? You're either all in or all out." She throws her coat and scarf onto her desk. "Who's her agent?" she bellows.

Keyboards are tapped and phones are scanned as the team around me races to be the first to give her the information she's requested.

"It's Mel Sheldrake," offers up the man opposite me, looking delighted with himself.

The woman, who I can only assume is Stella, groans. "OK, call up Mel and say you've just seen Yasmin's fabulous spread in . . ." She looks to me, snapping her fingers, and I rush to hold up the front cover, giving the tip of my nose a paper cut in my haste. Maybe the publication isn't as friendly as I first thought.

"*Better Living,*" Stella goes on, though I'm not sure whether she's speaking to me or someone else. I'm hoping it's the latter. "She's a tough nut to crack, but tell her we're running an article on the virtues of celebrities keeping their children out of the spotlight and we'd love to feature Yasmin's take on it. We'd be happy to give a big plug for the . . ." Stella looks at me again, catching me off-guard.

"Er, book," I say, fervently scanning the copy.

Stella rolls her eyes, clearly seasoned to the constant influx of newly crowned celebrities employing the services of a ghostwriter to exploit their fifteen minutes of fame.

"OK, get on with it," she says, snapping her fingers again in my direction.

I look open-mouthed at Lottie beside me as Stella saunters off in her high heels. "Was she talking to me?" I whisper.

She nods. "You need to stay on your game with Stella," she says, under her breath. "She doesn't suffer fools gladly."

"I don't understand," I reply, not taking my eyes off the woman I now know to be the deputy editor of the paper, and the person I report to. "She didn't sound like she was in agreement with celebrities who shield their children from public view."

"She's not," says Lottie. "But we've been after an interview with Yasmin for weeks, and Stella obviously thinks this might be an angle that gives us an in."

"But that's not the piece we'd run?" I ask dubiously, knowing *The Globe* well enough to realize that wouldn't be considered newsworthy.

Lottie laughs. "Of course not! But it's an opportunity to find another top line."

"But we'd give Yasmin the heads-up that's what we were doing, right?"

Lottie can't help but grimace as she looks at me. "You've not done this before, have you?" she says.

4

Stella

"Stella, you're looking as ravishing as ever," muses Peter as he passes her desk.

"Hello," she says, smiling as she stands up to kiss the owner of Global International on each cheek. His foul breath infiltrates her nostrils, and she has to force herself not to shudder as his chubby fingers linger on her waist. "I haven't seen you around here for a while."

His beady eyes travel up and down her body, unable to stop themselves from coming to rest on her breasts. "That's because up until now I've been reasonably happy with the way the paper's being run," he says.

Stella's smile tightens. She'd walked right into that one.

"I think we're in pretty good shape," she says, despite knowing that sales are down 9 percent compared to this time last year.

"Funny, that's exactly what Max has spent the last hour trying to convince me, but the numbers tell a different story."

"We're doing our best to get those figures back up," she says through gritted teeth.

"It's not *you* I'm holding accountable," he booms, with no regard for who might be able to hear. "Max is an experienced journalist and, I thought, an editor who could deliver. But perhaps it's time that he returns to his roots—does what he's good at." He raises his eyebrows as if expecting an answer, but as much as it pains her, Stella doesn't react.

She needs to bide her time, make her move when others are least expecting it. But until then, she'll toe the line and keep *both* sides happy.

"We're working on some really great stuff," she says, making it sound like a team effort, though she's sure that anyone with half a brain will know it's *her* stories that are keeping those sales from falling even further than they are.

"Glad to hear it," he says as his assistant taps on her watch to remind him that his time is too valuable to be wasting on Stella. "If you keep up the good work, who knows what will happen?" Despite herself, she can't help but picture herself in the editor's office, nailing a new name plaque to the door. It's nothing personal to Max of course, but Peter's right: he's a better journalist than he is an editor, and Stella fantasizes about the day he'll gracefully stand aside and let her take the job she was deprived of eighteen months ago.

She flashes her best smile, but Peter's already walking away, his bulk as evident from behind as it is from the front.

"Conference!" shouts Max from his office, and Stella can tell by the way he says it that he's seriously hacked off.

The Globe's top executives and senior journalists file into their editor's office, each of them, no doubt, painfully aware that he's just been hauled over the coals.

"Right, I haven't got the time or the patience to fuck around, so hit me with your best stuff," he says, in answer to anyone who might still be oblivious.

The less experienced would imagine that going first makes you either incredibly brave or ridiculously stupid, but most of them simply want to get the inevitable ball-crunching out of the way.

"It's Marache's last game as manager of Chelsea this weekend," pipes up Mike, the Sports editor. "So we could run a profile piece on his time there: his wins, his losses, some stats . . . ?" He looks at Max questioningly.

"Can we get a pre-match interview with him?" muses Max.

"Er, unfortunately not," says Mike quietly, as if wishing he had a different answer. "They're saying no one's getting access to him until after the game on Saturday."

"Well, what the fuck use to us is that?" roars Max.

Mike offers a resigned shrug of the shoulders.

"So *we're* going to run a shitty stats story, and the Sundays will get the big exit interview?"

"That seems to be the way it's looking," Mike offers.

"Well, that's not good enough. You're the Sports editor of Britain's biggest newspaper."

"Well, yes, but . . ." stutters Mike.

Stella can't help but feel sorry for him as she watches him squirming in his seat, wishing he were anywhere else but here. Like most of them in this room, he came into journalism to report the news, facts and figures—suffused with an innate sense of duty to highlight important topics and keep the public informed. But instead they find themselves peddling propaganda, forever conscious of staying on the right side of the political fence and sacrificing a good story if it dares to play into the hands of the opposing side.

Perhaps that's why mild-mannered Mike chose sport as his speciality, hoping that it was the one topic where he could avoid running the gauntlet. But to his chagrin, he's learned the hard way that there's *no* subject that escapes corruption and manipulation if it's in the public eye.

"Stella, have you got an in with Marache, or anyone connected to him?" Max snaps at her, though she learned long ago not to take it personally.

She saw this coming thirty seconds ago and has spent that time racking her brain for something to offer that might appease him. "I can speak to his wife," she says, silently asking herself whether they've run anything that Señora Marache would be unhappy about, since she last bumped into her at a cancer charity do a couple of months ago. Stella vaguely recalls being offered a kiss-and-tell that showed her husband in an altogether less charitable position: on his hands and knees, if she remembers rightly, being led around a hotel room like a dog on a leash. But she'd not run it, for reasons she can't quite remember—probably because it would have put their five million readers off their breakfast.

"Didn't we have something on him a little while back?" asks Max, deep in thought.

Stella wishes he didn't have quite as good a memory as he does, because she knows what's coming next.

"Er, yeah, I think it was a mucky dominatrix story . . ." she says, hoping that her disinterest will throw him off the scent, but knowing it won't.

"So, see if he wants to do a trade-off," says Max brusquely, looking between her and Mike, waiting for one of them to take the bait. Stella watches as Mike literally shrivels into his seat, like a slug that's had salt thrown at him.

A tightness pulls across her chest. Of all the questionable practices that come with being deputy editor on a tabloid newspaper, "The Trade-Off," as Max always likes to refer to it, is the one thing that pricks the very small conscience Stella has left. Despite making it sound as if there's an option, in reality it gives the target—or, rather, victim—absolutely no choice whatsoever. They either give the paper what it wants or their lives could be ruined within a few column inches. It's blackmail—pure and simple.

"Let me see if I can reach him via his wife first," says Stella. "Then, if that fails, we can look at other alternatives." She tries to catch Mike's eye, but his attention stays focused on the notebook in front of him.

"Get onto it," barks Max. "OK, Features, what have you got?"

Gilly, the Features editor, looks decidedly smug as she rolls her pen between her teeth. "Well, after Adrianna's groom jilted her at the altar, I've got three brides-to-be who were all left hanging on the big day, talking about how it felt, how they got over it—one of them even sold their dress on eBay." She looks around the room, laughing, but Stella can tell that Max has already moved on.

"Remind me who Adrianna is," he asks Stella, with a look of irritation on his face.

"They're saying she's the new Adele," she replies. "Started off in kids' TV in America, lost herself for a while, uploaded a few songs onto TikTok and everyone's gone wild for her." She knows to keep it to short, sharp soundbites when bringing Max up to speed on anyone new in the entertainment industry.

"And she's been dumped by *who*?" he asks.

"Some rapper she hooked up with a year ago," says Stella. "We ran a piece on how unsuited they were, a few months back—she comes from a religious family in the Deep South, seemingly using her wholesome image as a marketing tool, and then she meets this guy who's done time and is known to incite gun violence . . . The writing was on the wall."

Max sighs. "So we've got this melting pot going on and all we've managed to pull out of it is a spread on three randomers who have been jilted at the altar."

Stella can't help but savor the disappearance of Gilly's smug smile as it slides off her face.

"I know what you're going to say," retorts Stella. "And I've got people on both sides of the Atlantic working on it, but Adrianna's not playing ball. She's gone to ground."

Max's eyes widen. "*Everyone's* accessible, Stella—you know that."

"Yes, but . . ."

"I want the full low-down from Adrianna herself on their relationship, an exclusive on what happened—when she first knew he was calling it off, how she felt . . ."

"I'm trying, but like I say, she's gone to ground."

"Or has someone else got to her first?"

"I guess there's a chance," admits Stella, knowing full well that's exactly what's happened. "Though I've checked that it's nobody in the UK."

"So, if a US publication have got the exclusive, find out what it'll take to get it syndicated and get us first rights."

"I'm already on it," she lies.

How many pairs of hands does he think she has? She's been orchestrating the sting on the Labor MP all morning. She can't do that *and* follow up every other piece of minutiae that goes on in the world. There are simply not enough hours in the day.

"Well, then I guess we should all be thankful that the shadow home secretary is screwing a call-girl," Max booms. "How did it go this morning?"

"Good," says Stella, back on firmer ground. "As we hoped, we've got the pair of them sharing a quick kiss at the back entrance to the hotel." She looks around, revelling in what she's about to say. "But the money-shot was what went on inside."

Max looks at her questioningly.

"We've got them kissing in the lobby of the suite, Marianne giving Jacobs oral sex in the bedroom while dressed as Maggie Thatcher, and him on tape saying that the Labor leader secretly voted for Brexit while publicly proclaiming that the UK was better off in Europe."

Max throws his head back as his laughter booms around the room. "And we thought his wife was going to be the only thing he lost."

"Exactly," agrees Stella. "And did I forget to mention that this all happened after they'd snorted four lines of coke?"

Max rubs his hands together with glee. "How many pages do you want?"

"At least four," she says, knowing she's got enough material for six.

"Take as many as you need," he says, still chuckling.

She smiles. There's no better feeling than knowing that instead of having to magic words out of nowhere, manipulating the copy to make it worthy of its place in the paper, on *this* story she's going to have to cut it hard, pulling out the very best bits from a rich over-abundance.

"So right now Stella is single-handedly making *The Globe* the paper that its readers expect," says Max. "The rest of you need to pull your socks up."

"Yes, boss," murmurs Mike.

"Got it," beams Gilly through a fake smile, as if trying to convince herself of her optimism.

Stella watches the team file out of the office and shuts the door behind the last straggler.

"Can I have a word?" she asks, while looking through the slatted blinds toward Jess.

"Make it quick," snaps Max, looking at his watch. "I've got to get to Lord's."

It never ceased to amaze Stella how little work Max actually did. Sure, he put in long hours—even more than her—but they were invariably spent with the prime minister at a dinner party at Number Ten, lunching at Claridge's with a veteran Hollywood star or wangling a seat in the royal box to watch live sport.

When *she's* the editor, she's going to do exactly that—*edit*. She's had enough of rubbing shoulders with inept politicians and vacuous celebrities who think they can play the media to their own tune; who court them when they need something and accuse them of flouting privacy laws when they don't. She's already got a list, as long as her arm, of names she won't ever allow to be featured in *The Globe*. Mostly consisting of people who didn't think they needed her on their way up, but who'll be wanting to be her best friend on the way down. They forget that the puppy that will gladly roll over to be tickled will eventually get big and bite back.

"About the new girl . . ." says Stella, looking at Max with raised eyebrows.

"What about her?" he says, already distracted by something on his phone.

"Well, what's she doing here, and when were you going to tell me about it?"

Max bristles, his jaw tensing. "She's *here* because I want her to be," he says, narrowing his eyes. "We have to bring in more stories—*better* stories—and as much as I appreciate everything you're doing, you're not able to do it all on your own."

Stella doesn't know whether to feel angry or relieved. "She seems a bit wet behind the ears."

"That's because she is," says Max. "She's a rookie from a local gazette and I've brought her in to do the dirty work. If you get a lead, send her down the rabbit hole after it, let her gather all the salient information so that *you* can line up for the kill."

He makes Stella sound like an assassin. Maybe she is.

5

Jess

"Oh, hello, my name's Jess Townsend—is this Mel Sheldrake?"

"Yep, what can I do you for?" says the woman at the other end of the line.

I don't know why I'm so nervous, but as I've already discovered, dealing with celebrities is a whole different ball game from asking the friendly firemen in Chingford about their most hazardous job of the week.

"I'm calling about your client, Yasmin Chopra," I say. "I was wondering if she might be available for interview."

"How about you tell me where you're calling from first," says Mel, with more than a hint of derision.

"Oh, right, sorry, I'm from *The Globe* and—"

"Let me stop you there then," says Mel. "This isn't going to happen."

She sounds as if she's a nanosecond from putting the phone down and ending the call.

"But . . ." I start.

"Look, Jess, is it?"

"Yes, I . . ."

"It's nothing personal, but hell would have to have frozen before I subject any of my clients to the wrath of *The Globe*."

I slump back in my chair, with the last remnants of excitement and enthusiasm that had seen me skip toward the office this morning now seeping out of me. I thought working for the country's biggest newspaper was going to make it easier to get stories, not harder.

"Can I . . . can I ask why?" I venture.

Mel lets out a choked snort. "I'm not sure there's enough hours in the day."

I straighten myself up, hoping it will kick-start my resolve. "We'd only need fifteen minutes of Yasmin's time, and we'd be very happy to promote her book . . ."

"Fifteen minutes is more than enough to destroy someone's career," says Mel. "Mind you, Stella Thorne could probably do that in two."

I look over to Max's office, where the woman in question is pacing up and down in front of his desk, gesticulating in my direction.

"But *I* would be doing the interview," I say, daring to assume—especially if it makes the difference between getting it and not. "*The Globe* has journalists other than Stella."

Mel laughs cattily, making no attempt to mask that it's *at* me, rather than with me. "No disrespect, but am I right to assume you haven't been there very long?" she asks.

"Well, I . . ."

"Otherwise you'd know that Stella IS *The Globe*. She decides who, where, why and when to make or break careers."

"Can you be more specific?" I ask, needing to know exactly what I'm up against.

"Well, the fact that Ms. Thorne turned up at my late client's mother's house, claiming to be a nurse from the hospital, in the hope of getting an exclusive on her daughter's cancer battle will tell you everything you need to know. She hadn't even been dead for three hours."

I disguise a gasp.

"So thanks, but no thanks," she goes on. "Yasmin will be sticking with the publications that don't hound dead girls' mothers or set up elaborate stings to sell lies on the front page."

"What else have we got?" shouts Stella, taking me so much by surprise that I instinctively jump. "I've got a gaping hole on page eleven."

I murmur my thanks to Mel and put the phone down, feeling like I've been caught out.

"I've just taken a call from Tina Mowbray," says Lottie.

I can't help but feel aggrieved that it came to her instead of me.

"What's her story?" asks Stella, arching one of her impeccably shaped eyebrows.

"She's got bruises on her face and the intimation is that her boyfriend, Rex Macy, is responsible."

"Is she prepared to say that on record?" asks Stella.

Lottie shakes her head. "No, she won't even say it *off* the record, but she's taking the dog for a walk in Greenwich Park at four o'clock today."

I look between the two of them, waiting to understand the inference.

Stella nods thoughtfully. "OK, so get a photographer there. Tell him not to approach Tina—she may well be with the fella—but make sure he goes in with a long lens to get a good close-up of the injuries she's sustained."

"She's asked for a fee," says Lottie, through a grimace.

Stella snorts. "What a surprise! So she doesn't want to talk to us, but she wants everyone to know what he's done, leaving us to do her dirty work and get the flak for taking personal photos, while she keeps her powder dry . . ."

"Pretty much," sighs Lottie resignedly.

Stella tuts. "Fucking typical."

"Is that how you get most of your exposés?" I can't help myself from asking. "From the subjects themselves."

Stella looks at me with disbelief and laughs. "God, what rock did he drag you out from under?"

I look at Lottie with the first sting of tears pulling at the back of my eyes. I knew that working on a national newspaper was going to be brutal, but I had no idea I'd be crying before lunch on my first day.

"Her bark is so much worse than her bite," says Lottie, once Stella is out of earshot. "We've all been there. On my first day she sent me to the Chelsea and Westminster Hospital, where I had to pose as a relative of Josh Matthews."

"The movie star?" I ask, remembering my whimsical conversation with Flic.

Lottie laughs. "Yeah, he'd been involved in a car accident and was being treated for his injuries, but Stella was like a rat up a drainpipe, convinced he'd been under the influence."

I wait for the part that Lottie finds funny.

"So I turned up with a bunch of flowers, told the nurses I was his sister and, sure enough, they let me in. Luckily he was out cold, so I was able to go through the medical records in his room . . ."

I gasp. "Is that even legal?"

Lottie shrugs her shoulders. "I don't know—I didn't find anything anyway, but it gave us a great scoop the next day, highlighting the security lapses at the same hospital that the Duchess of Durham was due to give birth in later that month."

I shake my head.

"Look, it may sound terrifying right now, but believe me, being thrown in at the deep end by Stella will be the making of you. It will certainly toughen you up."

"What if I don't want to toughen up?" I ask.

Lottie looks at me, almost in pity. "Then you won't last five minutes."

6

Stella

Stella sighs as she slips her Jimmy Choos off at the front door of her apartment. As much as she wouldn't be seen dead in flats, the thought of giving her arches respite is increasingly appealing. She laughs at herself as her toes sink into the deep pile of the hall carpet, wondering when she became old. She'll be buying slippers at Marks & Spencer next. She shudders at the prospect. "Over my dead body," she says as she pads into the kitchen.

Last night's bottle of red is standing on the worktop and she greets it like an old friend. "Am I pleased to see you," she says, picking it up and pouring it into a large balloon glass.

She closes her eyes as the warm liquid trickles down her throat, imbuing her veins with its glow. It seeps into the hard-to-reach corners, taking the edge off another high-pressured day in the office.

She'd wanted the deputy editor's job so badly, busting her arse to get it, but this past year has been spent holding the hands of underqualified staff and dealing with the business end of running Britain's most successful newspaper. Sure, she was securing deals, and the adrenaline rush of getting one over on their rivals gave her a buzz that she wouldn't give up for the world, but she missed the written word. The days she spent banging out stories on her laptop in a toilet cubicle as she rushed to be the first to file copy from a celebrity party, or the times when she'd get a tip-off that a *Strictly Come Dancing* couple were no longer just dancing, and would book the hotel room next to them so that she could report on their torrid night of lovemaking. That's where the true thrill was: in following her nose and rooting out a story, not in negotiating drawn-out deals with people who always thought they were worth more than she was prepared to pay.

Still, it is the natural progression to being editor and one day, when Max finally falls on his sword, she will be perfectly placed to take over.

Speaking of the devil, his number flashes up on her phone screen and she immediately rejects it. Gone are the days when she'd take his calls at all hours.

It rings again as Stella unbuttons her blouse and reaches into the shower cubicle to turn the overhead jet on. The story-hunter in her wants to answer it, afraid that she'll miss the big one, but the slightly jaded forty-year-old, who's been doing this for far too long, knows that someone else further down the ladder will pick it up and run with it, if it's urgent. She's too tired and, frankly, too senior to be chasing stories at ten o'clock at night.

Groaning as she steps under the hot water, Stella closes her eyes as it washes away the debris of the day.

Her phone rings for the third time and she tuts in frustration, circling around the steamed-up glass with her hand to see who it is.

Harry's number shows up, under the name of Steve, and her irritation subsides. He's exactly who she needs right now and she reaches out of the shower, unable to get to the phone quickly enough.

"Are you nearby?" she asks, picking up.

"I can be with you in fifteen minutes," he says.

"I'm not sure I can wait that long," she replies, wrapping herself in a fluffy white towel.

"Make it twelve then," he says, before hanging up.

By the time he rings the intercom an impressive ten minutes later, she's rough-dried her hair and has poured two glasses of wine.

She buzzes him in and greets him at her door in an open silk robe and a pair of Manolos.

"Christ," he says, looking her up and down.

"What took you so long?" she asks, pulling him to her and pushing him against the hall wall.

She kisses him, her tongue meeting his as she reaches for the zip in his trousers. He holds her head in both hands, his soft caresses at the back of her neck becoming more urgent. Wrapping her legs around him, he picks her up and carries her into the bedroom, rolling on top of her as she falls onto the mattress.

A breath is snatched away as he enters her, and Stella closes her eyes. His fingers dig into her thighs as he quickens the pace, and within seconds he's calling out at the very same time as she is, leaving nail tracks down his back. The pair of them perfectly in sync, as always.

"You have no idea how much I needed that," she says breathlessly, rolling into him as he falls back onto the bed.

He brushes the hair away from her face and kisses the tip of her nose. "You and me both," he says, through a grin. "Though I could have done with a little more notice."

"Are you complaining?" she asks, propping her head on his chest. Just looking at him makes her want to do it again; those wickedly smoldering eyes, the suggestive smile, that dimple . . .

"No, I'm only saying that I can't always drop everything to come over," he says. "If we were able to plan things a little more, maybe . . ."

Stella pulls herself up and off the bed.

"Where are you going?" he calls after her as she goes into the living room to retrieve her glass of wine. She hadn't yet had the chance to give him his. "Why do you always do this?" he asks, coming into the room, doing his trousers up.

"Do what?" she asks sullenly, picking imaginary fluff off the turquoise velvet couch that she's sitting on.

"All I'm saying is that it would be a lot easier, and far more pleasurable, if we could plan when we're going to see each other, rather than me having to wait for you to call me when you want sex."

"You called *me* tonight," she says bitterly.

"Yes, but it wasn't because I wanted sex," he says, exasperated.

"Oh, I didn't realize it was a such an inconvenience to come and make love to me," replies Stella spitefully.

"It's not," sighs Harry. "It's one of my favorite things to do, but sometimes I'd quite like to take you out, first. We could go to a bar for a few drinks or a nice restaurant for dinner."

"You and I both know that's not a good idea," she says. "Imagine if we're seen together."

"I get that it might not be easy, but it's not impossible—not if we're careful."

"Most of my work is carried out in bars and restaurants," says Stella, staring into the bowl of her wine glass. "It's the last thing I want to do, when I get off."

"What about what *I* want?" asks Harry, turning in his seat to face her.

She can't help but laugh. "I would have thought this is the perfect scenario for *any* man."

"But have you ever thought to ask?" He looks at her intently, making her feel uncomfortable. She's under enough pressure at the office; she certainly doesn't need it at home as well. That's why what she and Harry have is all she wants.

She doesn't need to worry about where he is or what he's doing. She doesn't have to factor him into any decisions she makes. If she wants to stay in the office until midnight, she can. If she wants to eat cold baked beans straight out of the tin for dinner when she gets home, she can. There's no one to answer to, and no one to take up space in her bed. It suits her. She's happy.

"You make me feel as if I'm some kind of hired help," he says.

"You are," says Stella indignantly. "I pay you well."

"For privileged police information," he says. "Not sex."

"Well then, perhaps you should add that, as a *privileged* client extra, on your next invoice," she says acerbically.

7

Jess

"Well, would you look at that," says Dad, squinting at my tiny byline on page eleven of yesterday's edition of *The Globe*.

Mum grabs her specs from the kitchen table and peers through them, scanning the article.

"Oh my goodness," she squeals excitedly.

I flinch at the inflammatory headline the sub-editor deemed suitable for the picture-led feature: On the Ropes! Is this Macy's latest opponent? Underneath is a picture of Tina Mowbray walking her dog, but no matter how big her sunglasses are, they're unable to disguise the black-and-purple bruise that spreads across her cheekbone.

"What's happened to the poor lass?" asks Mum, looking even closer.

"She got beaten up by her boyfriend," says Flic, attempting to snaffle the smallest roast potato from the tray that Mum had momentarily left on the side.

"Serves you right, you greedy oik," I say, smiling, as Flic jumps around, fanning her mouth.

"Oh, leave her be," admonishes Mum, treating her, as ever, like the younger sister I never had.

Flic pokes her tongue out in a victorious one-upmanship and I shake my head. She can be so annoying at times, but I couldn't imagine life without her. She's been a part of the family since we met at senior school, even going so far as moving into my room when I went off to university. But I'd never begrudge her making my parents the ones she never had.

"Tina's become more famous than him, and I don't think his ego can take it," mumbles Flic. "So he lashes out because it makes him feel like more of a man."

"She didn't say that . . ."

"She didn't have to," says Flic. "You only have to read between the lines to see what's really going on."

No doubt that's exactly what the headline and the carefully worded article were meant to imply, but at no point did Tina say that her boyfriend had raised a hand to her. In fact, she'd concocted an elaborate story about how she'd come home drunk from a wrap party and fallen out of bed when she'd attempted to go to the bathroom in the middle of the night. But that version didn't satisfy Stella Thorne's warped desire to present Tina as an abuse victim, so I'd been instructed to drop the explanation from the article and let the pictures do the talking. And seeing Flic jump to conclusions, it seems to have created exactly the feeding frenzy Stella had hoped for.

"You're putting two and two together and coming up with five," I say.

"Well, in the absence of anything else, what are we supposed to do?" asks Flic.

I can feel Mum and Dad looking at me. *The Globe* isn't their newspaper of choice to *read*, let alone to have their daughter work for, and their disquiet speaks volumes. "I do hope you're not putting words into people's mouths," mumbles Dad as he pretends to check the rise of the Yorkshire puddings in the oven.

"I would never do that," I say. "In fact, I didn't report Tina's side of the story at all."

Dad pulls a face. "Leaving people to make up their own minds can sometimes be even more damaging."

"Well, maybe I'm in the wrong job then," I say, unable to disguise the hurt in my voice.

My phone starts ringing, from the pocket of my jacket hanging on the bannisters, and Flic turns to look at me, as if asking, *Who's that going to be?*

I shrug my shoulders, not really knowing *who* would be after me on a Saturday night.

"Maybe it's that hot guy that Tinder matched you up with . . . looking for a booty call," says Flic, as she follows me out to the hall.

"Well, seeing as 'hot' to you means he only has to be breathing, I think I'll pass."

She turns her nose up at the slight, but doesn't dispute the claim.

"And, anyway, I don't want a boyfriend," I say sanctimoniously. "I want to concentrate on my career."

"Career girls can still get laid," she whispers, smiling that infuriating sweet smile, which lets her get away with murder.

I stick two fingers up as I answer my phone. "Hello?" I say, and wait for a computer-generated voice to ask if I've been in an accident recently.

"Jess, get yourself to the Dorchester hotel, will you?" says a woman's voice.

"Excuse me?" I ask, fearing I know who this is, but praying I don't.

"We've got a big story about to go down, and Lottie's sick, so I need you there right away." If I was ever in any doubt about who I was speaking to, her clipped, acerbic tone confirms it.

"But . . . but, Stella, I can't," I stutter. "I'm just about to have dinner."

An icy laugh comes down the line. "The news doesn't wait for you to fill your stomach," she says. "How quickly can you get here?"

Even though I lived in this house in Essex for twenty-five years until renting a flat with Flic six months ago, my brain can't compute where the nearest station is or the quickest route from suburbia into town.

"Mmm, three-quarters of an hour, give or take," I say, as I mentally scan the London Underground map in my head, weighing up which station is closest to Park Lane.

"Try and make it less," barks Stella. "Call me when you get here and I'll come and meet you."

The line goes dead and, as I stare at the phone in my hand, a frisson of excitement ignites my nerve endings. A big story, Stella said. What could possibly have happened to warrant her needing me at such short notice?

My immediate thought is that it's a hostile situation: an explosion or perhaps a terrorist incident. I scan my phone for the latest news as I walk slowly toward the kitchen, but nothing of any note appears to have happened in or around the Dorchester hotel. But perhaps it's not reached the wires yet and it'll be us breaking the story. My heart thumps in my chest as adrenaline begins to pump through my veins, my body now desperate to move toward the action. *This* is what I came into the newsroom for. The chance to lead the narrative; the chance to make a difference.

"I'm afraid I'm going to have to take a rain check," I say, pulling on my jacket. "Something's come in at work—a really big story."

The three of them look at each other, unsure whether they should be excited or concerned for me.

"OK, well, be careful, won't you?" says Dad, pulling me in for a hug.

"If it's got anything to do with Josh Matthews, call me and I'll be there in a flash," says Flic, wide-eyed.

"I'll send home a plate for later," says Mum.

I can't help but smile; their responses sum up their individual personalities perfectly.

I spend the train journey checking all the news apps for the latest on the situation at the Dorchester, but still nothing's coming up and I'm almost too scared to go into the labyrinth of Tube tunnels, for fear of missing the headline when it appears. By the time I'm climbing the stairs of Green Park station I'm so desperate to know what monumental story I'm about to cover that it takes all my resolve not to call Stella and ask before I've reached the hotel.

"I'm here," I pant into my phone, out of breath, as I run the last few yards along Park Lane. I'm listening out for sirens, looking up for smoke—my senses on full alert to whatever the story is.

"OK, you need to go to the service entrance at the rear," says Stella, just as I momentarily entrap myself in the revolving doors at the front. "I'll meet you there."

I do a full three-sixty, coming out where I started, and head round the corner.

Unsurprisingly, the back of the hotel is at odds with the perfect facade of the front. There are no pretty flowers to mask the harsh exterior, no sound of gently trickling water from the fountain and certainly no green-suited doormen doffing their hats at my arrival.

I dodge the beeping delivery trucks as they reverse, and smile my apologies as I divide a group of kitchen staff on a cigarette break.

"Jesus," says Stella, as she looks me up and down before manhandling me into a loud and chaotic kitchen. "Have you got nothing else with you to wear?"

I scan my body, taking in my trainers, jeans and cabled jumper, quickly picking at the fluff bobbles stubbornly attached to the wool. "I was at my parents'," I say, as indignantly as I dare. "And it's Saturday night."

She tuts and rolls her eyes. "What do you take? A ten?"

I look down at myself again, as if double-checking. "Yeah, I guess."

"Right, follow me," she says, turning on her impressive heels. "We have to be quick, though, as we're running out of time."

"Where . . . I mean . . . what's going on?" I stutter as the delicious stab of excitement and nerves penetrates my veins. "What's the story?"

"Tilly Ashcroft is the story," she says in a hushed voice as I half run down the corridor to keep up with her.

"As in, the soap star?" I ask, grateful the service lift that we step into is empty.

Stella pulls her mouth tight in a half smile, half grimace.

I can't help but feel a little disappointed, because as exciting as this is, it's not quite the hazardous drama I was expecting or hoping for.

It then occurs to me, unfathomably, that perhaps Tilly's body has been found cold and unresponsive in one of the rooms. I shudder as the outlandish idea is slowly replaced by the unlikelihood of the press finding out before the emergency services.

Stella leads the way out of the lift and through a fire-exit door, which suddenly transports us into the decadent depths of the hotel. My trainers sink into the red-and-gold swirls in the deep-pile carpet and the sweet smell of vanilla permeates my nostrils. Wealth is imbued in these walls, seeping out from the William Morris wallpaper and wrapping itself around the gilded edges of the framed pictures.

"OK, get in here and stay out of sight," says Stella, swiping a card against a door handle.

"Wh-where are *you* going?" I ask.

"To get some clothes from my car," she snaps. "You can't work, dressed like that."

The door slams and I stand there looking after her, feeling like a naughty schoolgirl who's been sent to the corner to face the wall.

"Who are you?" asks a gruff male voice, making me jump out of my skin.

I turn toward what I thought was an empty room to be met by a pair of inquisitive eyes peering over the top of a mustache and bushy beard.

"I'm Jess," I offer. "I work for *The Globe*."

"Oh, right," says the man, adjusting his baseball cap. "I'm Boj."

He reaches for a bottle of beer on the table and it's only then that I see the bank of monitors set in front of him.

I watch in silence as people move around a room that looks like it should be on the pages of *Country Homes & Interiors* magazine. The over-plump floral sofas clash with the heavy stripes of the flock wallpaper, and the modern lamps are at odds with the swag-and-tail curtains, but somehow the sensory overload works.

"What's going on?" I ask, hoping that my ignorance is taken for casual small-talk.

"We're just getting the final touches done," he says, nodding toward the screens. "Then we'll be all set."

I want to ask, *"All set for what?"* but I hold back. I can feel the tension in the air, see the care and consideration that the people on the screens are putting into everything; the last thing they need is an uninformed rookie to unnerve them further.

I'm almost relieved when the door opens and I hear Stella barking orders. It's only as I turn to see her on her own that I realize she's talking to me.

"Here, get this on," she says, handing me a cellophane-wrapped garment on a hanger. "You're going to have trouble filling it out, but do your best."

I can't help but look at her full breasts contained within a bra under her silk blouse, and at the hourglass of her waist, encased in a tight pencil skirt. If she's given me an outfit of hers, my assets are going to woefully under-represent it.

"Quickly!" she snaps, looking at her watch. "We've got less than ten minutes until showtime."

I fall into the en-suite bathroom with all the grace of an elephant, tripping over the trailing plastic.

"For Christ's sake" is all I hear as I close the door behind me.

I catch sight of myself in the mirror as I kick off my scuffed trainers and instantly feel inferior. While Stella dresses like every day is London Fashion Week, with her signature red lips and perfectly formed curls, I look like I've spent the day in a mosh pit.

I splash cold water onto my face and wish I'd washed my hair this morning. As I lift my Nirvana t-shirt over my head, I also wish I'd put my graying bra through an express cycle in the machine.

"Get some slap on, as well," says Stella as she swings the door open and throws a makeup bag into the basin. I make an awkward attempt to cover myself up, but the corners of her mouth are already pulled tight in disdain. Or it may just be the thought of her designer trouser suit touching my mismatched underwear and unshaven legs.

I use the frayed belt from my jeans to pull the waistband in, relieved that the jacket is long enough to cover the unseemly ruching, though I can't imagine it's quite the look the designer envisaged.

Stella's make-up bag appears to hold the entire cosmetics counter of Harrods, with products that I don't even recognize. I rummage for something that resembles a mascara and work it through my lashes. I blanch at the redness of her lipstick, knowing that I'll look like a clown, but time to have a choice is not on my side. I obviously need to look the complete opposite of how I arrived.

Using water to push my hair back, I stare at my reflection and laughingly convince myself I look cool, in an alternative way.

Stella's face says otherwise as I step into the room, but she pulls herself up and forces a smile.

"OK, so what I need you to do is go down to the foyer to meet Tilly and take her to room five-four-five, which is next door to here."

I nod, but butterflies are fluttering in my stomach because Stella is making me feel as if there's more riding on this than simply an interview.

"OK, but what if . . ." I start, not knowing what I'm asking, but feeling as if I surely need more information.

"There is no 'what if,'" says Stella bluntly. "You do as I say and nothing more."

She hands me a key card. "David Phillips from Sony Entertainment will meet you there, but you can use this to enter. Leave him to do the talking, and just back him up whenever it's required. Imagine yourself as his right-hand woman and do everything he asks."

"Got it," I say.

Stella looks at her watch again and the light catches the faintest line of perspiration on her top lip. Maybe she is human after all.

The walkie-talkie in her hand crackles. "She's arriving at the front entrance," says a male voice. "It looks like she's on her own."

"Great," replies Stella, before pressing the side button. "OK, I'm sending someone down to meet Tilly now. Did you hear that, Rob?"

"Yep, roger that," booms a voice. "We're out of here."

There's a final burst of activity on the screens, before all the bodies in black clothes disappear, leaving only one man, straightening his jacket and adjusting his tie pin.

"OK, you're on," says Stella, ushering me out of the room.

I wobble on the shoes she's lent me and wonder how obvious it is that not only am I unused to my heel being three inches higher than the ball of my foot, but also there's a wad of tissue stuffed into the toes.

"Just do as I've asked," says Stella brusquely. "And keep her drink topped up."

I nod as I enter the corridor.

"Oh, and Jess . . ."

I turn to face her, concentrating all my efforts on staying upright.

"Whatever you do, don't let on that you work for *The Globe*."

8

Stella

No matter how many times she's done this and how impressive her strike rate may be, at this moment in the proceedings Stella is always reminded of the time she'd been summoned to a meeting in a hotel room, not too dissimilar to this one, which had almost been the undoing of her.

She goes into her own world as, frame by frame, the moving images of the woman who called, claiming to have just slept with the married captain of the England football team, infiltrate her mind. "The proof is still on the bed sheets," she'd said, rather crudely, on the phone.

In the minimal time Stella had to think, she'd run a quick check on the current whereabouts of the England captain and had felt a thrill rush through her when she discovered that the team was due to play a World Cup qualifier at Wembley the next day. It not only meant that it was highly likely he was in London and this woman's claims were true, but also that the headline would be all the more tantalizing if he was found to have been shagging someone other than his wife the night before a big game. His other half would be the least of his worries, if the fans found out he wasn't conserving his energy.

Stella had already amused herself by writing up the copy in her head by the time she knocked on the door of the hotel room. She only hoped that the woman was reasonably attractive, as it would make for more palatable pictures. So when an older woman beckoned her in, she didn't know whether to laugh or cry, because as stunning as she was, with her peroxide-blonde hair and brightly painted lips, she had to be at least twenty years older than the man she claimed to have just had sex with.

"Can I get you a drink?" she'd purred, gesturing for Stella to sit down on one of the suite's multiple sofas.

"I'm fine, thank you," Stella had said, wondering if she was an escort. There was definitely something off about her. Was it her hair? Her voice? Something didn't sit quite right, as if she was trying to be someone she wasn't. It didn't matter to Stella, because as far as she was concerned, the muckier the story, the better.

"So he was here earlier this evening?" she'd asked, tilting her head toward the bedroom. If she thought it was odd that the bed looked pristine, it wasn't enough to ring any alarm bells.

"Who's that?" asked the woman, smiling as she swirled ice cubes in a cut-glass tumbler.

"Leo Radcliffe," said Stella, wondering how she could have forgotten so quickly. "The England captain."

"I'm sorry, we must have got our wires crossed," she said, her thin lips sloping up to one side. "I'm afraid I don't know a Leo Radcliffe."

It was in that second that Stella had realized who the woman really was. Her fight-or-flight instinct had kicked in, one battling the other for supremacy, while all the time her brain battled against what it knew to be true. But why get Stella there under false pretenses? She didn't need to ask herself that question. She already knew the answer.

The woman seemed to know that her cover had been blown. It might have been Stella's terror-filled eyes, frantically jumping from left to right, attempting to assimilate the seriousness of the situation, or it could have been the tremor in her voice as she pretended that everything was fine. "W-what do you want?" she'd faltered.

"I wasn't quite sure which one of you would come," said the woman, settling into her high-backed chair, showing none of the vulnerabilities that were coursing through Stella. "It was a lucky dip between you and Max Forsythe. You, I could deal with on my own, but I couldn't take the chance if Max turned up."

It was then that two men had emerged from the adjoining room, stealthy and silent.

The moisture in Stella's mouth had instantaneously dried up and she'd stood on wobbly legs, in the half-hearted belief that she could get to the door without being manhandled back to where she was sitting.

One of the men, with a head like a bowling ball, had only needed to take one step forward to let her know that she wouldn't make it to the end of the coffee table, let alone the door.

"What do you want from me?" Stella had asked, her eyes darting between her tormentors as she fell down onto the sofa, defeated.

The woman had wordlessly slipped off the wig she was wearing to reveal the raven-haired bob that Stella had come to know well during the six-week court case a couple of months before.

Christina McAllister had smiled. "*I* don't want anything," she said. "But my husband, on the other hand . . ."

Stella had closed her eyes and pictured Ray McAllister standing in the dock, his head bowed as he awaited sentencing. When the judge had ruled that he should serve six years for conspiracy to kidnap, handling stolen goods and being in possession of an illegal firearm, his neck had straightened and he'd glared straight at Stella and Max in the viewing gallery and roared, "I'll fucking kill the pair of you."

Max had placated Stella afterward, jokingly asking her what she expected from a man whose crimes they'd single-handedly uncovered and exposed. "He's not going to invite you round for Christmas dinner, is he?"

"No, but I didn't expect a death-threat, either," she'd said, clearly rattled. Though if the truth be known, it wasn't the first and it was unlikely to be the last. It was, however, the most alarming. McAllister was, after all, the feared kingpin of a notorious gang, who thought nothing of taking something that wasn't his. Stella had spent the last couple of months wondering if that included her life. Now, it seemed, she was about to find out.

"It may surprise you to know that my husband is not a man who makes enemies easily," said Christina. "But it seems he's made an exception for you."

Despite wanting to present a strong, undaunted front, Stella's fear had been making itself felt. It was in her hands, her fingers unable to stop trembling, and her eyes unable to focus properly. Everything was blurry, making the heat that was wrapping itself around her all the more oppressive.

"So while I was hoping to put an end to all this here and now— was *happy to*, in fact—it seems he wants you all to himself, so he can savor the moment." Christina's eyes had danced with the twisted pleasure that her husband would derive from the act. Stella imagined that when that day came, his wife would be there, watching and cheering from the sidelines.

She had allowed her coiled insides to relax a little, grateful to know that she wasn't going to be killed there and then. And she had vowed that by the time McAllister was released, she'd have changed her life beyond all recognition, so that he'd never be able to find her again.

"But until that time comes," Christina had gone on, "he wants you to know that he'll not forget what you did to him. He'll not forget that you double-crossed him, and he needs to know that you'll not forget it, either."

Given the tenuous situation she found herself in, Stella could only numbly agree, knowing there was little point in attempting anything else. Though if McAllister's wife truly believed *she* was the criminal, then Christina was in denial of who her husband really was.

"So, just to make absolutely sure that you'll remember him until you meet again, he's asked me to give you a present—a little token, as a constant reminder of what you've done and what's to come."

Stella had pushed herself back into the sofa as the two men came toward her, screaming as one held her legs and the other fixed her shoulders in a viselike grip.

"What . . . what are you doing?" she had cried, struggling to free herself, knowing it was futile. "Get off of me."

She hadn't felt any pain at first, the adrenaline pumping around her body too potent to let her feel anything other than the innate need to get out of there alive. But as the blood had leaked from her wrists, spreading like ink on blotting paper as it made its way up the sleeve of her white blouse, the sting of the knife had made itself felt.

She hadn't remembered the immediate aftermath—thankfully, her protective mind had gone some way to block it out. But she'd called Max as soon as they let her go, not just because he was the only one who'd understand, but who else was there? He'd picked her up from a rain-soaked street in Marylebone and taken her home, where he bandaged her forearm and begged her to go to the police.

"No," she'd said resolutely. "Look what happened the first time we got the police involved."

"But we can't have this hanging over us for the next six years," Max had said. "Looking over our shoulder . . . wondering who's hiding behind every corner."

"I think the next six years are going to be the least of our worries," Stella said. "It's when McAllister gets out that we're really going to have a problem."

Now, as Stella fingers the double cross etched into her forearm, its crude scarring still pronounced through the silk of her blouse, she can't help but be thankful they've still got another two years to go.

9

Jess

Having watched *Granville Park* since I can remember—the fictional Red Lion pub being as much a stalwart in my childhood as the Royal Oak that Dad used to frequent most nights—I'd assumed I'd recognize its star, Tilly Ashcroft, instantly.

But as I turn full circle in the hotel's flamboyant lobby, all I can see is the continuous arrival of esteemed guests, and the assured front desk taking it all in their stride.

"Are you looking for *me*?" comes a tiny voice, seemingly from nowhere.

A young girl destined to blend in, wearing jeans and a t-shirt, smiles out hopefully from beneath a black baseball cap.

I go to tell her no, as I'm looking for the character we all know and love: the brassy barmaid who gives the punters more than a pint; the effervescent attention-seeker who glides effortlessly down the red carpet at award ceremonies, knowing which shoulder to look over and when, to give the waiting media her best angle.

But just as I'm about to pass her over, I see something that I recognize.

"Tilly?"

"Yes," she says breathlessly, sounding relieved.

"I'm so sorry, I wasn't sure . . ."

She smiles knowingly. "I'm not as tall as you'd expect," she replies, sounding as if it's a line she's used to reeling out.

I actually wanted to say that she's so much prettier in real life than I thought she'd be, but I couldn't decide quickly enough whether it was a compliment or an insult.

"It's good to meet you," I say instead. "If you'd like to follow me."

"I'm so nervous," she says as we step into the lift. "I can't remember the last time I felt like this."

I offer a warm smile. "You'll be fine. We don't bite."

She looks at me a little oddly and I clamp my mouth shut, remembering what Stella said. For some reason, she doesn't want Tilly to know that I work for *The Globe.*

As the windowless box ascends, the journalist in me wants to fill the awkward silence with so many questions, but I hold my tongue.

"Will you be staying with me?" she asks as the lift slows to a stop and the doors open.

"Of course," I say, taken aback.

"OK, great," she says, her tense face breaking into a smile.

"We're in here," I say, swiping the key card against the door of room 545.

"Ah, so good to meet you again," gushes the man I presume to be David Phillips, coming to meet us at the door.

"Yes, it seems like forever since we met in Dubai," says Tilly softly. "My schedule is crazy busy—sorry about that."

"It's not a problem," says David, in a soft-edged American accent. "We got there in the end. Now what can I get you? Tea, coffee, water? Or something stronger maybe?" He smiles and rolls his eyes toward a silver bucket on the coffee table, where a bottle of champagne is nestled into a bed of ice.

"I probably shouldn't, as I've already had a couple," Tilly says, taking off her baseball cap and ruffling her hair.

"And why not?" replies David, making a great show of popping the cork one-handed.

"I just needed a little something to settle the nerves," she says, laughing.

"There's no need to be nervous," says David, handing her a fizzing flute. He holds her embarrassed gaze a moment too long. "Please sit," he says, signaling to the sofa that I'd seen so perfectly framed on the monitors next door.

I can't help but speculate whether it's set up for an audition, and I wonder if Tilly's aware of what's expected of her. She doesn't look like she's come in character, but then that's the magic of actresses, I suppose: they can become whoever they're asked to become, in the blink of an eye.

David coughs to clear his throat. "So, as you know from our previous discussion, Tilly, Sony are preparing to shoot the first in the *Vortex* trilogy."

Tilly knocks back her champagne and nods enthusiastically.

"And we're finalizing our casting wishlist, which is the reason I wanted to talk to you again."

"OK," says Tilly hopefully. She raises her glass to her mouth before realizing it's empty.

I immediately remember my instructions and reach for the bottle to top her up.

"Thanks," she says gratefully.

"So we've secured Josh Matthews for the lead," David goes on. "And . . ."

"Josh . . . Matthews?" chokes Tilly, her eyes widening. "Gosh, he's huge."

"This whole thing is going to be huge," says David. "It's going to be one of the biggest movie enterprises the world has ever seen. We're working with a four-hundred-million-dollar production budget . . . We've got Greg Thompson directing."

"Wow," says Tilly, necking her second glass of champagne.

I can literally see the tension in her jaw begin to dissipate, and her tight neck and shoulders loosen, as the alcohol releases her inhibitions.

"And we're down to the last two leading ladies," says David. He waits to make sure he's got her full attention, before giving that Hollywood smile. "Tilly Ashcroft being one of them."

Her face immediately flushes with anticipation.

David looks at me and tilts his head toward her empty glass. I wonder if it wouldn't be easier to give her the bottle.

"We've seen what you can do; we only need to look at the difference between you and the character you play on *Granville Park*— you're a great actress."

"Thank you," says Tilly.

"*I'm* completely confident that you're right for the role, but our director, Greg, is going to take a little more convincing."

"Oh," replies Tilly despondently. "What do I need to do to prove I'm the right woman for the job?"

"I tell you what," says David, suddenly animated. "Why don't I see if I can get Greg over here? He's in town, and I know it will make for an easy decision if he meets you in person."

A sickening sensation coils itself around my insides as I imagine the sofa that Tilly's seated on turning into the casting couch I've heard so much about. Is that what the cameras are for? To capture every sordid moment of Tilly's "audition."

"Show him how much you want the job, and you'll have it in the bag," David goes on.

Tilly looks at me, wide-eyed, as she empties the last of the bottle into her glass, desperate to squeeze out every last drop of its Dutch courage. It's almost as if she knows what's coming.

I stand up abruptly, making sure to knock over the ice-bucket stand, splaying frozen cubes onto the deep-pile carpet. David jumps up and glares at me, as if to say, *What the hell are you doing?* I don't really know myself; I just know that I have to stop whatever is about to happen.

My head spins toward where I know the cameras must be, ready to give Stella my best "stand-off" face. But there's nothing there. Nor is there a single camera focused on the coffee table or on the chair that David was, until recently, sitting in. But that's impossible. I saw shots from all three viewpoints, transmitting real-time footage to the monitors next door. What the hell is going on?

As David talks animatedly on the phone, I want to ask Tilly if she's comfortable with what's happening, but I pull myself up. This may be how the movie business works: late-night meetings in hotel rooms, directors being called over at the drop of a hat; Tilly's probably found herself in this position countless times before. The fact that she's still here to tell the tale—and, seemingly, happily so—forces me to take perspective. Nothing has happened. Yet.

"So, it's great news," says David, coming off the phone. "Greg's at a function near here and he's going to swing by, to have a chat. Let's see if we can get this signed, sealed and delivered tonight."

Tilly smiles brightly as she takes her jacket off.

"I'd better call for a few more provisions," David goes on, rubbing his hands together. "It is Saturday night, after all."

"Please don't do so on my account," says Tilly. "I've had more than enough."

"It wasn't champagne I was thinking of," he says with a glint in his eye. He looks to me. "There's another bottle in the fridge—open it, will you?"

"I really don't need any more," says Tilly as I unwrap the cork. "I need to keep my wits about me if I'm to impress the great Greg Thompson."

I can't help but wonder if it's already too late for that.

"Are you OK with this?" I ask, as David goes back on the phone.

She nods. "As long as you promise to stay."

"Of course," I reply, smiling.

"Shit!" exclaims David, theatrically ending the call and throwing his phone on the sofa.

"Bad news?" asks Tilly, concerned.

I wonder if *I* should be too.

"It's nothing," he says, though everything about his body language suggests it's the very opposite. "I was hoping for something to get the party started—you know, a bit of the good stuff to get us all in the mood." He looks at her with raised eyebrows.

"Oh. Right," says Tilly, as my brow furrows, wondering if he's talking about what I think he's talking about.

"Yeah, but I can't get hold of my man . . ." David goes on, leaving it hanging.

"We can do without it," says Tilly.

"But I could really do with some," says David, suddenly agitated. "And I know that Greg would appreciate it, too—especially as I'm pulling him away from what already sounds like a good party."

Tilly looks at me and I shrug my shoulders.

"Is there any way . . ." he starts, before seemingly thinking better of it. "Fuck it—it could make all the difference between him liking what he sees and not."

He makes Tilly sound like a prized livestock at auction.

"Is there anyone," he starts, "anyone *you* might be able to call? I can give you cash, and my driver downstairs can take you to pick it up, if it's close by."

For a moment I think he's talking to me and I almost snort, but it's even worse—he's talking to Tilly.

"Erm, I guess I could make a few calls," she says eventually.

"Could you?" asks David, looking as if he could kiss her. "That would be amazing."

"Erm, let me see what I can do," she replies, fishing her phone out of her bag and taking it to the bathroom.

David looks at the TV screen on the wall and winks, as if he were staring down the eye of a camera. It occurs to me that maybe he is.

10

Stella

"What a coup," says Max as he leans back in his office chair. He's already contentedly nursing a whiskey in a cut-glass tumbler, even though it's not yet ten o'clock. "Why aren't all Monday mornings like this?"

"We struck gold," says Stella.

"That's why *you're* my number one," says Max, though she can hear the insincerity in his voice.

"I'm only as good as my editor," replies Stella, sounding equally phony. "In fact, you called this one in."

"But *you* chased it down," he says. "As only you can."

She smiles.

"And there's absolutely no room for doubt?" He raises his eyebrows questioningly.

"What—that Tilly Ashcroft procured drugs and supplied them to a third party?" asks Stella. "Absolutely not."

"But she didn't take any herself?"

"Unfortunately not, but then we've not suggested she did."

Max leans the tips of his fingers against one another and smiles. "I just want to make absolutely sure we're cleaner than clean on this one, as I don't need Peter breathing down my neck."

"You've got my word on that," says Stella confidently.

"Excellent! I can't wait to see what Subs come up with," says Max. "We're going to be spoiled for choice."

Stella's brow furrows. "Are they laying the pages out *now?*"

Max nods, already distracted by the next item on his "to do" list.

"Aren't we going too early?" asks Stella. "I thought we weren't running it until Friday."

"It's being kept well under wraps," says Max. "So even if any of our loyal and faithful staff *are* on the payroll of another newspaper, they'll have trouble sniffing it out. Talking of which, I've had a tip-off from someone over on the Sommersby Diary at *The Post.*"

Stella's lip curls involuntarily. She and Dane Sommersby have something of a checkered past. They'd met as rookie reporters on *The Globe* and, after a year of ending up at one another's flat every time they went out for drinks, they'd decided that their modest salaries would be put to better use if they were only servicing one tenancy agreement. Plus, it felt like the done thing at the time; all of Stella's friends were coupling up and having babies, and although a family wasn't high on her wishlist, she surprised herself with how secure she felt being one half of a team.

But a year down the line, Dane upended her newly found peace of mind when he pitched a story that she was working on to their bitter rival, *The Post.* They were offering a chance to step up the career ladder, which *The Globe* had, until then, failed to do, so he'd taken the leap, and the credit, and left Stella behind. No one would ever have known how heartbroken she was—not from the hole Dane left in her life, but because the story that the asshole had taken with him was a corker.

Stella's only retribution is that she now pays someone who works for Dane to tell her what stories *he's* working on. It goes a little way to address the karma.

"Oh yeah?" she says to Max nonchalantly. "Anything interesting?"

"She reckons she's got an in with Yasmin Chopra," he replies.

"The *On the Ranch* winner?"

Max nods and picks up three glossy magazines from his desk, before throwing them back down one by one. "Last month, this month, next month," he says. "And Yasmin's on the front cover of every single one of them."

"Mmm, she's hot property right now," says Stella, picking one up and flicking through it.

"So why haven't *we* got her then?" he asks, his voice brittle with indignation at being left out.

"She won't do tabloids," says Stella matter-of-factly. "We've spoken to her agent multiple times, and Yasmin won't budge."

"Apparently she was at a Tiffany event last night, drunkenly trying to schmooze them into loaning her some jewelry for the National TV Awards on Wednesday."

Stella tuts. "Everyone's certainly exploiting their fifteen minutes of fame for all they can get these days, aren't they?"

"I don't think it's ever been any different," says Max. "There are just more people at it."

"And they're all playing the game. So did she manage to persuade them?"

Max shakes his head. "Apparently not, and by all accounts she was devastated."

"First World problems," mutters Stella.

"Precisely, but it so happens that the CEO of Tiffany is a very good friend of mine."

Stella stops wondering when the pages in a glossy magazine became distinctly unglossy, and looks at Max, her interest piqued.

"What are you proposing?" she asks, with delicious anticipation.

"Well, suppose I could arrange for Ms. Chopra to choose all the jewelry she wants."

"In exchange for . . . ?" prompts Stella, even though she knows the answer.

"In exchange for an exclusive interview," says Max, taking a swig of whiskey.

"If she's plastered over every other publication, I'm not entirely sure there's anything more for her to say."

Max raises his eyebrows in surprise. "You know as well as I do that what readers *really* want to know is written between the lines. They don't care who inspired her to cook, what her signature dish is, or what she'd pull together if she only had chicken, a banana, mustard and chocolate in the fridge."

"Not when there are unanswered questions, such as how come one of her children was born two years before she met her husband? What happened to break up her parents' marriage? And why was she bullied at school by a girl called Chardonnay? All of which is alluded to in the monthlies, but not elaborated on."

Max grins. "No matter how good an editor you are, you're always a journalist, first and foremost."

Stella smiles, grateful that she's done her homework. "It's worth a punt," she says. "It sounds like Yasmin will do anything if she gets what she wants in return."

"Put the call in, then," says Max. "I'm sure Tiffany will give her whatever she wants, as long as they get a big mention."

Taking her phone into the private pod in the corner of the newsroom floor, Stella swipes down the screen to Yasmin's agent's number.

"Hey, Mel, it's Stella Thorne."

There's an audible groan of impatience at the other end of the line.

"I've got a proposition for you," says Stella, forcing a wide grin in an attempt to stop herself from telling this glorified publicist to go fuck herself *and* her clients.

"What is it?" asks Mel, sounding as if she's already doing something far more interesting.

"We've had an approach from a high-end jeweler looking to dress a high-profile celebrity at the National TV Awards. I was thinking it might be of interest to Yasmin Chopra."

"I don't think so," says Mel. "She's not the type to sell her soul for a couple of hours in someone else's diamonds."

"*Sell her soul?*" repeats Stella, unable to keep the vitriol from her tone. "Like she hasn't already done that in every magazine over the past month."

"But you'll want even more," says Mel. "Like you always do."

"Your client seemingly wants all the exposure she can get—why would you deny her the five million readers of *The Globe*?"

Mel laughs. "And of those five million, I'd hazard a guess that half don't even have a garden, and the other half grill cut-price sausages on a disposable foil tray. So they're not exactly the target market for a barbecue cookbook, are they?"

Stella tries to swallow her indignation, but the jumped-up snob's had it coming to her for months. "When your already low-rent clients become Z-listers, you will be begging me to put them in my paper to publicize the nightclub appearance they need to make to pay their bills. Just remember this conversation, so that you'll always under-stand why none of them will *ever* be given an inch."

"They wouldn't even wipe their arse with *The Globe*," says Mel, as Stella ends the call.

"Shit!" she says, looking up out of the pod and straight into Max's office, where he's staring back at her with a questioning thumbs-up.

Stella knows how much he wants this, and she's never been one to disappoint her editor. So she smiles and gives an encouraging thumbs-up straight back at him, knowing that one way or another she's going to have to get the deal done.

11

Jess

The headlines scream out from the subs' Macs as I make my way to the toilet, and I stop mid-step, too shocked to move:

GRANVILLE STAR's DRUG SHAME.

"I CAN GET YOU WHATEVER YOU WANT," brags Tilly Ashcroft.

Page after page is laid out, every attention-grabbing headline more salacious than the last.

"Oh my god," I whisper.

"What's that, love?" asks a gruff voice, turning round from his screen to face me.

"You . . . you can't run with that," I stutter. "That's not what happened."

The man and his colleagues on the back bench laugh and guffaw, making me feel stupid and vulnerable. "Whatever, darling," he chuckles. "If you've got a problem with it, you know who to see." He tips his head in the direction of Max's office.

Their sniggering follows me into the ladies' bathroom, and I feel like I'm running from playground bullies as I rush into a cubicle and bolt the door, holding back the hot sting of tears.

Tilly hadn't said it like that. She hadn't meant it like that. She was only doing what David Phillips had asked her to do. She would have done anything he said, if it meant she got the part in the *Vortex* trilogy.

But maybe therein lies the problem.

A putrid ball of poison collects at the back of my throat at the thought that Tilly had been so cruelly exploited and taken advantage of. I only hope that she got the part, but then I realize that even if she did, she won't hang on to it, once this comes out. Sony won't touch her with a bargepole, even though they were just as complicit as she was—perhaps even more so.

I'm suddenly overcome with the ridiculous notion that I need to warn Tilly that she's been entrapped. Should I call her agent? Or the *Granville Park* press office to warn them that their most popular star is about to be exposed as a drug dealer? What would they do? What *could* they do?

Nothing, I now realize.

With renewed vigor, I fastidiously wash my hands, as though I'm ridding myself of the scum lurking in every crevice, and splash my face with cold water, forcing myself to wake up to reality.

"Oh, sorry," says a man, as he's about to bump into me coming out of the toilets.

I look at him—my already-befuddled brain is short-circuiting. *"David?"*

His brow furrows. "It's Sean actually—sorry, do I know you?"

I honestly don't know. He looks so much like David Phillips from Sony Entertainment, but he can't be. Because what would *he* be doing here?

"I'm sorry—I thought you were at the Dorchester on Saturday night, but . . ."

"Ah yes, you were my assistant," he says, his eyes lighting up as the penny drops, although I'm still quite a way behind him. "I've lost the facial hair and the suit . . ." he prompts, as I look at him numbly.

Suddenly it clicks and, despite trying to keep my lip from curling and my nostrils from flaring, I'm clearly unsuccessful.

"I'm not as awful as you might think," he says, almost apologetically.

"You're not even American," I rasp, the magnitude of what I'd been a part of finally catching up with me.

He laughs awkwardly. "No, I'm from Manchester."

"So, this . . . this is what you do when you're *not* masquerading as an American TV executive?"

"I'm the Politics editor," he says. "But I can be whoever you want me to be." He says it as if he's proud of his cunning proficiency in hoodwinking young women into believing he's a famous producer.

"Oh my god," I say, pushing past him with my hand over my mouth.

"Come and say hello next time you're passing," he calls out after me. "I'll introduce you to the team."

I walk across the newsroom, feeling like a different person; I'm no longer in the shadows of the people I'd once looked up to, but am gliding above them, holding my morals high.

"Sorry, but he's . . ." says Gail, Max's assistant, as I push open the glass door of his office and stand expectantly in front of his desk. She follows me in, breathless from the exertion of the six steps it takes; or maybe it's fear taking hold of her airways. "I'm sorry, she just barged in—" she continues.

"It's OK," says Max, holding his hand up. He waits for the door to close again. "Jess, what can I do for you?"

"I have no idea why you wanted to employ me, or why you'd think I was a good fit for *The Globe*, but I am already one hundred percent confident that I'm not."

He smiles, more to himself than to me, as he pours what looks like whiskey from a cut-glass decanter.

"And I'll be leaving at the earliest possible opportunity," I add.

"Why don't you take a seat," says Max softly. "Perhaps you'd like to join me in a drink?"

I shake my head and remain standing. "Do you have any idea how corrupt this publication that you call a *news*paper is?"

"Reporting the news is steeped in corruption," he says. "It always has been."

"You're *not* reporting the news here," I say, struggling to keep the overwhelming frustration from my voice. "You're exploiting innocent people, misrepresenting them, making them out to be something they're not."

His expression doesn't change as my accusations run off him, seemingly like water off a duck's back.

"Do you have any idea what your staff—your *senior* staff—are doing?"

"I know they're bringing in first-class stories," he says. "Which is why *The Globe* remains the biggest-selling newspaper in this country."

"But the stories aren't real," I reply, exasperated. "Your journalists, if you can call them that, are using methods such as subterfuge and entrapment to create a story; they're making people do what they otherwise wouldn't do, putting words in their mouth . . ."

He sets his tumbler down on the desk and looks at me with a grave expression. "I do not condone that kind of behavior in my newspaper and, if that is happening, then I will endeavor to find out who is perpetrating this immoral practice and severely reprimand them for it."

I raise my eyebrows doubtfully. "Well, good luck with that—there's a lot of them to hunt down."

"Why don't you help me then?" he asks.

I feel as though the carpet has been pulled from under my feet.

"You want *me* to help stamp it out?" I ask incredulously.

He nods. "Peter's on my back. He's under pressure from the PCC for us to clean up our act. We still need to bring in the big stories, but we have to make sure that the *way* we get them is watertight. We can't take any chances—everything needs to be aboveboard, completely transparent, or it'll be my head on the block."

A frisson of hope runs through me. "So what do you want me to do?"

"Keep your ear to the ground and report back to me," he says. "If you see or hear anything that makes you feel uncomfortable, then I want to know about it."

"Are you serious?" I exclaim.

"Absolutely. Of course I want *The Globe* to be the biggest-selling paper in the country, but I also need our readers to trust us. If they think that our stories and methods aren't completely kosher, they'll start leaving in their droves."

"A newspaper based on truth will still sell," I say.

"That's exactly what we need to be striving for, but there are certain individuals who'll no doubt buck the trend . . ."

It feels as if we both know exactly who he's referring to. "I don't know," I say, shaking my head. "You're asking me to spy on my colleagues."

"I wouldn't call it spying," he says. "I don't want a day-by-day report; just be aware of what's going on and if there's something that doesn't feel right, I want you to tell me."

"And what am I supposed to do in the meantime? Go along with it all, as if I don't have a problem?"

He empties his glass. "I don't anticipate it taking very long to sniff out the rotten eggs. And once they're dealt with, you'll be in pole position to work on the stories *you* think are important, reporting them in the way *you* think is more ethically sound."

I can't help but smile—it's all I've ever wanted to do. "OK," I say. "You've got yourself a deal."

12

Stella

The phone gets answered more quickly than Stella was expecting and she has to force herself to swallow the granola she was munching on.

"Hi, Yasmin, I'm so sorry to bother you, but I understand you've shown an interest in wearing some Tiffany jewelry to the National TV Awards on Wednesday night."

"Er, yes, who is this?" asks Yasmin.

Stella purposely avoids answering the question. "Well, I'm calling to say that we're so incredibly flattered and would be absolutely delighted to offer you something from our new collection."

"Oh, wow," says Yasmin. "That would be amazing."

"What do you have in mind to wear?" asks Stella. "Just so I can present you with the best items to go with it."

"I can send you a picture of my dress—would that be helpful?"

"That would be perfect," says Stella. "Has my number come up?"

"Yes, hold on one second," replies Yasmin, clearly fumbling with her phone. "Sorry, I'm in the middle of feeding the baby, so I haven't got quite as many hands available."

"Ah, you never do when you're a mum," says Stella sympathetically, even though she has no idea what it's like to be a mother. She doesn't suppose she ever will.

"I honestly can't believe it," says Yasmin. "This is so kind of you."

"We're honored that you'd even think of us," says Stella.

"OK, so I'm sending the dress over by text to you now. Shall I stay on the line to make sure you receive it?"

"That would be great."

"I hope you don't mind me asking," says Yasmin, "but how did you get hold of my number?"

Stella draws in a breath through clenched teeth. She's offering Yasmin thousands of pounds' worth of jewelry, for God's sake. "I believe you left it with one of my colleagues at our event last night."

"Ah, I'm ashamed to say I had one too many champagnes," says Yasmin. "It was my first night out since having the baby, and I think it all went to my head a little quicker than normal."

Stella forces a laugh, wondering whether now would be a good time to say that Yasmin's not getting the gems for nothing. As the text pings through on her phone, she decides to make it that little bit more difficult for her to say no.

"Oh, it's a beautiful dress," she comments, without even looking at the picture. She can hear the faux admiration in her own voice and wonders when she became as fake as the people she hounds. "We have some incredible pieces that would really come alive alongside it."

"Perhaps an emerald?" says Yasmin excitedly.

"Yes, possibly," replies Stella, although personally she'd go for a classic diamond. "Why don't you take a look at the website and see if there's anything that takes your fancy, and I'll give you a call back later today to see what we can do."

"Yes, that would be amazing," says Yasmin. "My husband's due back shortly, so he can take care of the kids while I have a look."

"Great," says Stella. "I'll speak to you then."

As she strides back to her desk, Stella clicks on the photo Yasmin sent and is pleasantly surprised. Her dress is simple, elegant and understated, so unlike the over-the-top creations that are usually paraded on the red carpet by newly famous reality stars who will do anything to stand out from the crowd. Though Yasmin will no doubt be simultaneously congratulated for keeping it real with a high-street brand, and criticized for not being glamorous enough. As Yasmin herself said, "You just can't win."

"Have you seen who's in the boss's office?" says Lottie.

Stella expects to see Peter on the warpath again, so is slightly perplexed to see Jess standing surprisingly tall on the opposite side of Max's desk. "What's *she* doing in there?"

Lottie shrugs her shoulders. "I get the impression that she and *The Globe* aren't exactly a good mix."

"Is she resigning?" asks Stella, keen to see the back of Jess. If she's not a liability already, then she fears she soon will be.

"I don't know," says Lottie. "Maybe she's being fired."

"Fingers crossed," says Stella as her phone rings. Seeing *Steve* flash up on the screen makes her hesitate. She should probably change the name again now, as she wouldn't want anyone to think she's got a man on the scene, just as much as she wouldn't want them knowing that the foreign secretary's bodyguard is on her payroll.

"Yep," she barks into the receiver, hoping that her feigned indifference will let Harry know she's got the upper hand, before he even starts to speak.

She isn't used to not having the last word, and since he walked out on her the other night, she's been itching to redress the balance. Because, like all her other relationships, the scales weigh heavily in her favor if it's control and dominance she values. Though they're pitifully light on love, companionship and security.

It's not as if she hasn't tried the latter; there was Vaughn at university, Niall on the night desk and then Dane Sommersby. But every one of them had chipped off a little something inside her; she doesn't like to call it her heart. Maybe it was her empathy, her passion, her soul . . . Until, by the end, it felt easier not to have anything worth taking.

"Hey, it's me," says Harry in his warm and friendly voice.

Stella instantly relaxes, thankful that he's not calling to pick up where they left off. She's not in the mood to argue over something that means nothing to her.

"Are you busy?" he asks.

She laughs acerbically. "When am I ever not?"

"I'm just around the corner," he says. "And I've got a couple of hours off."

His words, and the thought of him, ignite a spark deep in her groin. She looks at her watch and wonders if she couldn't take the lunch hour that is, laughably, written into her contract. "Have you got a room?" she asks, under her breath.

He tuts, but she and he both know that's why he's called, despite his half-hearted attempt to pretend it was anything else the other night.

"Yes, but the foreign secretary's in a private meeting in the suite on the floor below, so I'm only here until she finishes."

Stella imagines what it must feel like to have someone like Harry protecting you 24/7. To have him at your beck and call, for all your needs. Despite herself, she can't stop wondering whether those needs extend to ones of a sexual nature. Just because his charge is supposedly happily married doesn't make it impossible. You only have to look at every other politician in living memory to know that.

"I've got something you're going to want," he says.

"Haven't you always?" she says, her voice husky. "I'll be there in ten minutes."

"Three-two-four at the Hollington," he says.

Stella hadn't thought she needed to see him. In fact, she hadn't thought about sex *once* so far today, but now that the offer is on the table and she's within fifteen minutes—max—of it being served on a platter, she can't think of anything else.

"I'm running out to meet someone," she says, snatching her laminated pass from her desk.

Her guilty conscience implores her to add more to bolster its authenticity, but she reminds herself that she doesn't have to answer to anyone apart from Max, and seeing as he's otherwise occupied . . .

"Cool," says Lottie, the only one on the desk to bother looking up, let alone respond.

Suddenly grateful for the bodycon dress she chose to wear today, Stella debates whether to slip her metallic gold mac on over the top. While it works wonders when greeting Harry at her flat with nothing underneath, it's rather conspicuous in the sombre gray light of a September morning in London. And, as unaccustomed as she is to it, being noticed is not what she wants on this particular occasion, although by the time she sees her reflection in the lift mirrors, she wonders who she's trying to kid, because her height and bright-blonde hair create attention all on their own.

It's only a seven-minute walk to the Hollington, but she's worked herself into a frenzy by the time she arrives, imagining Harry's hands roaming over her body, his tongue setting fire to her skin. Without even considering the camera in the hotel lift, she steps out of her knickers and throws them in her bag. Not only will it drive Harry wild, but it will also save time.

Hence she finds it hard to hide her disappointment, *and* irritation, when he opens the door to room 324 fully clothed. Does he not realize she's on borrowed time?

"Hey," he says, looking her up and down appreciatively.

Her mouth finds his as she pushes him back against the wall, kicking the door shut with her foot. Her hand is already on his crotch, desperately tugging at the zip that separates her from what she needs.

"Whoa," he says, pulling away. "Can we just talk for a minute?"

Stella stops abruptly and looks at him, astounded. "Are you serious? I haven't got time for this."

"I tried to tell you the other night, but . . ." he goes on.

"I'm too busy to play games," she says, going for his fly again.

"I need to tell you something," he says, holding her off.

She throws her arms down by her side, like a petulant child who's been told she has to eat all her greens before she can have a dessert.

"How much will it cost me?" she huffs.

"It's got to be worth a bag of sand," he says, his deep-blue eyes toying with her. She'd happily pay double that if he'd just give her what she came for.

She reminds herself that she pays him for information, not sex. Information that, she's recently noted, is not coming quite as fast and furious as the sex is.

Harry used to offer her a lead every other week, whether it was intel on a high-profile police case or privileged information on the private life of the foreign secretary he was supposed to be safeguarding. Both were equally valuable, and both were well rewarded, but these days their liaisons were more often spent in bed than discussing the secrets of the Cabinet. Maybe what he's about to divulge now will bring about a turn in the tide.

"OK, fine, what is it?" she asks, falling onto the bed resignedly.

He looks at her, as if weighing up the best line of approach. "McAllister has got parole," he says, going for the bold and direct option.

"*Ray* McAllister?" asks Stella needlessly.

Harry nods.

The tap that had turned her on instantly turns her off again, her arousal immediately doused with a bucket of cold water.

"Shit!" she says as her mind rehashes the ramifications that she's spent the past four years trying to bury.

Harry grimaces. "A release date's been set for Wednesday."

"*This* Wednesday?" says Stella, her voice high-pitched. "Could you not have given me more notice?"

"I tried to tell you the other night," he says.

"You should have tried harder," she replies. "I needed to know this the moment you found out."

"It's not always easy getting the information you want to know," he says.

"Why not?" asks Stella harshly. "I pay you enough."

Harry looks at the floor, his vigor suddenly diminished.

"In fact, I probably pay you more than the Met does," Stella goes on. "So you should be giving me the answers I want before I even know I want them."

"Do you have *any* idea what I'm putting on the line for you?" he says. "I could get sacked. I could even go to prison. *You* could go to prison."

Stella shrugs nonchalantly, though the thought unnerves her. Despite her devil-may-care attitude, she's spent many a night thinking about what would happen if she were caught conspiring to aid misconduct in public office—almost as many nights as wondering what Ray McAllister will do to her when he gets out.

"Don't pretend you're doing it for me," she says. "You give me privileged information because I pay you for it."

Harry sighs and puts his hands on his hips. "What part of this are you not getting?" he says, raising his voice for the first time. "Not everything has to be a business transaction."

Stella looks at him, knowing what he's trying to imply, but refusing to allow herself to believe it.

"What other type of transaction is there?" she asks harshly, though if he knows her at all, he'll be able to feel her resolve softening.

Harry kneels down on the carpet in front of her. "I'd give you what you want for free." He takes hold of her hand and she fears she knows what's coming. "If it gave me an excuse to see you."

In the loaded silence that follows, she feels compelled to laugh or issue a sardonic put-down, more out of habit than anything else, but as he strokes her cheek, she bites her tongue.

"Will McAllister be kept under surveillance?" she asks, feeling suddenly vulnerable. "Will he be tagged so that the police can monitor his movements?" She only has to look at Harry's face to know the answer. "So he can conspire to kidnap the Tory party leader, be armed when he was arrested, issue death-threats to me and Max throughout his trial and walk out of prison four years later, free to roam wherever he wants?" She stops herself, as she hears her voice start to wobble.

"He's served his time."

She scoffs. "He's served just over half."

"There'll be parole conditions he'll need to adhere to, and unless he wants to go straight back inside, he'd be stupid to darken *your* door again."

"That doesn't mean he won't darken somebody else's."

"There's always a chance," says Harry. "But the man he was conspiring to kidnap is now the prime minister. You can't get more high-profile than that, so he'd be wise to stay under the radar and keep his nose clean, because as soon as he sticks his head above the parapet, the police, the media and the government will be gunning for him."

Stella feels mildly placated to know that the country's most powerful agencies will all be on high alert, though if they're focusing on the safety of the prime minister, she can't help but wonder who's going to be looking out for her.

13

Jess

The pub that I know journalists frequent at all hours of the day is woefully empty when I arrive, and I immediately wonder if this is going to be a waste of time. Though when I check my watch and see it's not yet midday, I tell myself I'm never going to know if I'm not patient.

"What can I get you?" asks the smiling barmaid, happy to have something to do.

"Can I have a white wine, please?" I say, before adding, "Make it a large."

"Sure thing," she says.

"I expected it to be . . ." I start, looking around for the best place to sit. I opt for a seat at the bar, next to an oversized vase of flowers.

"Busier?" she asks.

I nod, watching as she pours the golden liquid into a glass. As someone who invariably prefers a soft drink over alcohol, I wouldn't want what she's about to serve on a Friday night out on the town with Flic, let alone sitting on my own in a bar on a Monday morning. Flic doesn't understand my reticence, but she accepts it and defends me when ignorant buffoons take offense when I don't accept their offer to buy me a drink.

"A *water*?" they mock, as if they've heard me incorrectly. "What are you—the fun police?"

"Hey, don't be thinking for a second that my girl's not up for having a good time," Flic will often interject. "She'll still be on that dance floor, long after your sorry arses have keeled over in the corner, and she'll be the one who wants to do it all again tomorrow, when the rest of us can't even lift our heads off the pillow."

The guys will shrug their shoulders, considering themselves suitably educated, although to date, my abstinence and their understanding still haven't garnered anything more than a couple of entertaining sleepovers and a one-night stand that turned into a three-week relationship, purely because the guy had lost his job and I felt sorry for him.

Maybe Flic's prediction that this new job will bring about a change in fortune will come true. At twenty-five, I know my mum and dad would like to think so. They'd love nothing more than for me to meet a fellow journalist, though he'd need to be of the broadsheet variety, of course. A hack from *The Globe* certainly wouldn't cut it, and nor would a columnist from *The Post*, which—seeing how handsome Dane Sommersby is, as he walks in and shirks off his blazer—is something of a shame.

"Hi, Dane, how was your weekend?" asks the barmaid coquettishly, equally enamored, it seems.

He flashes her a knowing smile, and I can't make out if the look they share is pre-or post-coital. If it's the latter, then it's blatantly obvious that she's looking for a repeat performance.

The split-second heat of the moment gives me the opportunity to upend my wineglass into the vase beside me.

"Can I have another?" I ask loudly, keen to get Dane's attention onto me rather than her.

"Sure thing," says the barmaid, unable to hide her irritation that their fleeting spell has been broken.

"Sorry, I didn't mean to interrupt anything," I say, half slurring, though even *I* know what a lightweight I'd have to be, if I'm mumbling my words after one glass. "It's just that I've had one hell of a morning . . ."

I leave it there, half hoping that Dane will be the one who feels the need to inquire further. But knowing the type of journalist he is, I doubt he'll be up-front enough to ask outright. He's of the weasel variety, predisposed to a slow and painful kill, even when his belly is already full.

"What's up?" asks the barmaid instead. She couldn't sound any more disinterested if she tried, but she's obviously so used to patrons sharing their woes that it's an automatic response.

"Urgh," I groan. "I've just started this new job and it's a nightmare." I let my head drop into my hands, snatching a glimpse at Dane to check that's he's listening. His head stays fixed, focused forward. "I've only been there for a week, but the moral bar is so low that I can't see how I'm going to make it to Friday."

"You in the print?" the woman asks absentmindedly.

I nod and tip my glass back, but I keep my lips firmly pressed together.

"I'm on the News desk at *The Globe*," I say, sensing Dane's head swivel round.

"Oh, that's a notoriously hard gig," she says.

Dane surreptitiously takes a seat on one of the bar stools, and I'm sure I can hear his brain whirring as he decides how best to play this.

"I'm only a junior, but I'm not sure I can stomach my editor for much longer—she's truly something else."

"A bad boss can be intolerable," pipes up Dane, his attempt to sound nonchalant pitiful. Every fiber in his body is itching to ask me more to get the low-down on exactly who I'm referring to, and it gives me no greater pleasure than to make him wait. If he thinks he's going to get the gossip on his biggest competitor, then he'll have to work a lot harder than that. Or he at least needs to think I'm not going to give him what he wants at the drop of a hat.

The sound of a glass breaking rings out, and as their heads turn to the corner table, I use the opportunity to pour three-quarters of my wine into the vase. The elegant snapdragons that stood so tall when I first arrived are already drooping.

"Can I get you another?" asks Dane, his eyes alight with a mischief that my naivety would normally confuse with flirtation.

"Sure," I say glibly, forcing myself to finish the dregs in my glass, if only to show I was willing.

"Same again," he says to the barmaid with a nod in my direction.

She looks at me with a nostril-flared grimace, her amiable attitude having quickly been replaced by the sense that she'd like to kill me.

Dane moves his stool ever so slightly closer to mine. "Do you wanna talk about it?" he says, laughably. "I can't lay claim to knowing what it must be like to work under that kind of pressure, but I've had my fair share of shitty bosses."

I will my eyes to narrow in consideration, or else I fear my wry amusement will give me away.

"I bet you've never met anyone quite like Stella Thorne," I say, raising my glass in thanks before taking a large glug. The acidic liquid courses down my throat like paint-stripper and I shudder involuntarily.

"Clearly not a seasoned drinker," he observes. "She must be quite something to have you knocking them back before lunch on a Monday."

"You have no idea," I say bitterly, though my research proves he knows her better than most.

"So you're a reporter?"

I nod, the simple act seemingly sending me off-balance, and I wobble precariously on the stool.

"Whoa there," Dane says, reaching out to hold me up. "How many have you had?"

I hold my fingers up and count. "Four or five," I state, lowering my voice so that the barmaid doesn't correct me.

"So what's happened?" he asks, with genuine interest.

"I can't even begin to tell you," I mumble. "If you—the general public—knew what she did to get stories . . ." I roll my eyes theatrically. "I mean, you'd never buy *The Globe* ever again."

"I'm more of a *Post* reader myself," he says.

I attempt a smile, though it probably looks more like a grimace to him. "That's a good thing," I reply. "They at least seem to have *some* scruples—a moral compass of sorts."

"I don't know about that," he says, laughing. "So what has your boss done that's pissed you off so much?" His eagerness to get to the crux of the matter is comical, though if I were as drunk as he thinks I am, I doubt I'd even notice.

I look at Dane as if weighing up whether I should trust him. "If I tell you, do you promise not to say anything to anyone?"

"Cross my heart and hope to die," he says, drawing lines on his chest.

"She's done a really bad thing," I whisper, peering around furtively. He leans in closer. "How bad?"

"She's framed someone for something they didn't do."

His eyes widen. "*Really? Who?*"

"I've had way-y-y too much to drink," I say, my words stretched out and garbled. "I shouldn't be saying anything. I'm going to regret it later."

"Your secret is safe with me," Dane says earnestly. "It might even be helpful to talk about it. I'm no expert and I don't know how the press works, but I might be able to give you an outsider's viewpoint."

I force my involuntary guffaw into a cough. Are all tabloid jour-nalists seriously this unscrupulous and shameful in their pursuit of a story that isn't theirs to tell? If that's honestly the case, what hope in hell do Max and I have of turning the narrative around?

"She set up a really famous actress . . ." I start, before pulling myself up. How much do I need Dane to know in order to get the job done, without running the risk of him printing the exposé in *The Post*?

"*Who?*" he asks, far too keenly.

I hadn't thought this far ahead, and I need to take a second before I throw caution to the wind. There's a fine line between needing to stop *The Globe* printing its salacious fake story, and protecting Tilly from the other piranhas that are circling in the waters below.

"Have you . . . have you heard of Tilly Ashcroft?" I ask hesitantly, unable to stop myself wondering what would happen if my grand plan were to backfire spectacularly.

His brow furrows, his face clouding over with confusion. "The name rings a bell," he says.

"You'd know her if you saw her," I offer, to help jog his memory, while knowing Dane doesn't need it. "She's the brassy barmaid on *Granville Park.*"

"Pretty young thing, with dark hair?" he says vaguely.

"That's the one!" I exclaim. "Well, my boss set her up on Saturday night, by luring her to an 'audition.' " I draw speech marks in the air, before forcing a wobble and reaching out to hold on to the bar. "But in reality she was being groomed to commit an illegal act."

"Wow," he says, trying to keep the corners of his mouth from turning up. "What did she do?"

I cup my hand around my mouth and lean into his ear. "She—" I break off, openly chastising myself. "I'm going to get in so much trouble for this . . ."

"It means nothing to me," he says encouragingly. "But it might make you feel better if you share it. I can tell you if I think you're overreacting."

How very noble of him.

"No," I say, shaking my head vigorously. "No, I should just cut my losses and get out of here, before I say something I'll regret."

"Come on," Dane says, placing a hand on mine. "One more drink for the road."

I look at him as if I'm seriously considering it.

"This one's on me," he continues, beckoning the barmaid over.

"No, I really should be going," I say, stumbling as I lift myself off the stool. "I fear I've said far too much already."

"What was the illegal act?" he calls out in desperation, as I weave my way through the bodies that have accumulated surprisingly quickly.

"You'll find out in Friday's paper," I say, without looking back. "Unless someone else beats us to it."

14

Stella

"Don't you *dare* answer that," pants Harry as Stella moves up and down above him, the pair of them so close to climaxing.

She throws her head back and closes her eyes, desperately trying to shut out the incessant ringtone, but the need to answer it is even stronger than the need for an orgasm.

As if sensing her distraction, Harry takes hold of her hips, locking her to him as he thrusts in and out with a sudden urgency. But Stella's mind is no longer on the matter in hand and as the desire fades, the only vibration she can focus on is that of her phone.

"Fuck!" says Harry, as she lifts herself off him abruptly.

"Stella Thorne," she says, breathlessly, into the phone.

"Where the fuck are you?" barks Max.

As she jumps off the bed, Harry moans in discontent, and she glares at him as she hurriedly steps into the dress that he unzipped her out of just ten minutes before.

"I'm following up on something," she says.

"Well, I suggest you get your arse back to the newsroom, because we've got a bit of an issue on our hands."

"OK, I'm on my way," she replies, using the sideboard for support as she slips on her Louboutin heels.

There's a sardonic "Bye, then" as she closes the door behind her, but Stella's already too much in work mode to care.

"Lottie, it's me," she says when she eventually gets service in the hotel lobby. "What's going on?"

"Where are you?" she whispers. "Max is going mental."

"What about?" asks Stella, desperate to know what's happened and trying to quell the hammering in her chest.

"I don't know," says Lottie. "But he's pacing the floor like a caged lion."

"OK, I'll be there in five minutes," says Stella, feeling ever so slightly sick.

She runs as fast as her heels will carry her, while desperately trying to work out what might have riled Max. He gets like this sometimes—and she's normally the one to calm him down—but there's something in her gut that's telling her she's the cause, and not the cure, this time.

By the time she walks onto the newsroom floor there's an uncharacteristic streak of sweat running down her spine. Not helped by the ambient temperature in the open-plan office feeling like it's risen another degree. Heads turn away and eyes avert as Stella makes her way across to the glass box in the corner, where Peter is pacing the floor, gesticulating wildly, and Max is sitting with his head in his hands.

"What's going on?" asks Stella as she opens the door, trying to keep her voice steady and measured.

"*What's going on . . .*" mimics Max in a high-pitched voice, "is that the whole world and his wife know our exclusive for Friday. That's what's fucking going on."

Stella looks from him to Peter. "What do you mean—the whole world?" she asks, trying not to let Max's histrionics cloud her judgment. At least not in front of Peter. "*Who*, exactly?"

Max pushes his chair away from underneath him. "*The Post*, the

PCC, who have been on the phone reminding me of the Editors'
Code of Practice."

"How did they find out?"

Max throws his arms up in the air, exasperated. "Take a wild guess."

"Max tells me it was *your* decision to lay the pages down early?"
says Peter, his eyes narrowing.

Stella's mouth drops open as she's thrown under the bus.

"Is that true?" asks Peter, looking at her.

She's stuck between a rock and a hard place, not knowing which
is the lesser of the two evils. Does she stand her ground and make her
position clear to the man who could ultimately make her editor? Or
does she appease the editor she has to spend every day with, and take
one for the team to save his skin?

"Well, I—" she starts.

"So, who's the leak?" Peter asks, cutting her off.

They all look out to the newsroom floor, where fifty or so staff are
trying to appear as if they are hard at work. Moving heads can be seen
just above half-height partitions, and a department meeting seems to
be taking place beside the vending machine. "It could be any one of
them," says Max.

"Where's Jess?" asks Stella. If she sounds suspicious, she hadn't
meant to, but now that she thinks about it . . .

"She's gone for a break," he says.

"Who's Jess?" asks Peter brusquely.

"She's a rookie," says Max. "And she's too wet behind the ears to
ruffle feathers to this degree."

"You say that, but she's only been here for a week, and all of a sudden we've got a breach." Stella looks between him and Peter, sensing
an opportunity. "What was she doing in here this morning?"

Max's eyes shift involuntarily, and he runs a finger needlessly
around the back of his collar. If Stella didn't know better, she'd hazard a guess that she's caught him on the hop.

"She was pitching me a story," he says. "But it's too low-grade for us."

Stella nods, but something's amiss. "Lottie thought she might be resigning."

"No, no, no," says Max. "Jess is still finding her feet and I think she just needs a bit of extra support."

"*Support?*" laughs Stella. "We're not in the business of hand-holding. If she can't hack it, she needs to get out."

"Give her a break," says Max. "You were a rookie once."

But I was a stalwart from the off, she thinks. *Committed and ferociously loyal from the very first day I started working here.*

It feels like only yesterday that she walked wide-eyed and naive onto the newsroom floor of *The Globe on Sunday*. Although the weekend edition comes from the same stable, it's an entirely different editorial team that produces it, and the two newspapers might as well be on opposing sides of a boxing ring, both of them baying for the other's blood.

For a graduate fresh out of university, Stella had found the underhand tactics both shocking and amusing, unable to comprehend why two publications in the same corporation were essentially at war with one another. But less than a month in, she found herself dressed as a cleaner, biding her time in a broom cupboard, waiting to glean the exclusives from their daily rival.

It was Max who had smoked her out and dragged her on a walk of shame to the editor's office. She'd envisaged him calling the police to report the thief in their midst, or at the very least calling her own editor and demanding that she be fired. But instead he applauded her chutzpah and offered her a job.

She and Max had been working together ever since, and for the most part they were a good team. But ever since he was made editor over her, eighteen months ago, it had felt like there was a power struggle at play. He wanted to assert his authority, and she admittedly went out of her way to push back against it.

She wonders, as she looks at him pacing up and down, if he's as aware as she is that the year and a half's head start that he had at *The Globe* before she joined is now more pertinent than ever.

The clock is ticking. Can he hear it as loudly as she can?

"If there's a leak on the news floor, I want it plugged. Fast," says Peter, his jaw twitching. He pulls on the cuffs of his shirt, signaling he's about to leave.

"Of course," says Max submissively. "But what do we do with Friday's issue?"

"Did the interview take place with this Tilly girl or not?" asks Peter.

"Yes, of course it took place," says Max. "We may sail a bit close to the wind sometimes, but we don't *invent* stories."

"And is it all on tape?"

"Yes, audio and visual," says Stella.

"So what's the problem?" asks Peter.

"The issue is more likely to be how we obtained the interview," says Max, looking at Stella with a grimace.

Peter stands there with his hands on his hips, waiting for one of them to elaborate.

"We set up a sting," says Stella quietly.

"Oh, for fuck's sake," he roars. "Whose bright idea was that?"

Max and Stella look at each other. "Well, I signed it off . . ." says Max, shrugging his shoulders. "But it was Stella's brainchild and she set it all up."

He immediately looks away, so he doesn't see Stella's eyes widen as he once again throws her to the lions. It's beginning to become a habit.

Peter rubs a hand roughly over his gray stubble. "What have I told you about this?" he asks, exasperated. "I'll need to talk to the lawyers, but if you don't hear from me, go ahead as scheduled."

"Right," says Max.

"Walk with me," Peter says to Stella, his voice commanding.

Shit! She's got between here and the lift to talk him into letting her keep her job.

With square-on shoulders and a set jaw, Peter's arms move rhythmically in line with his legs, marching with intention. People almost fall backward to let him through, loosening their collars once he's passed, grateful to have lived another day.

As Stella scurries behind him, she can't help but wonder what it must be like to be Peter Kingsley. To be fawned over and feared in equal measure, often simultaneously. Because regardless of what you may think of his business practices, you can't help but be in awe of the media empire he's created.

Owner of the world's biggest-selling newspapers, a multimedia sports channel that has the highest viewing figures globally and a film production company that is the toast of Hollywood, Peter has monopolized the industry for more than thirty years, although his critics would dare to suggest that his business brain isn't quite what it used to be; that he's getting too old to be spending half his week in London and the other half in New York. But when you're able to make the seven-hour commute in a private jet and be met on the tarmac in a chauffeur-driven bulletproof Range Rover, it's probably less stressful than Stella's fifteen-mile journey back and forth to Richmond.

Peter doesn't have to think about anything other than the business in hand, as all his other needs are catered for. Although with Mrs. Kingsley permanently ensconced in their chateau in the South of France, Stella knows that it's not only his food preferences that are satisfied elsewhere.

He calls the lift, only to call another when it arrives with somebody already in it.

That's because he doesn't want anyone to overhear him fire me, thinks Stella, as the ping of the next one sounds like the death-knell of her career.

"You've made a great impact on *The Globe*," he says as they step into the empty lift.

But . . . she waits for him to say.

"And I've been hugely impressed with your tenacity and ability to bring in the best stories," he goes on.

"Thank you," she says, wondering if now would be a good time to eulogize how much she loves what she does, and what *The Globe* means to her.

"This sting with the soap star being your best yet, if the headlines and pictures are to be believed." He looks at Stella for affirmation.

"It's all gold dust," she says, wanting to smile, but still unsure of where this is going.

"Can I level with you?" Peter says, looking at her.

Stella nods as her mouth dries up.

"All I care about is selling newspapers," he says. "But we're no longer *news* sellers."

She looks at him with a furrowed brow.

"We can't expect to compete with twenty-four-hour news channels and social media to report the news. Those days are gone. But what we *can* do is bring our readers the best *stories*—the ones other platforms can't get. I don't care where they come from or how you get them; what I do care about is not being able to print them. I'd rather spend a hundred grand putting a libel case quietly to bed than lose the million we would have gained in revenue, if we'd printed it."

The lift doors open onto the lobby, and those waiting part like the Red Sea as Peter steps out.

"So you need to find the mole," he goes on. "Because I will not have these stories—stories that need to be told—cut off at the pass because someone on my payroll is taking a backhander to leak them."

"Understood," says Stella, as a bodyguard in a black suit and redundant sunglasses steps out from the shadows of a pillar.

"Listen, I'm having my annual get-together at my place in the country this weekend—just a few of my top execs from the global corporation . . ."

"Right," says Stella, not knowing why he's telling her this.

"I want *you* there," he goes on, heading toward the revolving doors.

"M-me?" stutters Stella, blindsided by this turn of events. "Well, that would be lovely, but . . ."

He stops walking and turns to face her with a confused expression, clearly unused to an invitation being contested.

"What's the problem?" he asks.

"Well, I . . ." she starts, wondering why she's even pretending she's got anything on that can't be moved. Still, it won't hurt him to think that she might. She knows Peter doesn't respect a pushover. Perhaps that's why Max isn't doing quite as well as expected.

"So I'll see you on Friday," he says, striding off.

"OK, great, I look forward to it."

"Oh, and Stella," he says, turning to face her, "keep up the good work."

15

Jess

Sitting in the pod, looking out across the newsroom, I can't help but marvel at how my life has been transformed. Two weeks ago I was filing a story on how someone's toaster had burned Elvis's face onto a piece of bread, and now I'm about to call the shadow home secretary and put a very serious dent in the normal practices of a tabloid.

I have no idea how he's going to take what I've got to say, but Max is confident he'll be happier at the end of the call than at the beginning. "Just push on through," he said. "He'll loathe you and love you simultaneously."

I'd balked at the thought. I don't want anyone to loathe me, but Max had been reassuring.

"You're doing the right thing—a *good* thing. Isn't that what you want?"

My fingers play with the Post-it note on which he'd written down the personal phone number of Ned Jacobs's communications director, while I plan how best to say what needs to be said.

"Come on, Jess," I say out loud, in an effort to spur myself into action. "You can do this." Clearing my throat, I thumb the digits into my phone and press call, desperate for it to be answered before my reticence wins out.

"Yep," barks a voice down the line, belying his job title.

"Oh, hi," I say breezily. "It's Jess Townsend here, calling from *The Globe*."

"What do *you* want?" he groans.

I swallow. "It seems we have a bit of a situation," I start, playing for time. "We happen to have something in our possession that you should know about."

He sighs. "I haven't got time to play games—what is it?"

I'd expected to engage in a little more small-talk before getting to the crux of the matter.

"We have reason to believe that Mr. Jacobs is having an affair," I blurt out, not knowing any other way of saying it.

"Yeah, you and every other goddamn publication in this country," he says, sounding completely unfazed. "Have you actually got anything you'd like comment on, or can I get on with something more worthwhile, like sticking pins in my eyes?"

"We actually have proof," I say, as quietly as I can.

"OK," he says, humoring me. "Is it a copy of a receipt for the earrings he bought his wife for her birthday, or has a waiter got photographic evidence of Ned and his secretary having lunch together last week?" I can hear him tapping away on his keyboard, having already moved on to his next job, bored of our conversation.

"Er, we have video footage of him in a hotel with Marianne Kapinsky," I say.

There's an uncomfortable silence.

"And there's absolutely no doubt that their relationship is more than platonic," I add.

He kisses his teeth. "This sounds like a Stella Thorne classic."

"I'm not at liberty to name our source," I say, easing into the role of playing good cop, bad cop. "But what I will say is that the story we've been presented with is not the story we want to run."

"So you want to reverse-ferret?" he asks.

"Exactly," I say, not having a clue what he's talking about. "The images we have are not synonymous with how we would like to be portrayed. With how we'd like to portray Mr. Jacobs."

"That's not like *The Globe*, especially where the Labor party is concerned. You normally go for the jugular."

"Well, we're looking to change how we approach these kinds of stories," I offer. "We no longer want to associate ourselves with tawdry kiss-and-tells."

"Has anyone told Stella Thorne?"

"So I'd like to make a proposal," I say, ignoring his slight. As much as I'd like to get into a mud-slinging match, it'll only intensify his already hollow opinion of Stella, of *us*.

"Let me guess," he says wearily. "You won't run what you've got if we give you something better?"

"Well, yes," I say, feeling slightly put-out that he's beaten me to it. I'd wanted to revel in that good news for a while, hold it back, assuming he'd be delighted. But as it turns out, he sounds about as happy as a damp squib.

"So what do you want?" he asks tightly.

"My editor would like an interview with Mr. and Mrs. Jacobs and a photoshoot with the children—a really wholesome piece focusing on family values."

"And in return you'll not mention the indiscretion you claim to have uncovered?"

"Absolutely!" I say, my chest puffing out with moral fiber. "We want to take it back to basics. Give the British people politicians they can look up to."

I haven't seen the video footage Stella had obtained—probably illegally or, if not, then most definitely unethically. But I can't imagine it shows Ned Jacobs in any a worse light than every other MP the tabloids have tried to taint.

"We want to concentrate on policy and promises," I go on, sounding like a politician myself. "Not on what someone gets up to in their own free time."

He coughs awkwardly. "I'll have to speak to Ned and come back to you," he says curtly. "At the very least, we'll give you a holding response."

"Thank you, I'll wait to hear from you."

"Will you, or are you just going to run it anyway?"

"You have my word that we won't do anything until we hear from you."

"I appreciate that," he says, sounding genuinely grateful for the first time. "I'll speak to you soon."

Unable to keep the smile from my face, I end the call and immediately look up "reverse-ferret."

16

Stella

There's a knock at the door in the middle of the night and, expecting it to be Harry, Stella opens it without even looking through the peephole. A man stands there with a manic grin on his face, reminding her of Jack Nicholson in *The Shining*.

"Have you missed me?" he asks, as she stumbles backward into the hall, her hands grasping for anything she can use as a weapon.

"Wh-what are you doing here?" she hears herself asking.

"I told you I'd be back," he says, pulling on a pair of black gloves. "Did you think I'd forget?"

He backs her into the living room, his black eyes never leaving hers. "There's someone here," she lies breathlessly. "In the bedroom. He's a police officer."

The man throws his head back and laughs. "When have I ever been frightened of the police? Go get him—he can join in the fun."

It's the sinister sound of the unfurling duct tape that wakes Stella up with a start.

Her eyes shoot open and she looks around the dark room, desperately searching for the silhouette of something familiar to prove that she's in the safe haven of her bedroom. It's only when she sees the mirror of her dressing table gleam in the moonlight that she remembers to breathe.

"Fuck!" she says out loud, feeling the bed beside her, just to make sure she's on her own, although when she finds it empty, she almost wishes it wasn't.

The dampness of her back is accentuated by the cool air as she lifts herself up and swings her legs onto the floor. It's not yet 4 a.m., but as much as she wants to go back to sleep, she doesn't dare. Not if it means the return of Ray McAllister.

She thought these nightmares were a thing of the past, but knowing that this time tomorrow McAllister will be out of prison has brought it all rushing back.

She knew this day would come, but it had always seemed so far off. Another lifetime away. One where she'd left the profession she loved and had moved out of town to somewhere he'd never find her—where she could put it all behind her and start afresh. But she's never been one for hiding herself away, especially when she's done nothing wrong. That's why, four years on, she finds herself in the same job and the same flat . . . But instead of feeling her normal, secure self, knowing that McAllister can't reach her, she now feels like a sitting duck.

She has often wondered if she would have done anything differently if she had her time over again. But in all reality, she didn't have a choice.

When Max had told her that he'd received a tip-off about a plot to kidnap the leader of the opposition, Stella initially thought it was someone out to make a quick buck. They got calls every day from armchair detectives making up outlandish claims, so it was part of their job to sift the wheat from the chaff. But with the impending election, at which Jeff Greaves was expected to get a landslide victory for the Conservative party, it was too risky to ignore.

"They're going to do it in election week, while he's on the campaign trail, and demand ten million pounds ransom for his safe return," Max had said, coming off the phone from one of his trusted criminal sources.

"I'd give them fifteen if it means the Tory twat doesn't get to spout his right-wing rhetoric for the next four years," replied Stella.

Max had chortled. "Still backing Labor, even though they've brought this country to its knees?"

She'd looked at him witheringly. He should have known better than to question her left-wing stance; she might have been fast approaching thirty-five, but her socialist parents would kill her if she voted any other way.

"Do you honestly think it's a real possibility?" Stella had asked, suddenly serious.

"My contact says he's been brought in as the driver," Max had said. "It might be worth a meet?"

"OK," said Stella, feeling the first flutterings of something big.

On the morning they'd gone to meet the man named Akin Demir, they had sat on back-to-back benches on platform eleven of Victoria station, so paranoid was Akin that someone would see them together.

"I'm putting my neck on the line for this," he'd said.

"If it pans out, I'll make it worth your while," said Max.

"If it doesn't, either I'll be dead or Greaves will," Akin had said chillingly. "I want twenty-five K, nonnegotiable."

Stella had silently balked and shaken her head. They'd never paid that for a tip-off, and she wasn't about to start now. But Max had looked at her in a way that suggested he might, and as he was the News editor at the time, he had more clout to get a payment like that authorized.

"How do we know you're not bluffing?" Stella had asked.

Akin had kicked a holdall under the bench toward her. "Does it look like I'm bluffing?"

Lifting the cover of the canvas sports bag, she had peered inside. The color had drained from her face when she saw a gun.

"McAllister and his gang are scoping out the hotel tomorrow night," he had said, "working out the details of Greaves's stay there next week. That'll be your only chance to stop this from happening, because the next time will be the real thing and it'll be too late."

"What do you want to do?" Max had asked Stella, as the pair of them watched Akin walking away.

Knowing that he could use the gun in that bag at any moment had made Stella's hands perspire. A train was just pulling in, and throngs of people were stepping off it and walking alongside him on the platform. She could hear the chatter of tiny voices as a pre-prep class was being counted, before being led away to what was sure to be an exciting day out.

"Well, we can't let people like him carry on walking the streets, can we?" she said, turning to Max with raised eyebrows.

"So do you want to shop him now or get the story first?" asked Max.

"Oh, I wanna get the story first," she said, with a smile.

The next night, she, Max and a photographer were staking out a Premier Inn car park from the second floor of the hotel. An armed-response unit was undercover on the ground, waiting for the gang to meet Akin at the pre-arranged time.

When the van rolled into view, Stella's chest had tightened and she'd shot a look at Max, silently asking, *Are we doing the right thing?*

"Think of who we're saving," he'd said in response, knowing her better than she even knew herself.

Suddenly there was a rush of activity below them. Speeding cars, flashing lights and calls of *get on the floor*, which she could hear from all the way down there. As the police aimed their guns at the men's heads, she could see Max nudging the photographer, making sure he got every jot and tot for the next day's front page.

As it turned out, the exclusive ran across eight pages, with a grateful Jeff Greaves and his family giving Max an interview and a photoshoot on the sprawling lawns of his luxurious house in his constituency village of Burford.

When the high-profile case was expedited to the Old Bailey, Stella had expected it to be an open-and-shut affair. They had all the evidence: audio, visual and a sworn witness statement from Akin. There was no way McAllister could deny his involvement.

Except that he did.

He claimed he had been set up; that he'd been played by Akin and entrapped by *The Globe*.

What was scheduled to be a two-week trial had dragged out to six, with Stella's turn on the witness stand lasting three days alone. McAllister had glared at her the entire time, baring his teeth whenever she dared to look in his direction. It was terrifying to be questioned under his unrelenting, intimidating stare, but she was secure in the knowledge that every word she spoke was the truth and, thankfully, the judge and jury believed her.

She shudders now, wrapping her robe tighter around her, as she recalls the vitriol in McAllister's voice as he issued his death threat. She'd spent weeks looking over her shoulder at every turn, waiting for one of his henchmen to take her out at Starbucks or to show up at her parents' house and send her photos of her father's severed head.

As she fingers the double crosses carved into her arm, Stella can't help but think that she got off lightly.

Until now.

17

Jess

I can feel the damp of my armpits seeping through my blouse as I sit in stationary traffic in the back of a taxi with £50,000-worth of Tiffany jewelry on my lap. The iconic blue box is burning a hole through my bag, as I wait for someone to wrench open the door and snatch it from me.

"Is there no faster route?" I ask the driver, not because I'm late, but because I really don't want the responsibility of this on my shoulders for a second longer than necessary.

He doesn't hear me, as he's got the radio turned up too loud.

"Excuse me," I say, tapping on the glass that separates us.

"Oh, sorry, pet, I was just listening to the news," he says in a cockney accent. "I was rather hoping this Ned Jacobs fella was a good egg—would represent the values of his party—but he's been exposed as a sleazy love-cheat." He tuts and shakes his head. "They're all the bloody same."

I can see *The Globe*'s front-page exclusive in my mind's eye, can feel the indignation that had prickled every pore as I stormed into Max's office this morning. "You told me we were dropping this, in exchange for the family interview and photoshoot," I said.

He'd shrugged his shoulders despondently. "We had an editorial meeting with the board late last night and I was overruled."

"But I promised him we wouldn't run this if he gave us the interview. What was the point in sending Lottie and a photographer down there yesterday, if you were never going to stick to our side of the deal?"

"Stella stated her case for the sting," he said. "And, rather surprisingly, Peter went for it."

"So she wins, *again*?"

"She's very . . . persuasive," Max said, the intimation alluding to so much more.

"So what's the point in doing what we're trying to do, if we're flogging a dead horse?"

He'd looked at me resignedly. "The stable door may be open, but the horse hasn't bolted . . . *yet*. We'll splash the pics, and how much he loves his wife, in tomorrow's edition—I'd imagine he'll appreciate it."

I don't imagine Ned Jacobs will be in the least bit appreciative. I'd thought we were trying to shift the narrative; that this would bring about a sea change, but all the time we're battling against Stella it's going to be one step forward, two steps back.

I look at the map on my phone and see that I'm less than half a mile away from Yasmin Chopra's hotel. Running a quick risk-assessment, I scan the pavements of Knightsbridge through the window and quickly deduce that most of the pedestrians have got more bling on show than I've got hidden away.

"I'll jump out here," I say, unable to bear the upward trajectory of the fare-meter for a moment longer.

I quicken my pace as I walk along Kensington Gore, past the Royal Albert Hall, where tonight's National TV Awards are taking place, and on to the Royal Garden Hotel. A jogger rushes at me from the park and I clutch my bag to my chest.

The hotel lobby is awash with activity: porters pushing trolleys laden with oversized gowns, the concierge's phone ringing off the hook and guests queuing to check in, most of whom are women in bright-pink Juicy Couture tracksuits. I wonder if there's some kind of pageant going on nearby, but then I have to move out of the way as a soap star I recognize comes hurtling toward me while simultaneously telling his entourage to hurry up and berating someone on the phone for not picking up his dry cleaning.

I've always wanted to go to a red-carpet event, but if this is a snapshot of the kind of people who attend them, then I'd rather be at home, watching it on TV with a nice cup of tea.

As I ride the lift to the fifth floor I convince myself that the contents of my bag will have Yasmin eating out of the palm of my hand. But she doesn't seem nearly as happy as I would be if someone turned up on my doorstep with diamonds.

"Oh, hi," she says, forcing a half smile through gritted teeth when I introduce myself. "You'd better come in."

Her silky black hair is curled around rollers the size of Coke cans, and her skin is aglow with a shimmering powder. "Can we do this chat while the girls are finishing off?" she asks, sitting down on a stool in front of a dressing table.

"Sure," I say, laying my dress in its cellophane wrapping on the bed, before carefully taking the blue box from my bag and opening it as I hand it to Yasmin.

"Oh my gosh, it's stunning," she says, picking up the necklace from its velvet cushion. She places it on her chest, where the sunlight catches it, sending rainbows of color across the ceiling of the room.

"It will look amazing with your beautiful dress," I say, looking over to the emerald satin slip that's hanging from the door architrave.

"I'm very grateful, but I don't appreciate how you went about this." Her tone is acerbic and tension creeps across my chest.

"I'm sorry, I don't know what . . ."

"Are you Stella Thorne?"

"*Me?*" It comes out as a squeal. "No, no, I'm not," I say, making absolutely sure she's in no doubt.

"But you know what she did?" asks Yasmin. "To get this interview."

I numbly shake my head.

"Despite my agent telling *The Globe* several times that I wouldn't talk to them, this Stella woman somehow got hold of my personal phone number and proceeded to call me directly . . ."

I scrunch up my face, hoping that she's going to stop there.

" . . . Pretending to be someone from Tiffany, offering me whatever I wanted."

"Oh, I think there must have been some kind of miscommunication," I offer, while guessing there was nothing of the sort.

"And then, once I'd fallen in love with this necklace," Yasmin goes on, "she called again to say that they'd be delighted to loan it to me, just as long as I give a quick interview to *The Globe*."

As furious as I am at Stella for once again getting an interview under false pretenses, there's a tiny part of me that wants to say to Yasmin, *You could always have said, 'Forget it—I'm not going to be bought.'* Although I fear that's exactly what she's trying to say now, if I give her the opportunity.

"I'm sorry—that's not how we normally operate, but I can assure you that we will only discuss what *you* want to discuss and, if it makes you feel any better, I'll give you full copy approval as well."

I want to suck the words back in, knowing that the first unwritten rule of journalism is *never* to offer copy approval. But this is my first big interview—an interview that Max is desperate for and has entrusted me with—so I'll do whatever it takes to get it done, because going back to the office without it isn't an option.

"I've got ten minutes before I need to leave, so let's get on with it," says Yasmin tightly.

I ask the questions as quickly as I can, landing the innocuous ones first, in the hope that I can slip in at the last minute the ones Max actually wants the answers to.

"I'm going to need to get dressed now," says Yasmin, barely five minutes in, and so far I've got nothing other than what's her go-to dish for a weekday family dinner, plus a few lines on her idyllic childhood growing up in Slough.

"But didn't your parents divorce when you were young?" I ask in a rush, sensing that I have only seconds left.

She fixes me with an unmoving stare in the mirror. "My parents fought long and hard for their marriage, but in the end it wasn't meant to be. There was no drama—it was just how thousands of other couples break up, but they ensured that my sister and I always felt loved and protected. Now, if you'll excuse me, I really do need to get ready."

I smile tightly, knowing that the copy I've got to file won't even make a two-by-four-inch column, let alone a double-page spread.

But still I hurriedly type it up in the hotel bar, send it over to Max and wait for my phone to light up. I'm surprised that it takes as long as twenty seconds.

"Are you fucking kidding me?" he yells. I have to hold the phone away from my ears. "We give her a fifty-grand necklace and she gives us a recipe for sausage casserole?"

"She was on the back foot before we even started," I offer, in my defense.

"She had no right to be. I've called in a ton of favors for this."

"Yes, but Stella muddied the waters by pretending to be from Tiffany."

"She doesn't want to fuck with me," seethes Max. "Because it will be the last thing she does."

I daren't ask if he's talking about Stella or Yasmin.

18

Stella

Max is standing at the floor-to-ceiling windows of his corner office when Stella silently approaches. With one hand on his hip, and his shoulders set, she wonders if he's talking to his wife, Tanya. Either that or he's in full negotiation mode on a story. He's often said they're both as hard work as each other.

"So we're all set?" he says into the phone. "You know what you're doing?"

Stella knocks on the door and raises her eyebrows questioningly as he swings round.

"Fine, I'll speak to you later," he says, ending the call abruptly.

"Anything exciting?" she asks.

"Just Tanya organizing our silver wedding anniversary," he says.

"Oh, are you having a party?"

"Er, yeah, this weekend."

"Oh . . ." says Stella, unable to hide her surprise. "I didn't realize."

"That's why I'm going to be finding myself in a pub function room in Blackheath instead of spending the weekend with the world's most powerful men in media on a country estate near Bath," he says sardonically.

"Right," she replies, willing herself to pretend that her invitation must have got lost in the post. She'd always been invited to Max and Tanya's parties, even their children's celebrations, with Tanya often commenting, "You can't have Max without Stella." It wasn't meant as cattily as it sounded; it was simply a throwaway comment that alluded to the fact that they were always together. "Like partners in crime," Tanya would say.

"And while the boss may sack me if I miss *his* soirée," Max goes on, "Tanya will most definitely *kill* me if I miss ours. So I was left with no choice. Though, truth be told, I wouldn't be surprised if Peter had planned it that way, knowing this weekend would be tricky for me."

Stella doesn't know which part of that sentence she feels more put out by. "Is that why he's invited me instead then?" she asks.

"*What?*" says Max, looking like he's heard exactly what she said, but is hoping he's got it wrong.

"He's asked me to go," Stella says. "*Told* me, actually."

Max looks like he's had the wind taken out of his sails. "Well, are you . . . are you going?"

"Like you, I don't seem to have a choice," she replies.

"Right," says Max, battling to regain his composure. "Well, then I guess you'd better go."

"As long as you're OK with it."

He laughs sarcastically. "It doesn't seem as if either of us has a choice, does it?"

"It wasn't actually that I wanted to talk to you about," says Stella. "Have you got a minute?"

Max looks at the manic newsroom. "We're two hours away from going to press—*nobody*'s got a minute."

"It's important," says Stella, closing the door.

He checks his watch and falls heavily into his high-backed leather chair. "Make it quick then," he snaps.

As she looks at him, Stella wonders if she shouldn't just keep what she's got to say to herself. First, because she's not sure the information is of any use. There's nothing Max can do with it, and after last night's fitful sleep, she wishes *she* was still blissfully unaware. And second, because a part of her isn't sure he deserves to know.

The thought saddens her, another bitter reminder of how far apart they've grown. They used to share everything as they rose up through the ranks together; they'd pass leads to each other, pay each other's sources, split bylines. Most days they'd even go halves on a sandwich, not because they were watching their pennies, but because they never had time to eat a whole one.

Yet now they simply get on with the job, discussing nothing other than the leader on page seven or the picture caption on page twelve. She hasn't even been invited to his and Tanya's anniversary party. When had they become so divided? She suspects it was when one of them became editor undeservedly and the other was relegated to chomping at his heels.

The flicker of agitation that momentarily settles on Max's face, as she sits down, only makes Stella want to drag this out even more.

"So," she starts, "I was speaking with a police source . . ." She stills her shaking hands in her lap, unaccustomed to the sensation. "And it appears that McAllister is out on parole today."

There's an unnerving silence from the other side of the desk, but Stella knows, from the narrowing of Max's eyes and the pulsing in his jaw, that the words have hit home.

"How long have you known about this?" he asks, after what feels like minutes.

"I've only just found out," says Stella, knowing that it will serve no purpose for Max to know she's been sitting on this information for forty-eight hours.

"So we're back to having to look over our shoulders everywhere we go?" he asks—the question rhetorical.

Stella had rather hoped he was going to be slightly more optimistic in his outlook, even if only for *her* sake. She fingers the raised scar through her blouse. "Do you honestly think he's going to follow through on his threat?"

Max blows out his cheeks. "I'm hoping things have moved on in his world by now. They've certainly moved on out here. I'm running the country's biggest-selling newspaper, and when I'm not having lunch with the prime minister, I'm having dinner with the commissioner of police. Do you honestly think McAllister's going to come for *me*?"

Stella can't help but flinch, because the way Max says it makes it sound as if he already knows McAllister will come for her instead.

Her phone rings, and seeing *Steve* on the screen makes her hesitate to answer, fearing that it's about to change everything. But knowing that she can't hold off the inevitable forever, she takes a deep breath, looking at Max as she answers it.

"Hello," she says, hating her voice for the way it sounds.

"He's out," replies Harry, bluntly.

There's no other way of saying it, but Stella still wishes he'd somehow soften the blow, so that she at least had a *chance* of stopping the overwhelming fear from crushing her chest. The two words wrap around her vital organs, threatening to squeeze the life out of them.

"So he's just walked straight out of there?" she says, almost to herself. "He could be waiting outside the office right now. I could pass him in the street on my way home. He could already be in my flat . . ." The possibilities are endless.

"I think he's going to be doing more worthwhile things on his first night of freedom than risk being locked up again," says Harry.

If he'd meant to placate her, he's way off the mark.

"And what about *after* he's enjoyed a meal of kings with his family? *After* he's caught up with his gangster acquaintances? What happens in two or three days' time, when he's reflecting on *why* he's not been able to do either of those things for the past four years? What then?"

Harry's silence speaks volumes.

19

Jess

I survived the red carpet, largely because the bank of a hundred or so photographers didn't know who I was. Though it didn't stop them calling out, "Oi, over here, darling" or "What's your name?"

But it was out of the frying pan and into the fire, for as soon as I made it into the Royal Albert Hall in one piece, Max had called again to tell me he needed more from Yasmin.

"You need to go in again," he'd said. "I can barely fill a column with what you got."

"She could be anywhere," I'd told him. "There are over a thousand people here."

"So as soon as the ceremony's over, go find her," he said. "She will have had a drink by then and, with any luck, she'll be a little more loose-tongued. We go to press at ten, so get it to me before then."

I'd watched the clock ticking for the next two mind-numbingly boring hours, taking myself off to the toilet more times than I could count to scan the vast circular floor, hoping to see Yasmin. If Stella was here, she'd no doubt hunt her down, ply her with drinks and trick her into a conversation that Yasmin wouldn't want reported. But that's not the agreement Max and I have. He wants to promote trust between the paper and its contributors; make them feel that their words will be recited sympathetically. I've already let Ned Jacobs down—I don't want to let Max down, too.

But now, with just over an hour to go until the deadline, I have a horrible feeling I'm about to.

"Here she is," shrieks Yasmin, weaving her way toward me with her award for Best Factual Show held aloft. "This is Jess," she says to the bearded man that she's with, slurring ever so slightly. "And ssshh, don't tell anyone, but she's a reporter with *The Globe*."

"Yasmin! Can I get a quick picture with your award?" comes a loud voice over my shoulder.

The man steps out of shot as Yasmin giggles and poses with the golden statue.

"And give it a big kiss for me," says the photographer.

I watch a different woman from the one I met three hours ago pucker her lips, stick out her tongue and throw her head back against the wall, closing her eyes as she goes to slide the golden statue between her legs.

"OK, that'll do," I say, making a grab for the phallic-shaped award.

"I was only having fun," Yasmin says.

"Well, can you do it away from the flashbulbs of the paparazzi next time," I say, half laughing as she grabs my hand.

"Let's get a drink!" Yasmin shouts over the din of the DJ's trance mix.

I smile as she pulls me toward the bar and, against my better judgment, allow her to convince me to have a tequila shot.

"Jeez," I say, recoiling from the sour lime. "Why would anyone ever think this is a good idea?"

The second tastes better than the first and, by the third, I don't really care *what* it tastes like. I knock it back with all the confidence of a pro, slamming the empty shot glass down on the wooden bar.

"Woo-hoo!" shrieks Yasmin with her arms in the air. "Let's go dance."

As Flic has always attested, it turns out that hitting the dance floor with a little liberation-juice flowing through your veins is even more fun than when you're sober.

Yasmin and I spin around like whirling dervishes, throwing our arms in the air with wild abandonment. We attempt the *Thriller* routine and jump up and down to Calvin Harris's "Bounce," stopping for breath only when two milk circles appear on Yasmin's silk dress, spreading rapidly around her breasts.

"Erm, it's time for a visit to the ladies' room," I say, guiding her by the elbow and pushing her through the throng, now flashing their palms to Beyoncé's "Single Ladies."

"What are you doing?" laughs Yasmin, attempting to push back. "I love this song."

"Come on, I need a wee," I say, tugging her by the hand.

She sees it as soon as she's faced with the floor-to-ceiling mirrors in the cloakroom and instinctively wraps her arms around her chest.

"Oh my god!" she says, looking at me, horrified. "I had no idea. Do you think anyone saw it?"

"No, I don't think so," I offer. "It's only just happened."

"What am I going to do?" she says, sounding slightly panicked. "How am I going to get out of here and back to the hotel without anyone seeing me?"

"Does it really matter if someone *does*?" I ask.

"Of course it does," she replies, suddenly tearful. "If I was living my old life, then I wouldn't give a shit—it's the most natural thing in the world, after all."

"But in this life . . ."

"But in this life, every little thing I do is put under a microscope. I can't go to the shops without a photographer following me. Not a day goes by without an online debate about my post-baby weight;

strangers commentating on whether I'm looking too slim or too fat—because everyone has an opinion." She covers her face as she breaks down. "It all gets too much sometimes. And now *this*."

"Hey, it's OK," I say, pulling Yasmin into me.

"It is for you," she says as her head falls heavily onto my shoulder. "You can go about your life without being photographed, judged, bullied . . ."

"I'll tell you what we're going to do," I say into her ear. "You're going to stay here while I go and get my things from the cloakroom. I've got some clothes you can change into, or at the very least a coat you can cover yourself with."

She nods, sniffing.

"Hey, girl, why are you crying?" interrupts a woman as she crashes out of a toilet cubicle. Her pupils are dilated and there's a residue of white powder around her nostrils.

"She's fine," I say protectively.

"Do you want something that's gonna make you feel better?" she asks.

Yasmin's eyes widen as she looks at me, and for a moment I wonder if she's asking if she should accept the poisoned chalice that's being offered.

"We're absolutely fine, thanks," I say, guiding Yasmin into a cubicle.

"Hey, ain't you that chef chick?" asks the woman, attempting to follow us in. She puts a hand on the open door. "Yeah, it *is* you. My best friend's mum is your biggest fan. Oh, man, she's going to be so pumped."

"I think you're confusing her with someone," I mutter, under my breath, as I gently try to prise the door out of her grip.

"Nah, I don't think I am. Can I get a picture?" she says, already trying to position her phone in the air with her free hand.

In that split second I can see the resulting photo before she's even taken it. Yasmin, looking worse for wear, drunk and crying, with stains on her dress, being manhandled by a woman in a toilet cubicle, with clear evidence of drug use having taken place.

Even if it only ends up on social media, the fallout could be catastrophic. People with nothing better to do will ask where her newborn baby was while she was snorting coke.

Well, it clearly went hungry, one cruel keyboard warrior will comment.

She's not fit to be a mother, another will observe. *Where is she when her baby needs her?*

The kinder spectator will merely ask their followers to *Just look at the state of that . . .*

In a fit of pique, I shove the woman with my shoulder and grab the door with both hands, wrestling for control, before she lets go and it slams straight into her face.

"You fucking bitch," she calls out, banging it with her fist. "You're going to regret that."

Yasmin looks at me, wide-eyed in panic.

"Don't worry," I say. "She's bluffing."

Though we both know that if she managed to get a photo, she probably isn't.

20

Stella

"You might want to take a look at these," says Stella, throwing the pictures down on Max's desk.

His mouth turns upward. "Where did these come from?"

"They were sent anonymously," replies Stella.

"It's risky," says Max. "But if you think they're kosher . . ."

"I can't see how they can't be," says Stella. "I'll do some digging, but it's too good an opportunity to miss, surely?"

Max's smirk turns into a rictus grin. "So, it seems that Miss Goody Two-Shoes does have a dark side after all."

Stella nods. Of all the forms that celebrity comes in, it's *this* type that infuriates her the most. Those who are all too happy to exalt their virtues on the pages of the glossy monthlies, boasting about their ethical values, while in reality they're living the life they pretend not to have any part in: the *tabloid* life.

"You want to run them?" she asks.

Max taps his fingers on the desk. "It could work quite well with the copy Jess filed. Show the juxtaposition between what she says and what she does. The image she purports to have, versus the real Yasmin Chopra."

"I like it," says Stella.

Max looks at his watch. "Jess has got less than half an hour to get me better quotes, and if she gets them before we go to press, we'll swap them in. But in the meantime, write up what we've got and if you're as confident as you can be that these pics are the real deal, then we'll splash with them."

"No problem," says Stella.

"Great work, Ella, well done."

She doesn't know what's the most startling: the fact that he's praising her, or that he called her by her pet name. He hasn't called her that in months.

"Are you OK if I get going?" asks Lottie when Stella gets back to her desk.

"Yeah, we're splashing with Yasmin Chopra, so I'm just going to write it up and I'll be out of here myself." But even as she says it, Stella's not sure that she will be. This feels like the safest place to be right now. There's twenty-four-hour security in the lobby, pass-access barriers and thirty floors on which she could hide if McAllister comes looking for her.

"Anything I can do to help?" asks Lottie, blissfully oblivious. Stella can't remember what that must feel like, the events of the past few days having seemingly rendered her impervious to the life she had before.

"No, it won't take me long. It's late—go home."

Home. Her sanctuary. At least it used to be, until the thought of Ray McAllister had turned it into a place where she felt vulnerable and at risk. What would it take for him to find out where she lived? Has he already had someone staking it out, monitoring her movements?

Unable to stop herself, she opens up a search bar on Google and types in Ray McAllister kidnap trial.

YES, PRIME MINISTER! screams the headline from the top news item: the splash from *The Globe*'s coverage, the morning after his conviction.

Hardened criminal Ray McAllister was found guilty yesterday of attempting to kidnap the prime minister.

Following an undercover investigation by *The Globe*, due to which we were thankfully able to save the prime minister from a terrible fate, McAllister was also convicted of being in possession of a firearm and will be sentenced later this month.

The Globe's News editor, Max Forsythe, and senior journalist Stella Thorne, who alerted the police to the ill-fated plot, were never in doubt of securing a rightful conviction.

"This was a terrifying attempt to derail the election and coerce the Tory party into paying ten million pounds in exchange for Mr. Greaves's life," says Ms. Thorne, who was in court to hear the verdict. "It is a huge relief that *The Globe*, together with the police and the judicial system, have been able to rid the streets of this scourge."

Unsurprisingly, other publications weren't quite so biased toward the good work that *The Globe* had done, being far more eager to discredit their self-righteous claims than report on the indisputable evidence that was staring them in the face.

A FLAWED CASE FROM DAY ONE, screamed *The Sunday Chronicle*.

HOW FAR IN THE PRIME MINISTER's POCKET IS **THE GLOBE**? questioned *The Daily News*.

But it's *The Post's* exclusive interview with the woman who quite literally branded Stella a double-crosser that catches her eye.

HE DIDN'T STAND A CHANCE, she bleats across the front page of their bitter rival:

Christina McAllister, the crestfallen wife of the man convicted of attempting to kidnap the prime minister, has sensationally claimed that he was always going to be found guilty, because he didn't get a fair trial.

"How could he, when it was essentially the biggest media corporation in the country that was trying him?" she says. "This country isn't run by the government or ruled by law; it's controlled by the media. He was framed for their own purposes and, while he rots in jail, they've got away with it.

"But he won't take this lying down. He'll be back to avenge those who did this to him. He'll get his day of reckoning."

Stella lets her head fall into her hands, wishing she hadn't gone down this rabbit-hole, because the more she reads, the more last night's dream turns into a real-life nightmare.

21

Jess

"Are you going to be OK?" I ask as I deposit Yasmin back in her hotel room.

The debris from her getting ready six hours ago litters every surface; the potent smell of hairspray still hangs in the air.

"Will you stay and have one more drink for the road?" she asks, sighing as she steps out of her high heels. "Oh god, that feels better."

I look at my watch to see that there's only fifteen minutes until Max presses the button to send tomorrow's edition to print, if he hasn't already.

"I really should be getting home."

Yasmin smiles as she pours a glass of flat champagne and hands it to me. "Do you have a boyfriend who'll be missing you?"

"No, just an anxious flatmate who sends out a search party a minute after ten."

"Ah, so you've got it all to come," she says, all melancholic. "What must it feel like to be young . . . and so free!"

"You're not all that older than me," I say, laughing.

"Mmm, but I'm lugging all this baggage around," she says, falling onto the bed. "I've got a husband, kids, pets, a mortgage . . ."

"You make it sound as if they're things a person doesn't want. I can't wait to have all that."

She looks at me, her face pulled tight as if she might cry again. "Be careful what you wish for," she warns.

"But I thought you were happy," I say, confused. "You were waxing lyrical about your life a few hours ago."

"I lied," she says.

My heart skips a beat, wondering what she's going to say next and whether I'll have enough time to file it.

"I used to be happy, but these past few months I don't know . . . I guess things have changed."

I sit down on the bed beside her. "But that's only because of everything that's happened since winning *On the Ranch*. It's turned your whole world upside down and that'll take some getting used to."

"Mmm," she muses. "I guess so, but I get a real sense that something's shifted."

"In what way?" I ask.

"Krishan," she says. "He's changed. He's been cold and distant since this all happened. And with the new baby and all the demands that brings, I've felt strangely isolated, even though I've never been surrounded by more people. I know it doesn't make sense, but that's how it feels."

"But life's different for him too now, don't forget," I offer. "He's gone from having a stay-at-home wife to this jet-setting, bad-ass mother of three who's winning awards and fighting off mad women in toilets."

Yasmin laughs. "Well, when you put it like that . . ."

"It'll all work itself out," I say. "It's a big adjustment and it might just take him a bit more time."

She nods. "I'm sure you're right, but I've been here before. I can see the signs and I don't want to go down that road again."

"With your ex, you mean?" I ask, suddenly remembering the list of questions Max had wanted me to ask her. "What happened with him?"

She sighs and swings her legs up onto the bed, letting her head fall onto the pillow. "I was so young," she says ruefully. "And I honestly thought I'd struck gold when I met him. He was kind, funny, charming and ridiculously good-looking—everybody loved him, even my hard-to-please mother."

"So what went wrong?" I ask.

"Everything was fine until Maya came along, my eldest. I don't think he liked playing second fiddle."

"To a baby?" I ask incredulously.

She nods. "He was used to being the center of my world, but as you'll find out when you have kids of your own, *they* have to come first. He started staying out late, telling me I was a terrible mother—and generally undermining my confidence. I thought he just needed to get used to the new family dynamic, but when Maya was six months old, he came home drunk and hit me."

"Oh my god," I say, my hand shooting up to my mouth. "What did you do?"

"I did what any self-respecting woman should do and walked out, there and then."

"That was it?" I ask, marveling at her bravery. "You didn't give him a second chance?"

She shakes her head vehemently. "My mum gave my dad chance after chance, and it ruined our childhood and made me a different woman from the one I would have otherwise been. I wasn't going to let that happen to my daughter."

"You were very brave," I say, but she shakes her head.

"No, my mum was brave for putting up with it for so long, believing that it would be better for me and my sister if she stayed."

"So she left him in the end then?"

"Yes, when I was fourteen, but by then the damage had already been done. I was a frightened, broken girl and had so little confidence in myself that I was a sitting target for the school bully."

I remember Max mentioning that he wanted me to get to the bottom of the bullying story. Perhaps he's thinking of starting up another campaign for our readers to get behind.

"That must have been difficult to deal with, on top of everything else."

A tear falls onto her cheek and Yasmin wipes it away. "It was a tough time, and I don't think you ever truly get over being bullied. The things they say, the things they do . . . they stay with you. No matter where you get to in life, you're always reminded of what it felt like to be that scared and lonely fourteen-year-old."

"Did you ever see your nemesis again?" I ask.

"Yeah, funnily enough she got in touch with me straight after I won the show. It was like we'd been best friends at school, and she was reaching out to rekindle what we once had." She shakes her head. "Go figure."

"It's amazing who crawls out of the woodwork to ride on your coattails, isn't it?"

She smiles. "It did feel like good karma, I have to say. It felt like I was the more powerful one for the first time."

"You are!" I exclaim. "Look at you. You've come so far, and you've done so well to leave all those bad memories and negativity behind."

"Yeah, but it feels like I've just stepped straight into another hornets' nest."

"Because of the press and social media?" I ask.

She nods. "At least back then I could get away from situations, hide in my bedroom or go for a walk to clear my head. But now the insults and accusations taunt me wherever I go. They're on my computer, on my phone—they're there when I go to sleep at night and are still there when I wake up." Her shoulders convulse. "Oh god, I can't believe I've poured my heart out to a journalist."

Nor can I.

"Can I get your number?" she asks as I go to leave, with only a matter of seconds to get this bombshell copy over to the office.

"Of course," I say, feeling strangely honored. "Call me if you ever need anything."

"Thank you," she says, pulling me in for a hug. "You've restored my faith in human nature."

22

Stella

As soon as Stella is out of the relative safety of the Global International HQ, she feels as if she's on a stage with a spotlight beaming on her. Keeping her head down to avoid making unnecessary eye contact, she battles against the wind, which is making an ominous screaming sound as it whistles its way between the tall buildings. She's sure it's a noise she hears most nights when she leaves the office, but tonight it has a particularly sinister intonation.

Her paranoia is heightened even further when a man bumps into her and grabs her arm, though whether it's to steady himself or to protect her, she's unsure. Yet by the time he's walking away, she's convinced he's injected her with a substance that will knock her out by the time she turns the next corner, where a van will be waiting to bundle her away.

This sense of vulnerability doesn't sit well with her; she's unused to being reliant on someone else to decide whether she's safe or not. The thought of her empty flat—which she normally can't wait to return to—now fills her with apprehension, its dark corners goading her with what they might be concealing.

Seeing the weakness in herself is enough. Showing her shortcomings to someone else is unheard of, but she can't pretend that having a convicted criminal chasing her down is anything other than terrifying. Fuck McAllister!

Ducking into an office doorway to shield herself from the rain that is just beginning to fall, she fumbles for the phone in her bag and calls Harry's number.

It comforts her more than it should that he picks up on the first ring.

"Hello," he says.

Now that she's got him, she doesn't know what she actually wants. *Reassurance*, her subconscious calls out.

"I've been waiting for you to call."

She's immediately on-guard. "Why? Have you heard something?"

"*What?* No. I'm just at the NTAs with the foreign secretary and I thought you might be here."

"What are you doing *there?*" she asks, desperately trying to distract herself with thoughts of vacuous soap stars in taffeta, rather than face the very real predicament circling in her head.

"Don't you know that all MPs are actors in disguise?" Harry says, laughing. "She was invited to give out an award and she couldn't get here quick enough. Her security's been a nightmare, because all she wants to do is flit around the room and introduce herself to everyone. I don't know if she's looking for votes or their agents' numbers."

Normally Stella would laugh, but all she can think of is how she wishes she had someone like Harry to follow *her* around 24/7, keeping her out of harm's way.

"How long do you think it'll be until you get off?" she asks.

"Well, it all depends," says Harry. "There's a rumor that George Clooney's here somewhere, so I can't see me getting off until Harriet's tracked him down and auditioned for him."

A tiny part of Stella considers going across town, knowing that she'll surely feel safer at the Royal Albert Hall, in the presence of a thousand people far more important than her. But then she wonders why the hell she should. She wants to go home, have a glass of wine and relax.

"You OK?" asks Harry, as if he can hear her troubled brain whirring away. "You worried about McAllister?"

She shakes her head, hating the feeling that even his name evokes. "I'm all good," she lies.

"Well, if it's any consolation, I found out he's wearing a tag."

A little flash of relief momentarily lifts her. "What does that mean exactly?"

"Well, it'll mean that the control center will be able to see where he is at all times."

"The *control* center?" says Stella. "What use is that to me? I need to know that he can't come near me—not be notified after the event." She can hear the pitch of her voice rising.

"There might be a list of banned areas and addresses that he's not able to go near . . ." he goes on.

"And is mine one of them?"

"I don't know," he says. "I'll have to look into it."

Stella can't help but feel irked that he hasn't already. Can't Harry see how exposed this is making her feel? *Not if you don't show him*, says a voice deep inside her.

"Do you want me to come over later?" he asks hopefully. "Once I've managed to brush all these sequins off me."

"If you want," she says nonchalantly, even though she's feeling anything but.

"OK, if it's not too late I'll head your way," he promises, before hanging up.

As soon as she steps out from the doorway she hears the roar of a motorbike, the sound of its thunderous engine reverberating around the tall buildings surrounding her. The one-way street, now devoid of the hundreds of workers who pound its pavements like ants at lunch-time, is eerily still. But the noise is getting louder, making her ears hurt, and in that split-second Stella realizes that it's coming from be-hind her. Swinging around, she is blinded by a single beam of light that is racing toward her. If she doesn't move, it's going to mow her down, but she's rooted to the spot, frozen in fear. At the last second, as she feels a sudden rush of air, she moves, and the black machine skims past her body in a trail of heat.

Unable to breathe, she stumbles backward as the bike speeds away and, for a moment, she's ridiculously grateful for the lucky escape. It's only when she physically pats herself down to check she's OK that she feels the wetness. It's on her skirt, her blouse and, as her fingers hes-itantly reach for her face, it's on her cheeks too. Now that her senses have registered it, she can feel its warmth as the liquid sinks into her skin, but from what she can see in the muted glow of the streetlights, there's no blood on either her clothes or her trembling fingers. It's then that it occurs to her that it could be acid, thrown at her in a tar-geted attack.

Panic threatens to overwhelm her as she waits for the potency of the chemical to scorch the flesh from her bones. But there's no burn-ing sensation, and the silk of her blouse isn't fusing with her skin.

Falling against the wall of an office block, Stella feels hysteria set-ting in as she alternates between desperately needing to cry and the inane sensation of wanting to laugh. She does both, which makes her feel as if she's hyperventilating, unable to catch a breath.

She frantically rummages in her bag for the inhaler that she last used months ago, hoping it's still there and has still got something in it. Her breaths are coming short and fast now, and she needs that shot of Salbutamol to relax the muscles in her airways.

An instant calmness works its way through her nervous system and she allows herself to believe, just for a moment, that it was a one-in-a-million incident. That the rider had lost control. That it was a delivery driver who had got disorientated with his satnav. But as the thought settles in, she sees the face of the prime minister staring up at her from a mask lying on the pavement.

A sickening sensation swirls in the pit of her stomach as she tentatively bends down to pick it up. And as she turns it over, any notion of simply being in the wrong place at the wrong time is blown to smithereens.

23

Jess

I'm woken, well before my body is ready, by Flic slamming cupboard doors and making a racket with the saucepans, with no consideration for me or my banging head. I can't tell whether she's coming in or going out.

The smell of fried bacon both entices me and turns my stomach over; my assaulted senses don't know what they want or, more to the point, what they *need*, after a night of unprecedented alcohol intake.

"Oh god," I moan, pulling the duvet over my head, when she comes in and turns the light on. My eyes and ears physically hurt.

"You dirty rotten scoundrel," she squeals, falling onto my bed.

I half expect to turn and see an unfamiliar man lying beside me. "*What?*" I groan, relieved to see that I didn't pick up a stranger between Kensington and Hackney last night.

"So, what happened?" she asks excitedly, as she crosses her legs and settles in for the gossip. "Clearly the version we see on TV is completely different from what really goes on!"

"Can we do this later?" I plead.

"Oh my god, are you *hungover?*" she asks, throwing her full weight on top of me and tugging at the duvet, which is the only thing between me and a world that I really don't want to be a part of right now.

"I'm not sure," I say. "If that's what they call a throbbing head and a sickening swirl in the pit of my stomach, which doesn't know what to do with itself, then yes, maybe I am."

"So were you with her when she did it?" she asks, wide-eyed.

"With who, when she did what?" I exclaim, too tired to talk in cryptic code.

"That chef woman who you were interviewing last night," says Flic, sounding equally exasperated.

I reluctantly pull myself up against the headboard and attempt to open my eyes.

"Who, Yasmin Chopra?"

Flic nods intensely and rolls onto the bed beside me. "I can't believe it," she says. "I'd never have her down for that."

"I'm . . . I'm sorry, but I have no idea what you're talking about," I reply, rubbing at my pounding forehead.

"You'd better look at your phone then," says Flic. "Your social media will tell you all you need to know."

I slowly reach out to pick up my phone from where it's charging on my bedside table—my arms feeling like lead weights. My screen comes to life with a slide of my finger to tell me that I've missed three calls from Yasmin and one from Stella.

"Shit, it must have been on silent," I say out loud.

But as my brain slowly wakes up, I'm reminded of a dream I'd had, where I'd blindly reached out to my ringing phone, tapping at the screen to stop the noise. Or had that been real?

I close my eyes, forcing myself to remember, but either way, I'm unable to imagine why Yasmin would have called me at 3:36, 4:22 and 4:49. Had I left something there? Had I inadvertently brought something of hers home with me?

As I press my fingertips into my temples, willing my senses to return to normal, a tightness takes hold of my chest. *The necklace. Something's happened to the necklace.*

That's why Stella has called as well. Yasmin must have got through to her, told her the bad news and now Stella is onto me, needing to know exactly what happened and whether we're liable. Shit!

Wishing I felt better than I do, I try Yasmin first, hoping that she can give me the heads-up before Stella gets to me, but after five rings, it offers me her voicemail: "Hey, it's me. If I can't take your call, it's because I'm either in the kitchen, tied to the stove, or have three small children attached to my hip . . ."

"Or am frantically searching for a fifty-thousand-pound necklace," I say, as Flic looks at me quizzically, waiting for me to bring her up to speed.

". . . Leave a message after the beep and I'll get back to you as soon as I can."

I clear my throat. "Hi, Yasmin, it's Jess, from last night. Just returning your calls—hope everything's all right. Er, ring me back when you can. Thanks."

Avoiding the next job in hand, hoping I can hold out and speak to Yasmin before having to face Stella, I click onto Twitter and scroll through my timeline, trying to find what Flic's talking about.

I don't have to wait long, as one post after another makes lewd comments about a nameless chef.

You know what they say: a cook in the kitchen and a whore in the bedroom . . .

But I think you're meant to be that with your husband, not a randomer in a corridor, comes the reply.

And I thought it was just her cooking that was spicy, spouts another keyboard warrior.

I read the words and stare at the grainy images, unable to comprehend either. There is no way on God's earth this can be what my brain is telling me it is. It's not possible.

"Oh my god!" I gasp as I zoom in and out, the images becoming more and more pixelated with every magnification. I follow the leads to *The Globe*'s app, where I'm bombarded by X-rated images of the "friend" I left only a few short hours ago. A man's hand is cupping her breast, his lips are parting hers, but neither belongs to her husband, whose photo we've helpfully included, in case anyone is in any doubt.

My eyes run along the headline: TV chef can't seem to get enough of her main course. I wish they'd stopped before getting to the byline: Exclusive by Stella Thorne and Jess Townsend.

"What the hell?" I exclaim, as I read on:

TV darling and champion of *On the Ranch*, Yasmin Chopra seemed delighted with what was on the menu at her hotel following her win at the NTAs last night.

Despite her husband and three young children, one a newborn, being safely tucked up in their beds at the family home in Slough, Ms. Chopra was sampling all the delights London had to offer on a rare night away.

I feel as if I'm having an out-of-body experience. When did this happen? How had I missed it? Had the signs been there? Had Yasmin intimated that her marriage was so far gone that she'd have an affair? Or, at the very least, a sleazy liaison in a hotel corridor?

No, try as I might to see my way through the fog of my hangover haze, I can think of nothing to suggest that Yasmin was lining up anything more than an early night. But maybe that was all part of the ruse, and she's a better liar than I had her down for.

"This is all wrong," I say, stumbling out of bed in a daze. "I didn't write this."

Flic takes the phone from my hand. "But it's got your name on it," she replies, sounding confused.

"Because Stella-fucking-Thorne has stitched me up," I seethe, snatching it back and heading to the bathroom.

I jump in the shower, but am unable to wash away the dirty deceit that has worked its way under my skin. I can't be surprised by Stella's actions, but I honestly thought Yasmin was one of life's good eggs. I was even naive enough to believe that we'd struck up something of a friendship, but it looks like she pulled the wool over my eyes, along with everyone else's.

I dry myself off and call Max.

"Congratulations!" he says as he picks up. "This story is going viral."

"It's *not* my story," I snap.

"It's *your* words," he says. "*Your* interview."

"But you've taken it all out of context by putting it alongside those photos. It makes her sound duplicitous."

"It shows her for who she really is," he says.

"If I'd known for one second that you had those, I would never—"

"It's a great piece, made all the better by the quotes you got."

"But you've made it look like I was complicit . . . that I knew you had the photos." I read the damning copy again and an uncomfortable lump wedges in the back of my throat.

"I thought you did," says Max. "I told Stella to bring you up to speed."

"Well, she didn't. Where did the pictures even come from? This is so *not* the woman I met last night."

"Stella got them," he says. "I hate to say it, but she saved your arse. She was even unusually magnanimous in sharing the byline with you—allowing you a bit of the glory as well."

"*Glory?*" I rasp. "Is that honestly what you think I get from this?"

"You *should*," he says. "This will fly for days. Everyone will want to know more. We'll have to field calls from TV. It's going to be great publicity for *The Globe*."

I close my eyes and will myself to see the positives. I haven't done anything wrong—I only filed what Yasmin said to me—and I haven't made anything up or embellished it in any way. And *The Globe*, the newspaper that I am proud to work for, has only printed the photos that show what she got up to. We've not done anything wrong. So why do I feel so wretched?

"I'm going to need a top-up," says Max.

"What, today?" I exclaim.

"Afraid so. Yasmin's going to need to give us something to balance this out—to make the public understand why she did it. She's going to *want* to make the public understand to give herself half a chance of turning this around."

My brain whirrs and hums as his demands accost me, battering my senses, making me feel even more light-headed than I already do.

"Do you honestly think she's going to speak to any journalists after this?" I rasp.

"She's going to feel backed into a corner this morning and she's going to have to tell her side, because she *will* have a side to tell. And if she doesn't, then you need to narrate one, because she's going to want to turn this around at all costs . . . Not only for the sake of her marriage, but to save the TV projects she's got coming up and to allay the fears of her sponsors, who thought they were buying a wholesome family image, not this tawdry scene in a hotel corridor."

I sigh. "I've already tried calling Yasmin, but her phone is going to voicemail."

"So get over there then. She'll most likely still be at the hotel, contemplating her next move."

"OK, I'll pass by there on my way in," I say reluctantly.

"Good girl," he replies. "And don't leave without speaking to her. We've got a fair few pages to fill tomorrow, and an exclusive on how the nation's sweetheart has turned sour will gain us more than a few new readers."

I shudder. The only thing it gives *me* is a bitter taste in my mouth.

24

Stella

The morning light is just beginning to eke around the edges of the curtain and Stella instinctively unfurls from her fetal position and stretches her legs out under the duvet.

Peering out of one eye, she squints at the alarm clock on her bedside to see that it's 7:55 a.m. Shocked that she's actually slept right through, she pulls herself up onto her elbow to turn off the wake-up call that's set for five minutes' time.

She normally wakes with two hours still left to go; another 120 minutes in which to toss and turn, go over the previous day's events and worry about what the next day will bring. Some nights, when there are no foreseeable problems, she'll *invent* something that will start her mind racing, or else lie there panicking that she'll not have enough sleep to get her through the next day, when she knows that even after the worst night she somehow finds the mettle to push on through.

Throwing her hands above her head, she smiles, imagining this is what it must feel like when your baby sleeps through the night for the first time. She wants to wallow in the feeling, enjoy it for a few more seconds before whatever's lying in wait on her phone has a chance to get under her skin and into her bloodstream.

Then it hits her. Like a sledgehammer. Playing in full technicolor in her head, shattering the peace she'd inexplicably managed to find.

The noise, the lights, the mask, the warning . . .

"You OK?" comes a voice, making her jump.

Her mind frantically trawls itself back to last night, trying to find a reason why the man she had sex with is still in her bed. She hasn't allowed anyone to stay over since she and Dane split up eight years ago. It was easier that way: no strings, no expectations, no misconception that she is softer than she appears. But Harry is somehow slipping through the cracks.

This was supposed to be nothing more than a sex-for-favors relationship, though who's paying, and with which currency, is not as clear as it once was when they started this eighteen months ago. Back then it was nothing more than a bung of a few hundred pounds here and there for police information that benefited the paper. But somewhere along the way she'd thrown in a quick shag, making Harry feel as if it were a bonus when he gave her something good. Though if the truth be known, she found him ridiculously attractive—and why shouldn't she get something out of a work arrangement every once in a while?

But is that *still* what their relationship is? A work arrangement?

As much as it goes against every natural instinct in her body, Stella can't help but acknowledge that she feels more than she should for him. She doesn't want to admit it because it makes her feel exposed and vulnerable, but as she imagines being in Harry's arms, a sense of security instantly wraps itself around her, momentarily allowing the burden of being an independent woman to sit on someone else's shoulders. Because however far we like to think we've come, it's exhausting being everything to everyone.

As Jerry Hall's mother once crudely told her impressionable

daughter, a woman has to be a maid in the living room, a cook in the kitchen and a whore in the bedroom. Maybe that was enough fifty years ago, but now a woman is also expected to be as fearsome in the boardroom as she is between the sheets, while bringing up three children, caring for elderly parents, keeping physically fit *and* keeping a check on her mental health.

And although Stella isn't yet in the sandwich of mid-life, sometimes—*just sometimes*—she could really do with someone saying, "Is there anything I can do for *you*?"

Except that now Harry is asking *exactly* that, she fobs him off.

"I'm fine," she says, throwing the duvet off in a huff. "I need to get ready for work."

Closing the bathroom door behind her, she rests her hands on the sides of the basin and looks at herself in the mirror, trying to see past the panic. She thinks back to last night and the desperate call she'd put into Harry as soon as she'd seen what was written on the mask.

"It's not a direct threat," he'd said when he arrived at her flat an hour later. "I'm not sure the police are going to be able to do much."

She'd battled to control the fear that was snatching her breath away. "'Next time you look over your shoulder, we'll be sure to say hello.' How is that not a direct threat? It's implying that they're coming for me."

"It was probably nothing more than a reminder to watch what you print," Harry had said. "In case you were planning to run a damning piece on McAllister's release or something."

Stella had shaken her head in disagreement. "You don't throw liquid over someone as a reminder."

"It seems to have been water," Harry had said, as if that was supposed to calm her.

She'd snorted derisorily. "Water this time, but acid the next . . ."

"I won't let anything happen to you," he'd said, pulling her into him.

"You don't need to worry about me," she'd replied, shrugging him off, pretending that she'd not needed him to comfort her.

But when he'd made a move to leave an hour later, after they'd shared a bottle of wine and she'd bombarded him with a barrage of questions, she'd gone to kiss him. Had she initiated that in a bid to stop him from leaving? Used sex as a bargaining tool because she felt safer with him there? She can't help but admit that his presence must certainly have played a part in her sleeping so soundly.

"Are you going to be OK if I get going?" he asks now, through the bathroom door.

"Yes, fine," she snaps, because it's easier than admitting that she's scared half to death.

Hearing the front door shut, she falls onto the closed seat of the toilet to scroll through her phone to check for any emails or messages. Relieved to see nothing of any great importance, she clicks onto *The Globe*'s app to see what the online team has posted overnight. There'll be rich pickings at the award's after-party: a wardrobe malfunction or a bleary-eyed drunken stumble, both equally worthy of clickbait. But nothing can compete with this morning's top story. *Her* story.

Her phone rings, the lure of an unknown number making her answer it even quicker than if it were her own mother. It could be the next big splash.

"Stella Thorne?" asks the caller on the other end of the line.

"Yes, who's speaking?" she asks, walking into her bedroom.

"It's Michael Leith," says the voice. "I'm calling from *The Post*."

He doesn't need to announce where he's from, especially so modestly. Stella is more than aware that he's the owner of *The Globe*'s fierce rival.

"Mr. Leith," says Stella, her mind working at a million miles an hour, trying to predict what he might want. "What can I do for you?"

"Well, firstly, I wanted to congratulate you on *The Globe*'s splash today." There's a loaded pause. "As much as it pains me to say it, well done—great job."

Stella experiences a momentary guilty conscience that it wasn't her work alone, but it doesn't last very long. "Thank you," she says, feeling like a peacock cockily displaying its plume as she walks in front of the mirrored doors of her wardrobes.

"And secondly," he goes on, "I wonder if you'd like to come in for a chat sometime soon."

Stella's brow furrows. "What for?" she asks skeptically.

"I'd just like to talk to you, find out a bit more about where you see yourself heading . . ."

"Career-wise?" she asks, unnecessarily.

"Well, yes. We've got an opportunity coming up that I think you'd be the perfect fit for."

Stella almost chokes. "Are you offering me a job?" she asks incredulously.

"You might be jumping the gun a little," he says, laughing. "But yes, I think you would be good for *The Post*, and vice versa."

Now it's Stella's turn to laugh. "I'm very flattered, but it would be rather like asking Richard Branson to defect to British Airways. If you cut me open, you'd see an inscription of *The Globe* running all the way through me."

"So you'd not even consider a move?" he asks. "Not even for the editor's job?"

Stella clenches her jaw, questioning herself for a split second. "No, I'm afraid not," she replies.

"OK, well your loyalty is commendable," he says. "Much to my chagrin."

"I appreciate the call," she says.

"Let me know if you change your mind."

"I won't." She laughs.

Feeling ten feet tall, she puts in a call to Max as she turns the shower on. "This story is going mental this morning," she says glee-fully.

"I know—copies are flying off the shelves. I told you Yasmin Chopra was worth getting."

"Yep, you were right," agrees Stella. "We could do with a follow-up for tomorrow's issue."

"I've sent Jess back to the hotel this morning," says Max, "to see if she can get another chat with Yasmin."

"It's a risky move sending her on her own," says Stella. "We don't want to fuck this up."

"Mmm," muses Max. "You might have a point. Why don't you get yourself over there too, then—in case she needs backup?"

Once Stella's dressed, she heads straight for the Royal Garden Hotel, hoping that Jess has already made inroads toward speaking to Yasmin. But as she goes through the revolving door, she can see Jess standing aimlessly in the lobby, chewing on her lip and tapping her phone against her thigh. There is nothing about her body language that suggests she has achieved *anything*.

"Have you spoken to Yasmin yet?" asks Stella, making Jess jump.

"Wh-what are you doing here?" asks Jess, looking immediately flustered.

"Have you *spoken* to her yet?" repeats Stella.

"Er, no, not yet," says Jess. "I was just thinking about going to get a coffee in the restaurant and seeing if she comes down for breakfast."

"There's no way she's going to come to the hotel restaurant on a day like today," replies Stella impatiently. "She knows all eyes will be on her."

"She left the necklace for me at reception," says Jess. "So she must have come down at some point."

Stella frowns. "Well then, I'd imagine she's already checked out and gone home to face the music."

"I asked," says Jess. "She's definitely still here."

Stella's heart beats a tiny bit faster. "Do you know her room number?"

"Yes, I was there with her last night."

"You need to go up there," says Stella. "Knock on the door and ask her outright . . ."

"Oh no, I don't think so," frowns Jess. "That's crossing the line."

"That's what good journalists do. That's what *makes* them good journalists."

"I don't think she's going to be very happy if I turn up at her door," Jess says. "Not with everything that's going on. I'm going to be the last person Yasmin's going to want to see."

"We'll go together then," says Stella. "I want to make sure we get the story that everyone else is talking about." She takes Jess gently by the arm and guides her toward the lifts.

"This isn't right," Jess protests. "We can't just arrive unannounced."

"What floor?" asks Stella, ignoring her remonstration.

Jess reluctantly presses five and they ride in silence until the doors slide open onto a small lobby with two mismatched armchairs on either side of an armoire, deliberately designed to give the impression that not much thought has gone into the arrangement.

Stella follows Jess along the dimly lit corridor, almost relishing her obvious reticence and discomfort. Every time Jess looks round, as if questioning whether they really need to do this, Stella ushers her forward.

On seeing the *Do Not Disturb* sign hanging from the handle of room 504, Jess looks like she's about to abort the mission at the first hurdle, but as she makes an about-turn, Stella stands her ground.

"I'll knock, you talk," she says, leaving little room for choice.

She raps on the door and they both wait, although Jess can't seem to stand still.

"OK, she's not here, let's go," Jess says, shoving her hands into her coat pockets. The look on her face as she pulls them out again is hard to read . . . confusion, acknowledgment and regret cloud her expression in a split second as she looks at what she's holding. She quickly goes to put it back, shield it from view, but it's too late, Stella has already seen it.

"Is that the key card to *this* room?" she asks, unable to believe what she's seeing.

For a moment it looks like Jess is about to deny what is patently obvious. "I don't . . . well, yeah, I guess so."

"What are *you* doing with it?" asks Stella, her voice thick with suspicion.

"I guess . . ." starts Jess. "I guess Yasmin must have put it in here." Her eyes flicker as her brain races to catch up with her mouth. "She was wearing my coat last night—she must have opened the door and put the key card back in the pocket."

"So you came back here with her after the awards?" asks Stella.

Jess nods. "Look, she clearly isn't here. We should go."

"Give it to me," says Stella, holding out her hand.

Jess looks at her, wide-eyed. "We're *not* using it."

"Just give it to me." There's nothing about Stella's tone that suggests she should be defied.

"You can't—"

Snatching the card from Jess's grasp, Stella raps on the door one more time, harder and louder than before. She puts her ear close, listening for a hushed voice—perhaps Yasmin telling her lover to be quiet—but there's not even the slightest sound of movement.

She knocks again, calls out "Housekeeping" and swipes the card against the lock.

There's an audible gasp from behind her as she pushes the door open, but Stella doesn't look back. She doesn't need to see her lost conscience reflected in Jess's eyes.

The room is shrouded in darkness; not even the bright autumn sunshine is able to infiltrate the drawn blackout curtains. The pungent aftermath of aerosol gas hangs in invisible plumes: hairspray and deodorant clog the already-stale air.

Stella hasn't thought far enough ahead to know what she's going to do if Yasmin is lying in bed, nursing a hangover and a bucketload of regrets. That's probably because she already knows that's not what she's going to see. It's as if her eyes are already racing to protect her from what's there; to shield her from the reality of what, unfathomably, she already knows she's facing.

With her mouth formed into the shape of a scream, it's actually Jess that the noise comes from first—a blood-curdling howl that shakes the walls and makes the ceiling feel as if it's about to fall down.

Everything slows to a painful standstill as Stella attempts to absorb the scene in front of her. But as Jess rushes past, time suddenly fast-forwards as she lifts Yasmin's lifeless body up, taking the weight off the sheeted noose from which she's hanging.

"Help me!" Jess shrieks at Stella, who is rooted to the spot, paralyzed with shock.

They work together in breathless silence, both knowing that it's futile.

"Yasmin! Yasmin!" cries Jess, as they gently lay her still body down on the bed.

Stella watches numbly as Jess slaps her about the face and leans in, in the desperate hope that she'll hear a breath escape.

"W-we need to . . ." starts Stella, struggling to form a sentence. "The hotel—they'll know what to do. I'll . . . I'll go to reception."

"You can't leave me here with her," sobs Jess. "Call them, get an ambulance here—they might be able to . . ."

Stella looks at her, unable to hide her sense of hopelessness.

"It might not be too late," pleads Jess, pressing down on Yasmin's still chest. "If we just . . ."

Stella goes to Jess and gently pulls her away. "She's gone," she says. "There's nothing we can do."

25

Jess

"How the hell could this happen?" rages Max with his head in his hands. "I mean, was this even a remote possibility?"

I can see his mouth moving and can hear what he's saying, but it feels like I'm in a bubble, distanced from his words and the distorted faces, which look like they're staring at me through the bottom of a bottle.

"How will we ever know that?" says Stella, shifting from one leg to the other.

I couldn't stand, even if I wanted to.

"Well, how did she seem with *you*?" he asks me, exasperated. "Did *you* know she was capable of . . . of this?"

Does he not think I've asked myself the same question a million times already? Tortured myself for not seeing the signs. Scrutinized every single word Yasmin said. Analyzed every simple action she performed. Wondering whether it was the prelude to something she had always planned to do.

"That's not fair," says Stella, stepping in. "You can't possibly expect Jess to have known this was coming."

"Well, she was with Yasmin last night," Max says as if I'm not here. I wish I wasn't. "Surely she must have sensed something wasn't quite right."

I can feel him staring at me from across his desk, waiting for a response.

"Did she say anything to you—anything other than what's written in the paper?"

I shake my head numbly.

"If you were in the hotel room with her after the ceremony, she must have said something. *Think* . . ." He slams his hand down on the desk.

"What would you do with it, if she had?" I ask acerbically. "Splash it across tomorrow's front page?"

"No," says Max resolutely. "I'd give it to the police, as I'm sure they'll have to carry out an investigation."

My eyes widen as I look at him. "There'll be an . . . an *investigation*?" My voice is high-pitched, and the words catch in my throat. "Why would they need to investigate? It's clear what happened."

Heat prickles my skin, clogging my pores, as I imagine a forensics team combing Yasmin's hotel room, finding my hair, my fingerprints, my DNA all over the glass that I had drunk from. I shake myself down. I'd laugh, if it wasn't so goddamn tragic.

"They'll need a statement from you," Max goes on, as I shift uncomfortably in my seat. "They'll need to know exactly what she said, how she was—every little detail of the time you spent together."

"She took her own life because photographs of herself in a compromising position have been plastered all over the front page of a national newspaper. That's what this is about, pure and simple."

Despite myself, I'm once again confronted by what must have happened after I left Yasmin. I picture her arranging a clandestine meeting with the lover I never imagined she'd have, kissing him in what she thought was an empty hotel corridor, and her horror when she realized that she'd been caught on camera.

Had she called me then, desperate to be told that it wasn't as bad as she thought? Or had she called me earlier, hoping that I'd talk her out of doing it in the first place? Either way, I'd not been there when Yasmin needed me; to tell her that the husband she loved would forgive her, that the children she lived for depended on her, that the public she both revered and despised did not have the right to judge her, and that *nothing* was worth taking her life for.

No doubt she would have realized all that herself this morning, if she'd only given herself the chance to.

Max lets out a long sigh and runs a hand through his hair. "OK, so we need to treat this with real sensitivity," he says somberly. "We'll clear the front page and the inside spread, but I want a well-thought-out tribute to the woman we've come to know, from being in our front rooms every week—her best bits from *On the Ranch*, quotes from media personalities who knew her—"

"Don't either of you feel *remotely* responsible?" I ask, interrupting him.

Max fixes me with a steely glare. "Of those *responsible*," he says, drawing speech marks in the air with his fingers, "Yasmin is already dead, and the man she was with is no doubt in hiding. While I understand how distressing this must be for you, I have to emphasize that if it were not for Yasmin Chopra putting herself in this position, *we* wouldn't have the pictures to run . . ."

"Yes, but—"

Max holds his hand up. "That's the crux of the matter, and I won't have this turn into a witch hunt from one of my own people. There'll be enough of that going on, without your help."

I bite down on my lip, feeling the tug of tears pull at the back of my throat.

"Now, why don't you take yourself off home and try to put this behind you?" he says.

"Put it *behind* me?" I echo disbelievingly. "People's lives are being used for clickbait and you just want me to go home, have a cup of tea and shake it off, as if it never happened."

He looks at me with raised eyebrows. "What choice do you have?" he asks, somewhat condescendingly. "The world keeps turning, and you have to keep turning with it. People will continue to behave badly, and newspapers will continue to report it."

I snort derisorily. "And you can sleep well at night, knowing the part you play?"

"Jess . . ." Stella warns.

"It's the nature of the beast," says Max. "Now go and take some time out, and come back in tomorrow with a clear head."

I reach into my bag for my security pass, before throwing it onto Max's desk. "I can't even begin to understand how you can do all this again tomorrow to someone else," I cry. "I will *never* get Yasmin Chopra's blood off my hands, and I hope to God you don't, either."

26

Stella

Within an hour of Yasmin's death hitting the wires, Peter is marching across the newsroom toward Max's office. Stella sits at her desk, her shoulders uncharacteristically up around her ears, in the vain hope that she'll be rendered invisible. Because there's no way out of this for her; it's her name on the copy, so it might as well be her signature on the death certificate.

"Stella!" comes the raucous roar, though she's unsure which raging lion it's coming from. The office falls deathly quiet as she makes the thirty-foot walk along the plank—every step steeped in regret, guilt and resignation.

"I don't even know where to start!" barks Peter, his chest puffed up with frustration. He paces the floor in front of the windows. "I mean, does somebody want to tell me how the fuck this could have happened?"

Stella looks to Max, who's running a nervous hand through his hair.

"If we'd have thought for one minute . . ."

"But that's the fucking problem, Max," yells Peter. "You don't fucking think. The news works in twenty-four-hour cycles, and you've just proven how one day you're the cock of the walk and the next a feather duster. This morning everyone was lauding our stellar reporting, and tomorrow we're going to be vilified for causing someone to kill themself."

"In his defense," steps in Stella, even though every neuron in her brain is telling her not to, "the pictures were sent to me, and I was the one who brought them to Max."

"I don't give a flying fuck who did what, when—all I care about is salvaging the paper from the jaws of extinction."

The crushing words—from someone who won't ever have a bad word said about the institution that is *The Globe*—pull Stella up. She knows this is bad, but is it really *that* bad?

"Who spoke to this woman?" asks Peter, looking between them, with his hands on his hips. "Was it *you*?"

Stella almost wilts under his unrelenting glare. "It was a junior reporter," she says.

"Well, get her in here," says Peter.

"She's gone," says Stella, half hoping that he doesn't hear her.

"What do you mean, *gone*?"

"She wasn't able to deal with it," says Max. "She's only young and, in all honesty, she isn't made of the right stuff for this game."

"So why did you send her out, then?" asks Peter. "If you'd sent a more experienced journalist—like Stella—she would have got what we needed to make this look like it was this woman's problem, instead of ours."

"This woman's name is Yasmin," says Stella defiantly, unable to let the slight go. "And it wouldn't have mattered who we'd sent out; the outcome would have been the same."

"Yes, but *you* would have got something more," he says, jabbing a finger in Stella's direction. "*You* would have got something that would have proved to our readers that this woman was living a lie and couldn't deal with it anymore. Instead of making it seem that what *we* did was the only reason she's topped herself."

Stella can't help but blanch at his choice of words. She knows Peter's a ferocious businessman, but she rather hoped he had a semblance of compassion, somewhere deep down. If he has, it wouldn't hurt him to show it around now.

"I think she would have done what she's done, regardless," says Stella. "It's the pictures that tipped Yasmin over the edge, and I have to take full responsibility for that."

Peter's lips pull back, as if he has a sour taste in his mouth. "To be totally honest, I don't care what did or didn't make her do it. She means nothing to me. What matters is my newspaper and my reputation. It's all about damage limitation from here on in, so we need to get the rookie back in here. And don't let her leave until she gives us something that *proves* this woman had things going on in her life that made her do it."

Stella looks at Max with raised eyebrows. Peter clearly hasn't met Jess yet.

The mood on the floor is somber, the self-congratulatory bonhomie of a great issue now replaced by the daunting prospect of turning public opinion around.

For once in her life, Stella doesn't even know where to start.

"I've got a call for you," Lottie calls out. "He asked for you personally."

"OK, put it through."

"Sounds a bit pissed off," says Lottie, a little too late.

"Stella Thorne," she barks.

"You need to explain . . . and very fast," the man says in broken English. "I mean, how is this even allowed?"

Stella is not in the mood for a disgruntled reader, and throws Lottie a cautionary glance for letting him through the net.

"Would you like to tell me what the problem is, sir?"

"The problem?" he repeats, verging on hysteria. "The problem is that you use my photo without permission, without payment . . . That is not good business, where I come from."

Stella rubs her temples. "Then you need to take it up with the Picture desk," she says, going to put the phone down.

"But it is *your* name," he goes on. "You need to take the responsibility—because now she is dead."

Stella holds the receiver back to her ear. "Who is?" she asks, slowly and deliberately.

"The lady chef," he shrills.

"Are you talking about Yasmin Chopra?"

"Yes—is the one I'm saying about," he goes on. "She is not with me. I am not with her. Why you make it so?"

"I'm sorry, I don't understand," Stella says wearily.

"The man in the pictures: he is me . . ."

Stella's eyes widen as she assimilates this information. This was not what she was expecting from this call when she first picked up, but now that she has him, she needs to decide what to do with him— and quickly.

"OK, let's take this nice and slowly," she says, sounding as if she's trying to tame a rabid dog. "Can I start by taking your name?"

"Carlos Moreno," he says. "I can't have this on my head—it looks bad for me, you understand?"

"Yes, I understand," says Stella, still not knowing exactly how to play this.

"Is it true?" he asks. "Is she really dead?"

"I'm so sorry," says Stella, unable to believe that the burden of telling this man his lover is dead has fallen to her. "I can't begin to imagine how you must be feeling. Is there anything I can do?"

"Yes!" he exclaims. "You will have to be giving me money."

Stella lets out a long, slow breath. What is *wrong* with people? She's just confirmed his lover's death, and his first thought is of *money*?

"It's probably best if we could get together and talk," she says, sensing an opportunity to appease Peter. She's got more chance of getting something out of this man than out of their recently departed junior reporter.

"I'm talking now," he says a little more aggressively. It's as if he hasn't got time to talk about Yasmin—he's simply got dollar signs in his eyes.

"I think it would be better if we meet," she says, forcing herself to stay patient. "I'd be very happy to listen to you and get your side of the story across. Are you still in London?"

"*London?*" he laughs. "I'm in Brazil."

The cogs in Stella's brain stop turning. She's never been good at maths, but even she knows that he'd have to go some to have been in a London hotel last night and in Brazil a mere fourteen hours later. It's possible—but highly unlikely.

"I don't understand," she says as the pieces begin to fall into place. "Why did you leave London so quickly? Did something happen between you and Yasmin? Did you fight, after the pictures were taken? Did you know what she'd done before you got on that plane?"

She fumbles to get her Dictaphone out of her desk drawer. *Shit!* Maybe it isn't what they first thought. Maybe there's more to Yasmin's death—it would certainly make more sense. Jess's copy suggests a happy woman: the mother of three children, the youngest just a few months old; in love with her husband. Maybe this Carlos guy couldn't handle that. Maybe he . . .

But then she pulls herself up, because despite her best efforts not to return to what she saw in that hotel room this morning, she knows everything about it has the hallmark of a suicide. This was no cry for help, and there were no signs of foul play. It was what Yasmin intended.

"*Plane?*" he says. "I haven't left Brazil in three years."

"Wait—what?" exclaims Stella, losing patience. "How could you have been in London with Yasmin last night then?"

"This is what I'm saying! I know nothing of this girl. She is a complete stranger to me—we're separated by nine thousand kilometers, yet there I am with her."

Stella laughs, really laughs. Because if she doesn't, she'll cry. She's had some fruit loops in her time, but this guy takes the biscuit. She picks up the copy of *The Globe* with the offending front page, desperately trying to find the right words. "So you're saying you've never met Yasmin, never kissed her, but you'd like some money because this guy looks a bit like you."

"He *is* me!" he says as Stella puts the phone down.

"Another nutter?" asks Lottie.

"Afraid so," says Stella, absentmindedly moving her cursor onto the email that's just landed in her in-box from Carlos Moreno. When she double-clicks and the photos appear in all their glory, she gasps.

She'd almost rather he'd killed Yasmin than this.

27

Jess

The waves of regret wash over me as I lie in bed, tears soaking my pillow as I silently beg the clock to turn back. I don't want much; just a few hours to the time when I could have stopped this from happening.

Yasmin's words goad me on a continuous loop inside my head, showing me how I could so easily have realized what she was trying to say. It was all there, hiding in plain sight, so why did I ignore it? I was perfectly placed to help her wait out the storm, but I failed her. Not only when I left her alone last night, but when I ignored her desperate cries for help in the early hours of this morning.

I pull the duvet over my head to ward off the glare of the afternoon sun that is streaming in through the window. I hate wishing it were gray and gloomy, but nothing about today is remotely sunny. I doubt it ever will be again. The ringing of my phone interrupts my maudlin thoughts, and I'm grateful for its shrill tone rescuing me.

"Oh my god, Jess," shrieks Flic. "Have you seen the news? It's that woman, Yasmin . . . She's—"

"I know," I say, unable to hear her finish the sentence. "I . . ." My voice cracks and I cough to clear my throat. "I . . . I found her."

"*What?*" she exclaims. "Are you serious?"

I rub my head, wondering what part of Flic would think I was joking.

"It was so . . . so . . ." I can't stop myself picturing Yasmin's lifeless body hanging there, and my pathetic attempt to save her. "Oh god, I can't even . . ." Tears roll down my face faster than I can wipe them away.

"Where are you?" she asks.

"I'm at home," I sob. "But I don't know what to do with myself. I can't believe it's happening. It's so horrific and it's all *my* fault."

"Now listen to me. This isn't your fault."

"I quit my job," I cry. "I can't carry on working for an industry that does this to people."

A sob catches in my throat as I begin to think about how many other lives have been destroyed by the toxic tabloids. God knows, I've seen enough in the short time I've been working at one.

"How can this be allowed to go on? I thought Max was on my side. I believed we were stamping it out."

Flic sighs. "But isn't that what tabloids do? This poor woman gave them an opportunity and they ran with it. It's what they've always done."

"She's dead!" I shout. "How is that OK?"

"I'm not saying it's OK," says Flic. "I'm just saying that her indiscretion was deemed to be news, and in the public interest."

"What someone does in their private life shouldn't be cannon fodder for the masses . . . Not without their permission."

"Come on," says Flic, not unkindly. "You know how it works. You can't be surprised."

"But this hounding of people needs to stop," I say. "It can't be allowed to carry on."

"And who's going to be brave enough to take them on?" asks Flic. "It's not going to be the government or the police, because they're up to their eyeballs in it as well."

My mind races, desperately trying to imagine a sea change whereby the tabloids are held accountable for their actions. But Flic's right, everyone's running scared of them, lowering their own standards to get into bed with them, throwing their morals to the wolves if it means keeping on their right side.

"I'm coming home," she says as my brain continues to whir. "You shouldn't be on your own right now."

By the time she arrives thirty minutes later, I'm drowning in the depths of the internet, entrenched in the lost causes of former celebrities who have found themselves on the front pages for all the wrong reasons:

Hollywood Star in Hooker Shame

MP in Drug Orgy

Premiership Footballer's Cocaine Deal

Name after name, sting after sting, careers and lives ruined—all for less than the price of a coffee to you and me. Few have fought back. All have lost.

"Look at all these people," I cry as Flic wraps her arms around me.

"Are you going on a one-woman crusade?" she asks gently.

"I've got to do *something*," I say. "None of these poor people deserve what's happened to them."

She looks at my computer screen, where a staunch anti-drugs campaigner is pictured at a party with a powdered nose. "Mmm, well, maybe some of them do."

"I don't mean the likes of *him*," I say, sniffing. "I'm talking about the Tilly Ashcrofts of this world. I stood by and watched them ply her with drink, lured by the promise of a multi-million-dollar movie contract, then ask her if she could get hold of any drugs." I wipe my nose with the back of my hand. "They courted her for months. Giving her first-class plane tickets to Dubai. Putting her up in the best suites. All to reel her in, gain her trust, make her feel she was indebted to them."

"So what are you going to do?" Flic asks.

"I'm going to put a stop to it," I say, aware of how naive I must sound. "I'm going to make them accountable—make them realize they're destroying people's lives."

Flic frowns. "Look, you're my best friend," she starts, "and I love you to the moon and back, but you can't possibly change the media landscape all on your own."

"They're killing people, Flic!"

She pulls me close. "I know, and I can't begin to imagine how you're feeling, but this has been going on since the start of time, and there is nothing you, I or anyone else can do about it."

I narrow my eyes, knowing she's probably right, but refusing to accept it.

"You can't change the world all on your own," she says gently.

"Just watch me," I say, defiantly.

28

Stella

It has felt like the longest week of her life, and all Stella really wants to do is go home. But to do that will mean making herself vulnerable to whatever is waiting for her there. She shudders involuntarily at the thought. If only she could see into Ray McAllister's world; know what he's planning to do, because the anticipation is killing her. She'd almost rather he simply inflict the damage he's intending *now*, so that she doesn't have to live in fear waiting for it.

Even as the car that Peter has sent for her weaves its way through the narrow lanes of Wiltshire, she can't help but imagine a van coming out of a side road, with four hooded men jumping out, ready to ambush her. What will McAllister do with her, once he's got her? she wonders.

As the driver looks at her in the rearview mirror, his once-friendly eyes appear sinister in the narrow reflection, shrouded in the shadows of the passing trees as their branches tap against the bodywork of the car.

"Nearly there, Miss," he says as Stella forces a tight smile, pushing away the picture of a derelict barn in the middle of nowhere, with McAllister lying in wait. It's only when she hears the sound of gravel under the car's tires, and sees the welcoming manor house at the end of the drive, that her coiled insides begin to relax.

Standing at the front door, she adjusts the crossover neckline of her jumpsuit, wishing she'd worn something more conservative. It doesn't show anything, apart from the top crease of her cleavage, but still, if this party is going to have the ratio of men to women that she expects it to have, it would have been wiser to have thought it through more. But then she wonders why the hell she should.

When she pulls the gold decorative handbell, the double doors swing open and a man standing in a full white-tie service suit greets her with a nod and a sweep of the arm.

"Welcome to Chiltern Place," he says. "Mr. Kingsley is waiting for you in the drawing room." He makes it sound as if she's the only guest they're expecting.

Stepping onto the black-and-white checkered tile floor, Stella wonders if she'd got this all wrong. Had Peter actually said it was a party or is she about to walk into a cozy one-on-one dinner? Although in this house she'd imagine it would be the pair of them seated at either end of a twenty-foot-long gilded dining table.

She's relieved to hear voices drift down the hallway, and the gentle hum of small talk and imposed pleasantries, although it's Peter's voice that she can hear holding court, regaling his minions about his close friendship with the prime minister.

"Aha, our guest of honor has arrived," he bellows, throwing open his arms.

All heads turn toward Stella, each of them no doubt checking out the next recipient of Peter's well-rehearsed routine.

"Peter," she says, bending to give him a kiss on each cheek. "Wow, this place is really something."

"Only achievable by your hard work," he says, without an iota of irony. He takes a cut-glass flute of champagne from the tray beside him and hands it to her. "Come and meet my other esteemed guests."

Stella forces a smile as she scans the ten or so faces of Peter's inner sanctum, feeling disappointed, but unsurprised, that there's only one other woman.

"Paul, come on over here," says Peter, beckoning to a balding man who looks exactly like a stretched-out version of him. "This is your counterpart over in the States," he says, turning to Stella, with his arm around her waist.

"Well, not quite," she replies, knowing that Paul Hogarth is the fearsome editor of *The Oracle*.

"Who knows what's around the corner," teases Peter, his hand moving ever lower.

Stella purposefully moves out of reach when a waiter carrying a silver platter of hors d'oeuvres passes by. "Thank you," she says gratefully.

"Terrible business about that young chef," says Paul, his eyes glancing slyly toward Peter to make sure he's listening. "It seems to have caused national outrage."

"It's deeply regrettable," says Stella, taking a long slug of her champagne, its chilled bubbles fizzing as they hit the back of her throat.

"Regrettable that you ran the pictures or that she took her life, because of them?" asks Paul.

"I don't regret running them for one second," butts in Peter.

Stella imagines he'd eat his words, if he knew what she knew.

"But somebody has to be held accountable," says Paul, clearly out to make a point. "You can't have young women taking their own lives because of something that's written in a newspaper."

"It's a free press," says Peter, putting his arm around him in a power-play move. A gentle reminder of who's boss. "And the UK are pretty damn good at reporting the facts, compared to the fake news peddled on certain US outlets." He arches his eyebrows in an attempt to distance himself from being party to any such organization, even though everyone who's anyone knows he's currently trying to buy one of them. "But I, for one, happen to believe that if somebody in the public eye does something that is deemed in the public's interest, then it should be printed."

Stella swallows the acid reflux that burns the back of her throat.

"We sold more copies yesterday than any other edition in the last two years," Peter continues, his expression less in party mode now, and more like the pit bull Stella is used to in the office. "Every TV channel I turn to, they're talking about *The Globe*. Every social-media platform is hashtagging *The Globe*."

Stella wants to tell him that it's not in a good way, but Peter's not stupid. He must know what's really going on—he's just going on the defensive, and she doesn't blame him. It's a terrible position for them to be in, but he doesn't know the half of it yet. She swallows, knowing she's got to tell him sooner rather than later.

"Peter, could I have a word?" she says. "Privately."

"Of course," he says, his eyes widening.

Pinpricks of sweat jump to the surface of Stella's skin as he guides her out of the room and down a mahogany-paneled hallway, turning the corner at the end so that they're hidden from view. Of all the rooms that must exist in this house, she wonders why they're standing in front of a bookcase in a dead-end corridor.

He takes a book half out of its place and, in true James Bond style, the wall moves silently inward, opening onto a windowless room lined with bookcases adorned with awards, plaques and framed photos of Peter with American presidents, British prime ministers and Nobel Prize winners.

"Welcome to my trophy room," he says, sweeping his arms open. "I'm glad of this opportunity as there's something I need to talk to you about as well, somewhere we won't be overheard." He smiles, but it only makes Stella all the more uncomfortable. She looks around surreptitiously, checking for an escape route, but it's already impossible to see the door that she came in through, the walls all refusing to give up their secret opening.

She holds her clutch bag in front of her, a metaphorical barrier to ward off any unwanted advances.

"I wanted to get the latest on all this nasty business with the chef," he starts, propping himself up against the desk that sits in the middle of the room.

Stella bites down on her tongue, wondering why everyone is finding it so difficult to say Yasmin's name. Or maybe it's not important enough for them to bother retaining it. But as she pictures Yasmin's lifeless body, hanging from the ceiling of that hotel room, she knows she'll never be able to forget it—even if she wanted to.

"Well, it's actually Yasmin Chopra I wanted to talk to *you* about," she says, her mouth drying up. "There's been a development that I think you should be made aware of."

"Is it the rookie?" Peter asks impatiently. "Have we managed to track her down yet? What was her name again?"

"Jess," she says.

"So where have we got to with her?"

Stella takes a deep breath, grateful for the reprieve. "I've called a couple of times," she says. "But she's not picked up and, to be honest, I don't think we'll get much out of her."

Peter nods thoughtfully as he takes a cigar out of a polished wooden box and taps its end on the leather-inlaid desktop.

"So," he says, striking a match, "nothing further that would help us build a case to strengthen our position?"

Stella shifts from one foot to the other, sensing a change in the atmosphere. Peter's jaw has tightened and his eyes have narrowed, as if he's hatching a plan.

"Even if Jess had something, she isn't likely to tell us," she replies, trying her best to manage his expectations. "Her moral standards were set pretty high to start with, so if she did have something that might allude to why Yasmin did what she did, then you'll have the devil's own job getting it out of her now."

Peter closes his eyes and purses his lips around the rolled tobacco leaves, making Stella's stomach churn with the sucking noises that he makes.

"Well, something's going to have to give, because I'm not going to let my newspaper bear the brunt of a woman's selfish actions."

Stella tries hard to disguise the look of abject horror that she knows is on her face, but then she wonders why she should. Whether he's Peter Kingsley or not, how could *anyone* be so blatantly merciless?

"No disrespect, Peter, but I think we need to let things settle a little before looking to apportion blame to Yasmin, or heap the responsibility on a young reporter to find something that isn't there. The public need time to accept what's happened and the part we played."

"What the public *needs*," says Peter, "is to know that *The Globe* is in no way accountable for a woman taking her own life. We need to prove that she would have done it anyway."

"We can't magic up something that doesn't exist."

"Maybe that's *exactly* what we need to do," says Peter, looking at her intently.

Stella shakes her head. "I'm sorry, I don't understand . . . What are you suggesting?"

He narrows his eyes, as if weighing up whether or not he can trust her.

"You have real potential," he says. "You know that, don't you?"

"Thank you," she says, looking at the floor.

"Max is not performing as well as I'd hoped—as I'm sure you're already aware. He's making silly mistakes that are costing me, and the company."

Stella is tempted to ask for specifics, but she doesn't want to break Peter's flow. She rather likes the sound of where this is going.

"So, in the not-too-distant future, I'm going to be needing a new editor."

Stella's stomach somersaults and her fingertips tingle. This is it! This is what she's been waiting for.

"And you would be the natural first choice."

Stella smiles. "I'm very flattered."

"I can make all your dreams come true, but I expect a pound of flesh in return."

She swallows and nods. "I'm prepared to give you whatever you need," she says. "I give my word that I'd work twenty-four-seven to ensure that *The Globe* is the best newspaper it can possibly be. I won't let you down."

He makes that vile sound with his mouth again.

"So why don't we see how well you do with this rookie reporter," he goes on. "Go pay her a visit and see what you can do to turn this around."

Stella's chest tightens, knowing that it's an impossible task before she's even started. She's doomed to fail.

"As I said," she starts, "Jess wouldn't give it up, even if she had something."

"Well then, it's up to you to change her mind," he says matter-of-factly. "Find a way to help her remember something the chef woman said that will change the narrative."

Stella looks at Peter as the enormity of what he's suggesting sinks in. "And if she doesn't 'remember something'?" she asks, drawing speech marks in the air with her fingers.

"Well then, I'll be bitterly disappointed," he says. "And I'll have to find another way to convince her that it'll be in her best interests to give us what we need."

Stella nods, as if in agreement, but a sickening sensation is swirling in the pit of her stomach at the veiled threat. She pushes the feeling away, along with the notion that telling him about Carlos Moreno is a good idea.

"Rest assured," she says, "I'll do whatever it takes to make sure *The Globe* gets what it deserves."

29

Jess

I can see the throng of people outside the modest semidetached house as soon as I turn the corner and my heart sinks. There are vans parked up in the dead-end of the cul-de-sac, their crews milling around with headsets and boom microphones, ready to pounce as soon as the front door opens.

It's the first time I've witnessed the cause and effect that a news story can have, and the fact that I played a large, albeit unknowing part in this witch hunt makes me feel sick to the pit of my stomach.

"Is anyone in?" I ask one of the reporters loitering at the end of the short path leading up to the house.

"Yeah, we've got reason to believe that Ashcroft's in there," he says absentmindedly. "We've seen a shadow at the window."

I look at the house, its occupants thankfully shielded from view by white net curtains, yet while we may not be able to see them, they must certainly see us, having set up equipment on their neatly manicured lawn, trampling over their flowerbeds as if we have a right to be here.

Taking a deep breath, I push my shoulders back and head toward the front door.

The other journalists bristle as I walk past them, their body language reeking of indignation and pity. "There's no point knocking, love," one of them calls out. "Someone came out earlier to say they'll be making no further comment."

"So what are you all still doing here then?" I snap, without looking back.

I ring the bell, and my stomach lurches at the thought of the reaction I'm going to get if Tilly Ashcroft opens the door. Is she going to recognize me? If she does, and I don't get the chance to say what I need to say, then she's going to hate me more than all the other hacks put together.

The tiniest crack appears in the door, and a puffy pair of eyes looks me up and down warily. "I've got nothing to say, so will you please go away and leave me alone."

"Tilly, I need to speak to you," I say, instinctively wanting to put my foot in the door to wedge it open, although I think better of it.

But as the tiny gap begins to get smaller, I can't help but put my hand out to gain myself a couple more seconds. "Remember me? I was there that night," I say, the words rushing to come out. "I know what they did, and I want to help you."

There's an excruciating pause when all I want is for the ground to open up and swallow me whole. But then the door opens wider and she silently beckons me in.

There's a rush of discontentment behind me; huffing and tutting as the reporters no doubt ask themselves how I managed to cross the hallowed threshold.

"You've got one minute," she says, crossing her arms as we stand in the hallway.

"What they did was wrong and I'm so sorry I was a part of it, but I didn't realize . . ." A woman who looks to be Tilly's mother eyes me with grave suspicion from the kitchen. "I didn't know it was a setup. I didn't know what they were doing. I thought they were genuinely offering you a movie role."

She scoffs. "So did I."

"I'm sorry. I truly am. I tried to stop it. I let slip what they were planning, in the hope that it would stop them in their tracks, but . . ."

"You can't stop the juggernaut once it's rolling," says Tilly.

"But I have to try—after what's happened to you . . . after what's happened to Yasmin Chopra."

Tilly bites down on her lip, but it doesn't stop the tears from falling.

"I suppose I should thank her," she says cynically. "If it weren't for Yasmin, I'd be on the *front* pages today instead of on page six."

The clatter of the letterbox is followed by a loud thud that makes us both jump.

Tilly looks at the offending item, sitting idly on the doormat. "Every hour they add another thousand to get me to talk," she says disdainfully. "*The Post* will double the highest offer if I talk to them today."

"I'd imagine you could name your price if they smell a chance to get the scoop and discredit *The Globe*."

Tilly nods, but her eyes are still full of wariness. "So what's your plan?" she asks.

"I'll be honest with you, I'm not quite sure," I say. "But I cannot stand by and let women like you and Yasmin be treated in this way."

She laughs bitterly. "But we both did what they said we did. I was caught supplying drugs, and Yasmin was caught with someone other than her husband. We both made a choice, which *The Globe* was more than happy to exploit and report on. In a perfect world, I'd rather they hadn't, but I'm guilty of what they're accusing me of."

"But you were coerced," I say. "If I remember rightly, you actually said that you didn't need anything."

She shrugs her shoulders. "I didn't. I've never done drugs, but I got the impression that wasn't the person they were looking for. The role we'd talked about was gritty and bold—neither of which I'm known for—so I thought if I could just turn myself into that character, they'd not think twice about offering it to me." She looks at me imploringly, as if willing me to understand. "I really wanted the part—or at least thought I did, and I was prepared to do anything to get it."

"Including supplying cocaine?"

"If that's what they asked for, yes. They'd gone to such lengths to court me that I didn't think to question their motivation. If they wanted drugs, and all I had to do was find someone who was prepared to sell them to me, then what did I have to lose?" A tear rolls down her cheek. "Everything, it seems."

"So you got what they asked for and came back to the hotel?" I query.

She nods. "But by then the party was already over. Greg, the supposed director, hadn't shown, and David said he'd gone off the idea of getting wasted."

"So that was it?" I ask incredulously. "Nobody even took drugs? You just left?"

"Yes, but obviously only after they'd got their money shot of me, with a bag of cocaine sitting on the coffee table."

"What about the money?" I ask. "How did you pay for the cocaine?"

She shakes her head, as if unable to believe she could have been so stupid. "David gave me one hundred and fifty pounds and sent me to go and pick it up." She laughs pitifully. "But the problem was, I'd pretended to speak to someone on the phone in the suite—I didn't have a clue where to get drugs from." She looks at me. "So that's where Trevor came in."

"Trevor?" I ask, confused.

"He was the driver David so graciously offered me. Who, when I got in the car, panicking to the point of crying, told me that he happened to know a guy who could get me what I needed."

My mouth drops open. "So not only were you coerced into supplying drugs, but you were also literally driven to pick them up by someone who, directly or indirectly, was employed by *The Globe*?"

"So it seems," says Tilly. "Though, funnily enough, his part in the story wasn't reported."

I clench and unclench my hands, unable to believe the level of subterfuge used to ensnare a woman who, at worst, can only be accused of being foolish.

"Do you know who he was?" I ask. "Maybe we could find him; get him to say what really happened that night. These people have to be brought to justice."

Tilly laughs cynically. "Don't you think others haven't tried before you? People like me, who have nothing left to lose." She looks me up and down with an air of suspicion. "Why are *you* so keen to see the ivory tower crumble anyway?"

I want to say that when Yasmin died, so too did any respect I might have had left for the media. I want to say that I won't allow her to have died in vain.

But instead I ask, "Why do you think they targeted you? Were you just in the wrong place at the wrong time, or do you think there was more to it than that?"

"Be careful, Tilly," says her mum, coming out of the kitchen and putting a protective arm around her daughter. She looks me up and down with suspicion. "You can't trust this girl."

"Does it really matter anymore, Mum?" Tilly asks tearfully. "What else can they do to me?"

"They can still put you in prison," says her mother. "You supplied Class A drugs—and if you're found guilty, a judge won't hesitate to put you away, to make an example out of you."

I look from one broken woman to the other—each of them channeling such hurt and betrayal, but it's the mother who looks like she has the fight in her to seek revenge.

"They targeted me because they knew I was about to go public," says Tilly quietly.

"Go public?" I ask. "On what?"

She looks away, as though the memory is too painful to recall. "I went to a casting for a part in a new drama last year. I was trying out for a few different roles and the auditions went really well. The owner of the production company was in town and so he dropped by to watch the final takes."

I nod, not yet seeing where this is going.

"He liked what he saw and asked me to meet him in his hotel suite to discuss which of the roles I thought best suited me."

I close my eyes, unable to stop the ugliness of the situation showing on my face.

"When I got there, he handed me a glass of champagne and told me we had cause to celebrate."

Her eyes fill with tears, which balance precariously on the edge as she battles to stop them from teetering onto her cheeks.

"He said they wanted me to play the lead—a part I hadn't auditioned for . . ." Her voice trails off and she twists the tissue in her hand. "It was mine if I wanted it; all I had to do was . . ."

I bite down on my lip as I watch Tilly convulse.

"Of course I told him to stick it where the sun doesn't shine, and that's the last thing I remember."

"The last thing you *remember*?" I repeat. "Until when?"

"Until I came round a few hours later, feeling sick and confused. He'd left a note to say he'd had to go to a function and that I was to let myself out."

I hold on to the bannister to keep me from swaying, as the enormity of what this girl has been through sinks in.

"So this sting was to stop you from talking about that?" I ask incredulously. "To discredit you?"

She nods. "I'd been trying to get some momentum building on social media—I wanted to know whether anyone else had experienced the same thing. But I couldn't name names, because I didn't actually know what had happened to me. All I knew was that I was fine one minute and out cold the next. I didn't know what he, or anyone else, had done to me in that time."

"Well, you were certainly drugged without your consent," I say. "Did you go to the police afterward?"

She shakes her head. "No, but I wish I had, because then *The Globe* probably wouldn't have done *this*. It would have been too risky for them."

"Did anyone else come forward on social media?"

Tilly stares at me and I can almost hear her asking herself whether she can trust me or not.

"I'm on *your* side," I say in answer to her silent question.

"Nine women messaged me," she starts. "All of them saying the same thing had happened to them."

"*Nine?*" I ask, aghast.

She nods and swallows. "Those who did what he asked were spared the added humiliation of being drugged and waking up semi-naked, wondering what the hell had happened to them. But, for the likes of me and Sasha Peterson, we'll always wonder what he did to us when we weren't able to defend ourselves."

"Sasha Peterson," I repeat. "The singer?"

She goes to nod, but her mother pulls at her arm in warning.

"Erm . . . that's not public knowledge," says Tilly, wide-eyed in panic. "We've spoken privately."

I stiffen as a sense of unease works through my veins, knowing that the question is just waiting to be asked. I look at her, so suddenly fragile and frightened.

"Who was it, Tilly? Who was in that hotel room with you?"

Her nostrils flare and she swallows, as if trying to get rid of the bad taste in her mouth.

"Who was it?" I ask, desperate to know.

She looks me straight in the eyes as a single tear falls. "Kingsley," she says. "It was Peter Kingsley."

30

Stella

Against her better judgment, Stella had more to drink than she intended at dinner and is feeling the effects as she goes to stand up to head to the bathroom. She'd wanted to stay sharp and aware so that she could keep one step ahead, but the wandering hand on her leg throughout dessert had her reaching for the wineglass more often than she should have.

"Please, madam," says the butler, pulling her chair away. "This way for the ladies' room."

A dedicated toilet for the ladies? thinks Stella as she follows the suited man down the corridor. *There are only two of us here.*

The other woman had been seated at the opposite end of the table from her and Peter, but it hadn't stopped her throwing derisory looks their way all night. When Stella had asked Peter who she was, he'd said she was the newly promoted president of Global Pictures. But from the way she was acting, Stella wouldn't have been surprised if he'd said she was his *wife*.

"So you're the big hotshot that Peter's telling everyone about?" says that same woman as Stella emerges from the bathroom at the end of the corridor. She's pretending to admire a painting on the wall, but Stella would hazard a guess that she saw her heading this way and followed her.

"I don't believe we've been properly introduced," says Stella, offering her hand.

"I'm Elaine Simmons, president of Global Pictures."

Stella nods and widens her eyes, keen to pretend she's in awe, because she gets the impression that it's important to this woman. "I've heard so much about you, too," she lies.

The woman looks at her like she has a bad smell under her nose. "It appears Peter has set his sights on you being the next big thing," she says.

Stella fixes a smile on her face. "Well, that's good to hear. I only hope I live up to his expectations."

"Be careful what you wish for," warns the woman.

Stella can't help but be taken aback by the veiled threat. Aren't women in business supposed to back each other up?

"We don't get where we are on merit alone," the woman goes on.

"What other way is there?" Stella asks icily, offended by the mere suggestion that she's only got to where she is now by sleeping her way to the top.

"If you don't know by now, you soon will," says the woman cryptically.

"Ah, there you are!" exclaims Peter, coming toward them. "What plan are you two hatching?"

Elaine's eyes follow Peter's arm as it snakes toward Stella, settling around her waist. The look she gives Stella is one of pure disdain.

Playing on the woman's insecurities, Stella can't help but place her hand on top of Peter's—a silent gesture to let them both know where they stand.

It gives him all the encouragement he needs.

"I've got some business to discuss with you, Stella," he says with a smug grin. "If you wouldn't mind meeting with me upstairs?"

Stella gives the darkened landing above a cursory glance and smiles. "Of course," she replies.

As Peter heads up the stairs, Elaine grabs hold of Stella's arm and fixes her with a steely gaze. "Whatever glass he offers you, take the other one," she whispers into her ear.

Stella abruptly pulls away and looks at her questioningly, but the woman stands there, unmoving in her attempt to be taken seriously.

"What's keeping you?" Peter calls down.

Stella wavers at the bottom of the stairs, not knowing how to respond. Peter is reprehensible in his opinions, and his wandering hands need to be constantly managed, but would he really do what this woman is suggesting? He respects her, sees her as his deserving protégée. He would surely know better than to think she would fall for an underhand tactic like that. Other women—more *desperate* women—maybe. But *her*? She laughs to herself as the thought leaves her mind as quickly as it entered.

"If you do it even once, you'll always be beholden to him," says Elaine. "Is your career really worth that?"

"Trust me, I don't have to sleep with someone to get where I want to be."

"That's what I thought, too," says Elaine. "You can make yourself believe it if you really try hard enough."

Unable to determine whether this woman is warning her or insulting her, Stella follows Peter up the stairs and into an opulent suite.

A round bed stands on a platform in the center, draped in midnight-blue silk sheets. Its gold inlaid headboard reaches up to the ceiling, meeting a circular mirror that perfectly reflects the mattress below it.

"Welcome to my *real* office," says Peter, spreading his arms. "*This* is where all the big deals get done."

Stella disguises a shudder as she watches him walk over to an ice bucket, where a bottle of champagne and two glasses await.

"It's as if you knew I was coming," she says, wandering over to where he's standing.

"I was hopeful," he says, popping the cork. "You and I are very alike. *The Globe* is in our blood, and we will do anything to save it from harm."

"*Anything?*" she asks.

"*Anything,*" he says, handing her a glass. "We can't let a rookie make the difference between its success and its failure."

"So you want me to do whatever it takes to make sure Jess gives us what we need?" she asks to make absolutely sure she fully understands the brief.

"I've got . . . How shall I put it?" He looks at her intently. "Resources at your disposal—if you feel it will make a difference between her cooperating or not."

Stella pictures herself and two of Peter's henchmen lying in wait for Jess; prepared to inflict whatever damage is necessary to get what they need. How much would it take for Jess to go on record saying that Yasmin was in a fragile state? That she was sitting on a ticking time bomb. That she'd spoken of her guilt at the illicit affair she was having . . .

Stella sucks in her breath. Is she honestly prepared to put another woman through the same fear and intimidation that she has spent the past four years running scared of?

A loud *no* resounds around her head.

The shrill tone of Peter's phone shatters the loaded silence and, irritated, he snatches it from his pocket before looking at the screen and tutting. His fat finger jabs to decline it, and Stella swallows her regret that it hadn't given her the get-out she needed. But no sooner has he put it back in his pocket than it's ringing again.

He tuts and looks at Stella apologetically.

"Elaine, I'm in the middle of something," he snaps, turning and pacing across the bedroom.

Despite herself, Stella can't help but wonder why Elaine would be interrupting them when she knows they're in a meeting. But as she presses the champagne flute to her lips she knows *exactly* why. What if Elaine's right? What if she's looking out for Stella, knowing that she's about to be treated the same way as every other woman Peter's taken into his bedroom under the pretense of a meeting? What makes Stella think she's any different?

In that split second she makes a grab for Peter's untouched glass, quickly switching it with hers, before taking a hesitant sip.

"I don't know why you're bothering me with this now," snaps Peter into the phone, turning back toward Stella. "This can wait until tomorrow morning." He hangs up and grins wolfishly.

"A problem?" asks Stella, silently thanking Elaine.

"She wanted to let me know the box-office receipts for the opening of *No Limits* last night," he says. "But why she thought she needed to interrupt me, I don't know."

Stella offers a smile. "Let's not worry about anyone else," she says as she hands him the glass that was meant for her. "Tonight's about us."

She raises her glass, knocking back its contents, hoping it will encourage him to do the same. But as the effervescent liquid hits the back of her throat, she can only pray that she's picked the right poison.

31

Jess

I hadn't expected Max to be in on a Saturday afternoon, so am ill-prepared to justify my about-face.

"It was a knee-jerk reaction," I offer in my defense. "I was in shock and I wasn't thinking straight."

"That's completely understandable," says Max. "But I can't promise you the rose-tinted version that you seem to have of how a newspaper should be run. I'm trying my best, but it's not always going to pan out exactly how you'd like it to."

"I appreciate that," I say. "I just want to know that I'm making a difference—however small—for the better."

He nods thoughtfully. "But if we want to bring about a change, I fear we haven't got much time. Because the way things are going, Stella is going to be running this show in a few weeks."

My mouth drops open. "What? How come?"

"I'm not stupid. I know where this is heading and what Stella's up to. I wouldn't even be surprised to find that she's actively sabotaging my attempts to make this a paper that you and I would be proud to publish."

Max sighs, looking out across the newsroom as he wanders round to my side of his desk.

"She's hungry," he goes on. "Hungrier than I ever was, and she'll do anything to knock me off my perch. She's no doubt convincing Peter right now that she's the better person for the job."

"Where is she?" I ask, unable to stop my nostrils flaring in disdain.

"Spending the weekend at his place in the country," says Max bitterly. "Nailing the lid on my coffin, I suspect."

"And you're just going to sit here and let her do it?"

"What choice do I have?" he asks, looking at me with narrowed eyes, as if sizing me up, questioning whether I can be trusted with what he's about to say next. "We both know the kind of paper this will become if Stella is editor," he says, slowly and deliberately.

I can't help but shudder as I think of how many more lives will be ruined if she and Peter are allowed to continue with their abhorrent and devious, underhand methods of manipulation and entrapment.

"I'll do whatever it takes to ensure she doesn't get the chance to inflict any more damage," I say.

He offers a satisfied smile. "You're already my eyes and ears on the ground. But I need you to go further to find out what Stella's doing, what she's planning, who her next victim is. And how she's intending to snare them. Because I can't risk any more fuck-ups."

"How am I supposed to do that?" I ask. "She only lets me see what she wants me to see and, by then, it's already too late."

Max stops shuffling papers on his desk. "Get on her computer," he says. "See if there's anything on there that might incriminate her."

"But it will have a password."

He scrolls through his phone, jots down a long number on a pad and tears the page off before handing it to me. "That's the code that will override access to any of the monitors—I'd do it myself if I thought I could get away with it, but . . ."

A surge of fervor pumps around my body, boosting my wavering belief that I might ever begin to take on the Goliath that is Global International. In the darkness of the night I'd laughed out loud, berating myself for thinking that little old me could overturn Peter Kingsley's empire. But with Max more onside than ever, I'm beginning to think we might stand half a chance.

He starts transferring papers into his leather holdall. "I need to get going," he says. "It's my anniversary party tonight and if I'm late . . ." He pulls a grimace. "It'll be my balls on the spit-roast instead of the pig."

I half smile. Max's reputation may be feared—and so it should be—but it all seems like an act that he puts on to garner the respect he rightly deserves.

"I'll see you tomorrow," he says, waving a copy of today's issue in the air.

The change in atmosphere as he steps into the lift is palpable. Great sighs of relief are exuded from executives as they stretch their hands up in the air. The incessant chatter across the newsroom, from which Max deems the loudest voice to be working the hardest, quietens to a soft lull as the competition subsides. Even the notoriously diligent sub-editors, who rarely peer over their screens, push back from their desks and look around the office as if for the first time.

"I thought you'd left," says Lottie, appearing at the door of Max's office, with a puzzled look on her face.

I'm not sure whether she's happy or pissed off. She's tricky to read, constraining her emotions to such an extent that you'd never know whether she loves or hates you. I guess she's learned that particular skill from her mentor, though there's no doubt how Stella feels about me—it's written all over her face.

I wonder what irks Stella so much. Can she see that we're polar opposites, playing for opposing teams? Is she threatened by my moral high ground, aware that it only highlights her deficiencies? Or does she know that I'm onto her and determined to make her pay?

To that end, I spend the rest of the afternoon discreetly researching Tilly Ashcroft's social-media accounts, looking for anything that alludes to her call to arms. She doesn't name names and she doesn't mention anything that makes her alleged perpetrator identifiable, but those in the know will *know*. And certainly those who have been through what Tilly's been through. Several high-profile names sit behind the vapid "Like" button, but none are brave enough to actually comment.

None apart from Sasha Peterson, that is, who replies with a photo of her hands in a love-symbol, her face obscured by the portrait mode.

It's a clear sign of solidarity and I trawl Sasha's own accounts, reading between the lines to see if she gives any clue as to when the same thing had happened to her. But knowing the duplicitous way Global International works, it's impossible to work out how she might have been lured into the clutches of its depraved owner.

I'm having to invent things to do by the time the last of the backbenchers switches their monitor off, and my eyes are so tired and heavy that all I want to do is go home to bed. But there are things to do and, with Stella back in tomorrow, I won't get this chance again.

Sidestepping the cleaners' Hoover cables, I make my way to her terminal with as much confidence as I can muster. Sitting down and wheeling myself into the desk, I try to make it look like the deputy editor of Britain's biggest-selling newspaper wouldn't have a problem with me going through her computer. But then I wonder if the cleaners would even know that I wasn't the indomitable Stella Thorne herself.

I work quickly, tapping the nine-digit code into the password box that instantly flashes up on the screen the moment I move the mouse. My throat dries up as I watch the circle painstakingly rotate, deliberating whether or not to let me in. What will I do if it doesn't? How will I tell Max I let him down?

I let out the breath I've been holding as the screen springs into action. It's only a second later that I realize just because I have access to

Stella's computer, it doesn't mean I'm necessarily going to find what Max wants or needs.

Her desktop is littered with the icons of write-ups past and present, all neatly labeled with the subject's name and date of publication. Tears automatically spring to my eyes as I see one marked "Yasmin Chopra" and I stop myself clicking on it, knowing that seeing the pictures that made her kill herself will only stoke up more pain and regret.

However, I can't help but click on Tilly Ashcroft's folder and watch as the transcript of her meeting with "David" fills the screen—word by word, lie by lie. I want to call out to her between the lines, tell her not to do what I know she's about to do. Reading her downfall in black and white, knowing that her life is about to implode all around her, is like watching a car crash in slow motion. At the end of the document, there's a call sheet with all the details of the meeting. The time, place, confirmation of the suite reservation, the driver's name and contact number . . . Wait . . .

I backtrack. Tilly said that the driver was the man whose story, if he were allowed to tell it, would absolve her of any wrongdoing. It would prove that she was coerced and manipulated into doing something she would never normally do. His word could save her career, restore her reputation, even keep her out of prison.

"Trevor Menzies, you might be just the person we need," I mutter under my breath, as I make a note on the pad beside the keyboard.

I scan the rest of the folders, but see little point in looking into them further. They're all stories that have been and gone, and I haven't got time to go over old ground—I need something new. So I open up Stella's emails, hoping they'll give me more of an insight into what she's planning next: whose life she's about to destroy, for the pound the paper sells for. Whose life is worth that little? *Everybody's*, as far as Stella Thorne is concerned.

Her in-box is plea upon plea from PRs hoping to hook her into promoting their products, whether that be a new cereal bar or a human being. Stella hasn't responded to any of them.

I spot an email with the subject heading "You owe me" and my interest is instantly piqued. This is the sort of thing we need: a disgruntled contact with an axe to grind. My heart thumps as I open it up and start reading:

> After the conversation, here is the pictures I was talking about . . . I cannot be the person with that woman, as I said. Yet here I am, looking exactly the same . . . do you want to tell me how this is possible? You have more explaining to do, or I will call the police. They will surely be interested to hear what you have done.

My brow furrows as I try and make sense of the words. English is clearly not this person's first language, or perhaps it's some kind of code, specifically designed to keep people like me from finding out Stella's business.

I scroll down to find the pictures that the sender mentions, but there's nothing at the bottom of the email. Checking that the cleaners aren't looking at me with suspicion, I speed up to the top and see an attachment, hesitating before double-clicking on it, questioning whether there is any way Stella might be able to know I've gained access. A hotness creeps into my extremities as it occurs to me that she may not have even read the email yet. I hadn't noticed whether it had already been opened, but I have to assume it had, as it was sent the day before yesterday, and even though Stella's away, there's no way she would leave her emails unattended for so long. Especially if she's doing things that she shouldn't.

I swallow my paranoia as I open the attachment and am instantly bombarded with a dark-haired man in a variety of sultry poses. In one, he's looking moodily away from the camera, staring far into the distance, in a classic catalog stance. In another, he's lying on his back in the surf, his perfect six-pack rippling along with the froth of the ocean. But it's the shots of him with a woman that cause me to take a sudden intake of breath; not only because they're more than a little steamy, but because there's something familiar about them . . . about *him*.

Looking as if they're shooting the cover of a 1980s erotic novel, the couple are captured as they cavort in different positions, in various states of undress. With a well-oiled torso and faded jeans, he nuzzles her neck. She responds by throwing her head back in ecstasy.

It unsettles me, but I don't know why. Eight photos on, the niggle is becoming something I can no longer ignore. Fully suited in a tuxedo, the same man is pinning the woman up against a wall, kissing her deeply while lifting her dress up her thigh.

I've seen this photo before, but I can't remember where.

I go back to reread the email, and I'm only halfway through it when the most ridiculous notion bears down on me, wrestling with my conscience like a rag doll.

No, it can't be. I'm not sure if I say it out loud or not.

My legs don't feel like my own as I half walk, half run to where the archive copies of *The Globe* are kept. It's only two down in the pile, but as I pull out the issue with Yasmin's indiscretion adorning the front page, my knees buckle and I have to hang on to the desk to stop myself from falling. I race back to Stella's terminal and hold the offending page up against the screen.

It's the same man. In exactly the same position. But with a different woman.

I fight to breathe as I click on the email again and read it one more time:

I cannot be the person with that woman, as I said. Yet here I am, looking exactly the same.

So this man didn't know that his image was being used on the front of a national newspaper; he hadn't given permission for it to be Photoshopped; or for the woman to be swapped in for another, unknown to him.

I look at the pictures of Yasmin, with a wry smile parting her lips, ready to be kissed, and I'm immediately taken back to the awards night when she'd been drunkenly posing for the photographer. Except that in place of the golden statue she'd held between her legs, her hand is perfectly positioned on this man's crotch.

On the inside spread, Yasmin's arms are held high with abandonment as the same man pins her against the wall of the hotel corridor—just like the woman in the images in the email. Except I know that photo of Yasmin was taken when she was dancing, in front of a thousand people.

My hands jump off the desk, as if jolted by an electric shock, and I push myself as far as the wheels of the chair will carry me.

This can't be happening.

I trip over myself in my effort to get to the ladies' bathroom as a rancid heat envelops my entire body. I battle to lock the cubicle door, the unwanted adrenaline coursing through me, making my extremities tremble.

"Fuck!" I shout as I fall onto the closed toilet seat with my head in my hands.

I want to scream, call out Yasmin's name, in an attempt to ward off the horrific images that flood my brain. I can still smell the death in that hotel room, see her body hanging there, feel the desperation as I willed my breath to become hers. But it was too late—she was gone.

And for what?

She'd *known* she'd done nothing wrong, but the shame of everyone else thinking she had was enough to make her believe there was no way out. And all for a rag that would be the next day's fish-and-chip paper.

How could Stella do it? I knew she was rotten to the core, but *this*?

Clenching my fists, I punch at the flimsy walls in blind fury, venting my anger in the only way I know how. Tears of frustration fall onto my cheeks, every one of them crying for Yasmin and the injustice she suffered.

If Stella thinks she's going to get away with this, she's very much mistaken. She *has* to pay, and I will make sure that she gets everything she deserves, if it's the very last thing I do.

Splashing cold water on my face in an attempt to douse my rage, I wonder if it's too late to call Max; he'll know what to do—he'll be even more incandescent than I am.

I stare into the mirror, loathing the person who looks back, so ashamed by what she's let happen, right under her nose.

But no more.

I wipe the mascara away from under my eyes and puff my cheeks out, determined to take back control.

Just at that moment, there's a loud clunk and all the lights go out, plunging the bathroom into complete darkness. My pulse immediately accelerates and no matter how hard I try to keep it steady, convincing myself there's nothing to worry about, the thriller-reader in me automatically jumps to sinister conclusions.

I search blindly for the handle on the door, sure that once I get back out into the newsroom, normal service will be resumed. But as I peer gingerly through the gap, my eyes racing to adjust, I see that the entire floor has been blacked out, save for the dim emergency blue lighting on the floor.

I take a tentative step and look out across the vast space; the eeriness of the empty desks, with their personal effects outlined in the shadows, makes my mouth instantaneously dry up. I wait for the chatter of the cleaners, sounding confused by the outage, but there's nothing but an alarming silence.

"Hello?" I say, taking tiny steps in the direction of Stella's monitor, its light-glare shining brightly next to all the other "sleeping" screens. "Is anybody there?"

The gentle hum of suddenly icy-cold air-conditioning units is the only retort.

"Hello?" I ask again as I bump into a chair, grateful for the wheels that gently shunt it out of my path.

An uncomfortable tightness takes hold in my chest as the lights above the lift show that it's on the move, mechanically rising through the central column of the Global International Tower.

Quickening my pace as much as I dare, I move toward Stella's desk, desperate to log out of her computer, so that nobody knows I was on it. I alternate between watching the processing circle go round, agonizingly slowly, and the lift's swift ascent. The announcement of its arrival pings at exactly the same time as the screen goes dark, and I don't know whether to hide or stand my ground, pretending I'm working late on a story that can't wait.

When I see Stella emerge, I instinctively fall to the floor, my knees giving way out of shock or fear—I don't know which is the most powerful, but I know I feel both in equal measure. Fuck! What's *she* doing here?

Crawling on my hands and knees, I move around the back of the News desk, squeezing myself between Lottie's chair and ducking into the cubbyhole underneath her workstation. I clamp a hand to my mouth in an effort to stop my panicked breaths from making themselves heard.

"Shit, what's going on with the lights?" Stella snaps, her voice getting closer with every syllable. She must be with someone.

I imagine that she's with Peter; I can all too easily picture their surprise when the lights come back on and they find me hunched under a desk.

"Yeah, I'm fine," she goes on and I dare to hope she's talking to someone on the phone. "I managed to get away. I couldn't bear to do another night."

I strain my ears, waiting for another voice to respond, but there's only a momentary pause before Stella talks again. "So how did it go?" she says.

Another pause.

"Right, OK . . . and there's no way he could have known it was you?"

I listen to the silence that follows, wishing I could hear what the person at the other end is saying.

"Was his wife with him in the car?" asks Stella.

I so desperately want to know who she's talking to, knowing that by the sound of the conversation, it will work against her, though I don't imagine I'm going to need much more than I already have.

"OK, so you think it was enough to stop him from coming into the office tomorrow?"

What the hell is she talking about, and to whom?

"Shaken is good," she says. "Well done—I owe you one."

I dare to let out the breath I've been holding in, knowing that the conversation is coming to a natural end. Then I'm not sure how this is going to pan out. What possible explanation have I got if Stella finds me here, like this?

The silence stretches out and I risk peering out from beneath the desk, because if I don't take a chance, I could be here all night.

I see Stella's back as she retreats toward the toilets and I dart out of my hiding place, staying low on my haunches, in case she looks back. I collide with a wastepaper basket and stop, knowing that the noise will have her turning round.

"Hello?" she says. It's more of a question, and I have to suck in the breath that was already halfway out.

She only needs to take six or seven strides back to see my shadowy outline crouched on the floor. She doesn't even know I work here still, let alone that I'm hiding in the office at close to midnight.

I wait, my heart thumping, convinced that she's silently heading my way, but then I hear the bathroom door swing open and I make a dash for the lift. It's only as it pings its arrival that I realize I left the note with Trevor Menzies's name written on the pad on Stella's desk.

32

Stella

The call that Stella is waiting for comes in just as she's about to step into the shower.

"It's me," says Max gruffly.

"Oh, hi," replies Stella, as breezily as she can manage when she knows what's coming.

"I won't be in today," he says.

"Oh?" questions Stella. "What's up?"

"We had an accident last night," he says. "The car that Tanya and I were traveling home from the party in was involved in an . . ." There's a pause. "An . . . incident."

Stella sucks in a breath, because that's what Max would expect. "Oh my god—is everyone OK?" She can hear the fake sincerity in her own voice and wonders if he can hear it, too.

"Yeah, yeah, I think so," he says. "Tanya's a bit shaken up, but none of us are physically hurt, thanks to the quick reaction of our driver."

Stella would like to leave it there, but his words lend themselves to requesting further information. "So what happened?" she asks, sounding as genuinely interested as she can muster.

He lets out a deep sigh. "A motorbike was playing Russian roulette with us and, unfortunately, we lost and ended up in a ditch."

"Jeez, I hope he didn't get away with it," she says, already knowing that he did.

"Of course he did," snaps Max. "He rode off into the sunset without a single scratch on his leathers."

"Well, have you informed the police?" asks Stella, keeping everything crossed that he hasn't. It will only complicate things.

"I don't see any point in that, do you?" The question is heavy, loaded with a mutual understanding that only they could appreciate.

"Wh-what do you mean?" asks Stella, playing devil's advocate. "Why not?"

There's another slow release of breath. "It was a warning," he says. "Of things to come."

"Are you . . . are you saying you think Ray McAllister had something to do with it?" asks Stella, her voice raspy, as if in shock.

"It had all the hallmarks," says Max dourly. "He was dressed head-to-toe in black, completely unrecognizable and was careful to inflict just enough damage."

Stella makes a funny noise at the back of her throat—a half laugh, half gasp. "I think you're letting your imagination run away with you," she says. "It was late at night, he was most likely on his way back from the pub, having had one too many drinks, and he misjudged the situation."

"It was McAllister," says Max, matter-of-factly.

"B-but how do you know?" asks Stella, raising the pitch of her voice to sound panicked.

"He left a calling card," he says, coughing to clear his throat. "A photo, taken of everyone at the party, was lying on the road."

"I don't understand," says Stella naively. "How does that prove anything?"

"Everyone in it had a red dot in the middle of their head, like the laser sight from a gun, trained on its target."

Stella takes a sharp breath inward. "Oh my god. D-do you think McAllister was there?"

"I don't know," says Max gravely. Stella can imagine him at the other end of the line, holding his head in his hands, his thumbs rubbing at his temples as they pulsate with stress and fear. "But if it wasn't him, it was certainly someone who works for him. He clearly wants to show how close he can get to me and my loved ones."

Stella shudders involuntarily. While this might not be quite what Max thinks it is, it's only a matter of time before it is. McAllister is after revenge and he's keen to make his presence felt—Stella can lay testament to that.

She asks herself if now would be a good time to tell Max about her own run-in with a motorbike, but then she wonders why he shouldn't feel alone in this for a little while longer—like she has these past few days. She immediately pulls herself up, banishing the evil thought from her mind. She wouldn't wish that on her worst enemy, and although she and Max haven't been as close recently, he doesn't deserve to think he's being personally and solely targeted for any longer than she needs him to be.

"McAllister's made his intentions clear to me as well," she says, under her breath, as if hoping that he might not hear her. "A motorbike mounted the pavement as I was leaving the office the other night."

There's a loaded silence at the other end of the line.

"I wasn't going to tell you," she goes on. "I was hoping against hope that it was a random event, but the fact that he also left a calling card, and now this . . ." If she was hoping the admission would make her feel better, it doesn't. It just makes her feel even more alone.

"I'm not going to have him threatening my family and friends," hisses Max. "He needs to realize who I am and what I'm capable of, and back the hell away."

Stella feels oddly comforted.

"If he thinks I'm an easy target, he's got one hell of a surprise coming his way, because if he so much as touches a hair on Tanya's or my kids' heads, I'll kill him with my bare hands."

Fear momentarily grasps its tentacles around Stella's chest as the line goes dead, but she pushes it away. She hasn't got time to question the consequences if this all goes wrong. And anyway it won't. *It can't.*

33

Jess

I haven't slept a wink—unable to close my eyes without seeing Yasmin, feeling her utter desperation as she realizes that she is the victim of the cruellest hoax. Had she called her husband to assure him that what was all over the internet was a vicious attempt to derail their marriage? Had he believed her? I imagine the argument that must have ensued as she went all-out to try and convince him that the woman in the emerald-green dress, with dark glossy curls, whose diamond-adorned décolletage was being nuzzled by a man who was not her husband wasn't really her.

How had it been left? Had he told Yasmin not to bother coming home? Had she managed to convince herself that she would never see her babies again? I lift my head from my tear-stained pillow, unable to shake the thought that I might have been able to convince her otherwise.

If I feel as utterly wretched as I do for not taking her calls, how will her husband feel when he finds out he'd accused her of doing something she hadn't done? But then why would he think for a second that a newspaper would report a wholly untrue story, fabricate pictures—even go so far as setting the whole thing up?

Giving in to insomnia, I get up and go into Flic's room. I have to tell her what I've done, admit the part that I've played, or the guilt will consume me whole.

"Wh-what is it?" she mutters, through half-closed eyes.

"I need to tell you something," I say in a rush, before I have second thoughts. "If I don't tell you, I think I'm going to go mad."

She sleepily pulls herself up against the headboard, squinting as I turn on the bedside lamp.

"This is so much worse than I first thought," I say, feeling my chest crush a little more with every word. "Stella—she . . . she . . ."

Flic looks at me expectantly, waiting for the part that warrants me waking her up in the middle of the night.

"She Photoshopped the pictures of Yasmin . . . She faked them. Yasmin didn't do anything wrong—Stella took stock photos of a model shoot and replaced the woman with Yasmin." I'm crying by the time I've blurted the words out.

"*What?*" she exclaims, her voice high-pitched as she sits up straighter. "But, I mean, how is that even possible?"

"Anything's possible if Stella's involved," I say, unable to stop tears pooling in my eyes.

"Hey, hey," says Flic, reaching up to me. "Come here." I fall into her empathetic embrace as my shoulders convulse.

"Yasmin spoke to me when we got back to the hotel—told me things that *The Globe* would have splashed on the front page. How she felt like her marriage was falling apart, that she was overwhelmed by the constant attention the TV show brought on . . ."

I can't bear to look at Flic.

"It was exactly the stuff that Max and Stella wanted," I go on. "But I didn't file it because I felt I was being disloyal to Yasmin. I didn't want her to think I'd regurgitate a private conversation to five million strangers. I wanted to do right by her—I thought I was doing a good thing."

"So your conscience is clear then," says Flic matter-of-factly.

"No, no, it isn't," I cry. "Because if I'd done the dirty work that was expected of me, Stella wouldn't have faked the photos. Not only did I fail Yasmin by not answering her cry for help, but I also let her down by not telling her truth, and instead allowing someone else to tell a lie. *That's* what killed her."

"Listen to me," says Flic, holding me at arm's length. "You've done nothing to be ashamed of. You stayed true to yourself—true to *her*."

I nod, but deep down I know there's only one way I can do right by Yasmin, and that's to finish off what I started.

34

Stella

Stella feels more in control as the lift carries her up through the core of the Global International Tower. With Max banished to the sidelines, at least for today, she can do what needs to be done, in the knowledge that nobody is going to be aware of it until it's too late.

But she hadn't expected to see a familiar, yet unwelcome face as she walks toward the News desk that she's come to call her own.

"What the hell are *you* doing here?" she almost spits at Jess, who's sitting at her desk with a smug look on her face. Stella has made allowances for a lot of scenarios, but having Max's little sidekick back in the office isn't one of them.

"Oh, hasn't Max told you?" says Jess. "He's brought me back on the team."

Stella struggles to keep the involuntary spasm from locking her jaw.

"Max isn't coming in," says Stella, keen to state her authority. "So I'll be editing the paper today."

"Oh," says Jess, her eyebrows shooting up. "He didn't mention taking the day off."

Stella considers lying to her, saying that he'd booked it off to get over the party, but then she'd have to carry on that story with everyone. "He was involved in a car accident last night," she says matter-of-factly.

Jess's hand flies to her mouth. "Oh my god! Is he hurt?"

Stella waves a hand in the air dismissively, an attempt to make light of the situation. "He's fine—he's just looking after his wife."

"Oh, poor Tanya," says Jess, so quietly that Stella thinks she must be talking to herself. But she's sure she heard her call Max's wife by name.

"I-I'm *sorry?*" says Stella, shaking her head as if it will improve her hearing. "What did you say?"

"I said 'poor Tanya,'" says Jess with what can only be described as a superior grin. "I should give her a call."

Stella's mouth twitches. "Could I see you in my office?"

"*Max's* office?" questions Jess, at pains to correct her.

Just having this girl around is making Stella nervous. One slip and she'll be running to Max and reporting back.

"Can I ask what you're working on?" asks Stella, trying her best to hide her irritation that she's still here, making everything more difficult than it needs to be.

Jess closes the door behind her, unnerving Stella even more. She stands there with her arms crossed and fixes Stella with an intense glare.

"Max has asked me to look into something for him," she says, side-eyeing Stella as if daring her to question what. "A special project."

"Well, as I'm acting editor today, I would appreciate you sharing with me what that is," says Stella. "Perhaps it's something we could consider for tomorrow's issue?"

"Oh no," says Jess obstinately. "I don't think what I'm doing is intended for public consumption."

Stella can't help but raise her eyebrows questioningly.

"Max has asked me to look into the exact circumstances surrounding the Tilly Ashcroft story."

"Why?" barks Stella.

"She's threatening to sue us," says Jess. "She believes she was set up."

Stella smirks. "She got caught supplying Class A drugs—it is what it is."

"She could go to prison," says Jess. "Are you happy to have that on your conscience?"

"If you're asking whether I'll be able to sleep at night, then yes, I'll sleep like a baby."

At least that used to be the case. But if the truth be known, Stella's not sure she'll be able to sleep through the night ever again—not while McAllister is out there. She shakes herself down as his gnarled face, shouting threats from the dock, infiltrates her troubled mind.

"We only reported the facts," Stella goes on. "We didn't force Tilly to do anything. We didn't hold a gun to her head and tell her she *had* to buy cocaine."

Jess laughs falsely and shakes her head. "You're in denial. I was *there*, remember. I saw exactly what happened."

A sly smile crosses Stella's face. "If my memory serves me well, you'd already gone by the time Miss Ashcroft procured the services of my driver, instructed him to drive to London Bridge, where she met her personal dealer, who she'd phoned from the car, and bought three grams of coke, *on account*."

"But you and I know that's not what happened," says Jess.

"Well, that's what the driver said," replies Stella. "Who happens to be someone I'd trust with my life."

That's not entirely true, but Trevor Menzies has been a loyal member of the team for the past five years, and Stella has always been able to rely on him for the behind-the-scenes stories—the golden nuggets that her cameras aren't able to capture.

"So is he in on it as well?" asks Jess, fixing Stella with narrowed eyes. "Is he part of the coke set-up that entrapped Tilly, in an effort to stop her from going public?"

"Going public on *what*?" Stella snorts.

"On what Peter Kingsley did to her," spits Jess.

It takes all of Stella's resolve not to flinch, but her chest tightens and her stomach turns.

"I . . . I don't know what you're talking about," she manages, her voice breaking as her mind drags her back to the events of last night.

"Sure you do," Jess goes on, though Stella really wishes she would stop. "But you think you can just brush it all under the carpet—use Peter's power and influence to simply magic it away." Jess studies her, as if trying to work her out. "What has he got over you that makes you think that's an acceptable way to treat the women he's abused?"

The ground beneath Stella's feet suddenly feels uneven and her heels wobble precariously as her body sways. This wasn't how today was supposed to go. She was going to tell *her* story, but Jess is trying to force her down a road she doesn't want to go down.

"You need to leave this alone," she says, falling onto Max's chair.

Jess shakes her head, her indignation at the suggestion making her normally soft features harden. "You *could* be looking out for these women, calling out those they accuse of assault, and yet you . . . you sit here in your ivory tower, pretending to be a women's advocate, all the while protecting the ones who abuse us."

Stella sighs, wondering how best to play this. Maybe this turn of events could work in her favor. Maybe someone else's story would be even more powerful than her own. "Have you actually spoken to Tilly Ashcroft about this?" she asks, as she studies Jess, careful not to scare her off.

Jess's eyes narrow. "Yes, but if you think I'm going to share anything she said with you, you've got another thing coming."

"Look, maybe there's something in this," says Stella. "Maybe we can work together to bring it to the forefront."

Jess tsks condescendingly. "Do you think I've lost my mind? I wouldn't trust you if you were the last person on Earth."

Stella pulls herself up at the slight. She might be used to people *thinking* that, but for someone to actually say it to her face . . .

"I know we've not always seen eye to eye since you've been here."

Jess laughs. "That's something of an understatement. You've not wanted me here from the get-go. You've made that much clear."

"I'll admit that we've had a few teething issues," says Stella. "But just because we got off on the wrong foot doesn't mean we can't work together for good, now."

"What, now that I have something that threatens the very foundations of this whole corporation?"

Stella can't help but blanch at the threat. "Do you think Tilly Ashcroft would be prepared to go on record? Might she be prepared to talk to us about her experience . . . with him." She can't quite bring herself to say his name.

"She won't talk to *you*," sneers Jess. "Nor will any of the others."

"Others?" repeats Stella with raised eyebrows.

"Nine women have come forward so far," says Jess.

Stella can't help but gasp. "*Nine?*"

Every fiber in her body is alight with the shock that she's not the only woman to have found herself on the receiving end of Peter's reprehensible actions. She'd always known he had trouble keeping his hands to himself, and there'd long been whispers circulating in the depths of the rumor mill that his intentions weren't always honorable. And now, after last night, she knows that to be true, but to think that nine other women have suffered the same fate . . . She shudders.

"We have to move fast," Stella says, needlessly moving things out of the way on Max's desk, as if she is metaphorically clearing the decks and getting ready to roll up her sleeves.

Jess doesn't move and Stella wonders why she isn't as fired up as she is. Perhaps it's because she hasn't been through what she and these other women have.

"I mean it," says Stella. "We have to get these women's stories and go to print with them—like now, *today*."

"What, so you're going to expose Peter Kingsley for who he really is, in his *own* paper," asks Jess incredulously. There's no part of her that looks like it believes Stella would do that. Why would she?

"If Peter Kingsley is the predator these women say he is, then I'm prepared to put my neck on the line to expose him."

Jess can't disguise her skepticism as she frowns.

"But we don't have a lot of time," Stella goes on. "Max will be back tomorrow and we will have lost our only opportunity."

Jess crosses her arms in an act of defiance. "I'll take my chances," she says. "You seem to have forgotten that while you've been fraternizing with the enemy, spending the weekend at his country estate, Max has been *here*, trying to be a force for good."

Stella bites down on her lip, as she fights between desperately wanting to tell Jess what very nearly happened to her and the shame of being a woman who would have put herself in that position in the first place. She shudders as she silently thanks Elaine Simmons.

"Max won't run these women's stories," says Stella, fixing Jess with an intent glare. "If you want to get this out there, it needs to be done on *my* watch."

"Once he knows what these women are accusing Peter of, Max will do the right thing," says Jess assuredly.

Stella can't help but scoff. "Do you honestly think he's got the balls to stand up to Peter Kingsley?" she asks, her voice high-pitched.

"If he's got the likes of Tilly Ashcroft and Sasha Peterson onside, then I think you'd be surprised by how deep his moral code runs."

Stella stops dead in her tracks. "Sasha Peterson, the singer?" she asks, trying desperately hard to keep her voice level.

Jess's eyes widen, as if she's said too much, but Stella already has the bit between her teeth. Tilly Ashcroft's account against the owner of a newspaper who ran an exposé against her two days ago won't be seen as credible, but *Sasha Peterson*? She's a global superstar, whom the world can't fail to believe.

Stella allows herself a small smile.

35

Jess

From the look on Stella's face, I felt as if I'd inadvertently given her *new* information about the queue of women lining up to accuse Peter Kingsley. She seemed surprised, bewildered even, at the potential scale of the avalanche that could be about to hit, but then I'd pulled myself up, reminding myself that she must already have chapter and verse on every single one of Kingsley's victims. No doubt he furnishes her with all the abhorrent details, so that she's ever ready to jump into action, primed to intimidate and entrap any of those who threaten to blow the whistle.

But now that she knows the tide is turning, Stella's going to have to move fast to shoot down anyone who dares to put their head above the parapet. That's why I have to move even faster, so that Tilly's story, at least, is absolutely watertight and is one that neither Stella nor the behemoth that is Peter Kingsley can wriggle out of.

So in my effort to get one step ahead of them, I find myself in Peckham, South London, on the estate where I'd gleaned Trevor Menzies lives, from *The Globe*'s accounting system. Seemingly still naive, I was shocked at how much money he'd been paid in the last twelve months, though with all the remittance advice only ever referring to "chauffeuring services," it was impossible to know exactly what he'd been involved in. Perhaps now's the time to find out.

As I step off the bus, a group of unsavory characters eye me with interest, making me feel as if I should have left my watch at the office. I pull the cuff of my coat over my wrist and try to look as if I know where I'm going, keeping a tight grip on my handbag as I stride into the depths of their domain. One of them shouts something, but I can't be sure it's aimed at me, and even if it is, I'm of a mind to keep walking.

The concrete jungle towers above me, casting long, cold shadows on the bleak landscape below. Even the bright-yellow slide and the sound of laughing children in the barricaded playground do nothing to lift the dispirited atmosphere of unemployed teenagers who have nothing better to do with their time than peddle their wares openly on the skateboard ramps.

"Hi," I say to the only woman in the recreation area who watches me approach without eyeing me up and down with suspicion. "I'm looking for Hogarth House—can you point me in the right direction?"

"It's the big one over there!" declares the little guy sitting on the bench beside her. He points to the tallest tower block and my heart sinks.

"He's right," says the woman, who I assume to be his mother. "I hope the flat you're looking for isn't too far up, as the lifts have been out of order for weeks."

"Thanks," I say, groaning inwardly.

She smiles, almost in pity, though I can't tell whether it's because of the uphill climb I have ahead of me or the welcoming committee that she knows awaits.

Boys circle me on bikes as I make my way across the concourse, seemingly doing their best to try and intimidate me. I roll my eyes and tut at their efforts, in an attempt to pretend I'm used to it; convince them that I'm a local—*one of them*—though I fear my patent loafers and plaited hair screams that I'm not.

Feeling suddenly vulnerable and a little out of my depth, I call Max to at least let him know where I am and what I'm doing. I don't expect him to pick up, knowing he'll be recovering from the aftermath of what I fear Stella set up last night. I've tried to shake the absurd thought from my mind, but with what I heard her say on the phone, coupled with Max and his wife being involved in a car accident, I can't help but put two and two together.

Maybe Stella wants his job more than either he or I has given her credit for.

Unsurprisingly, his phone goes to voicemail and I wait for the beep before recording my message.

"I think I might be onto something," I say in a hushed tone. "I'm in Peckham, looking for Trevor Menzies—he's the driver Stella used for the Tilly Ashcroft sting. I'll let you know if it comes to anything. But call me back when you can. I need to tell you something about Yasmin Chopra."

Even though I've ended the call, I keep the phone to my ear to deter any of the kids from trying anything. But the only incoming attack is on my senses.

The smell in the stairwell makes me want to retch and I hold my sleeve to my nose to try and stave off the stench of stale urine, but it still forces its way to the back of my throat. Holding my breath, I jump over the puddle at the foot of the stairs and take them two at a time, not stopping until I'm on the second floor. I'm pretty sure the flat I'm looking for started with a three, so I keep heading upward, while rooting around in my bag for the piece of paper with Trevor's full address on it.

I'm nearly there, just one more floor to go, but as the rousing echo of men hollering up the cavernous stairwell pushes me on, I have no way of knowing whether where I'm heading for is a safer alternative.

I'm out of breath by the time I reach the graying front door, where the three is hanging on for dear life by the bottom screw. The bell doesn't work, so I bang on the door with the heel of my hand.

I do it again, louder this time, when I hear nothing from the other side.

"All right, all right, I'm coming," says a gruff voice eventually, shuffling ever closer. There's the sound of a chain being slid across, and then half a ruddy face peers through the crack. "Who are *you*?" he barks.

"Trevor Menzies?" I ask, unable to believe that this unkempt, unshaven man could have chauffeur-driven Tilly Ashcroft in a limousine just a week ago.

"Who's asking?"

"Erm, my name is Jess . . . Jess Townsend," I stammer, unsure what he'd want to hear. "I'm . . . I'm from *The Globe*."

His eyebrows shoot up. "You got my money?" he says, eyeing my bag.

I nod, playing devil's advocate. If I have to lie my way in here, I will. This is far too important to walk away now.

The chain rattles and he swings open the door. "You'd better come in then," he says, standing there in a stained vest and studying me with beady eyes.

The air is thick with a cloud of marijuana, its distinct funk curling its way into the back of my throat. I resist the urge to cough.

"So where is it then?" he asks, falling heavily into a worn armchair. "You promised me a monkey if I gave you what you needed."

A monkey? My brain scrabbles to remember whether it's cockney slang for £500 or £1,000. From memory, a grand is a bag of sand, so it's likely to be £500, which, looking around this place, will still go a long way. It would certainly pay the rent and keep Trevor's substantial drug habit in the style to which he's clearly become accustomed.

He lights a spliff and inhales it deep into his lungs. "And I more than delivered on my side of the bargain. So you don't want to be mucking me around, because I'll talk if you don't pay like you promised. In fact,

I might even request a little more . . ." Smoke furls from the slightest gap between his lips.

I shift from one foot to the other, wondering how best to play this. He clearly knows something was amiss that night and is being paid to keep quiet about it.

"What would you say?" I ask, half laughing, so he doesn't feel threatened.

"I'd tell 'em everything," he says, turning it back on me. "If you think I won't, just try me."

"Who would you tell?" I ask, chancing my arm.

He takes another long draw on the roll-up and looks at me through narrowed eyes. "Do you not think *The Post* would pay me thousands to know what you've done?" He stares, waiting for a response. "*The Globe* would be dead in the water if the public found out what you'd done to that poor girl."

I will my face to remain expressionless and my body to stay still, fighting against every instinct to leap forward, snatch him up from the chair and demand that he tells me everything he knows. If I'm to get the best out of Trevor, I need to make him think I'm on his side.

"It would put us in a very uncomfortable situation," I say.

"*Uncomfortable?*" he snorts, laughing to himself. "You'd be hauled across the coals."

"You don't honestly think we deserve that, do you?"

He gives a sinister lopsided grin. "I think you deserve everything you get. You and I both know that that girl didn't know her cocaine from her heroin. She certainly didn't know where to get it from, which is another reason why you should be giving me more money."

"If we could have avoided getting you involved, we would have," I say, making it sound as if it were deeply regrettable.

He chortles. "If I wasn't involved, you wouldn't have got what you needed . . . what you *wanted*. If you didn't have me telling her I knew someone who could help, taking her to the pick-up, then you wouldn't have had a story. And if I wasn't there to stop her stressing about what she was being asked to do, she would never have gone through with it. She was shitting herself; she'd never taken drugs, didn't agree with it, but if it meant she'd get the job, then she was prepared to listen to what I told her to do and hoped God would forgive her."

I clench and unclench my fists, in a futile effort to stop the onslaught of his words from feeling like bullets.

He shakes his head. "Man, if people find out what you did . . ."

"What about what *you* did?" I hiss. "You're the one who claimed Tilly told you where to go. That you believed she had a relationship with the dealer. That you saw her handing money over."

He kisses his gums. "I told Stella what she wanted to hear. What she paid me for."

Burning bile forces its way up into my throat as I'm forced to acknowledge how far Stella's gone to entrap Tilly. How could I have believed, even for a second, that she was on our side?

"*The Post* won't believe a word you say without proof," I bark, playing devil's advocate again.

Trevor hauls himself out of the armchair and lurches over to the old sideboard in the corner of the room. Pulling the drawer open, he takes out a Dictaphone and holds it up, with a crooked smile on his face.

"You're bluffing," I say, as my heart races at the prospect that he isn't.

"Test me," he says, raising his eyebrows defiantly.

When I say nothing, he pushes play as if he were detonating a bomb. When I hear the voice on the tape, issuing detailed instructions on how Tilly Ashcroft must be left with no choice but to supply drugs, I realize that the explosion is going to be far greater than either of us could possibly imagine.

36

Stella

Stella feels a sense of unease in her chest before she's even reached the Landmark hotel on Bayswater Road. Never before has she risked so much on a story, and the palpitations are making her short of breath.

Not wanting to draw attention to herself, she bypasses reception and heads straight for room 246, knocking lightly on the door.

A pair of suspicious eyes, already on high alert, peer around the smallest gap.

"Hi, Sasha, I'm Stella Thorne."

The door opens and the woman looks her up and down, no doubt trying to make a snap last-minute decision as to whether or not she can trust her.

"I meant what I said on the phone," says Stella, by way of trying to reassure her that she can.

Sasha gingerly beckons her in and gestures to an armchair by the window overlooking Hyde Park.

"Would you like a tea or coffee?" she asks, her timid voice unrecognizable from the power ballads that she's famous for belting out.

"A coffee would be great, thanks," says Stella, as she slips her coat off and lays it over the back of the chair. She imagines she's going to be here for quite some time.

"So . . ." says Sasha hesitantly, as she pours a freshly brewed coffee from a cafetière that she'd obviously ordered from room service ahead of Stella's arrival. "You said on the phone that you knew what I'd been through?"

Stella grimaces, knowing that the only reason Sasha has agreed to see her is because she thinks they're both victims of Peter Kingsley's depraved abuse. Stella doesn't want to appear disingenuous by admitting that, actually, she had a lucky escape.

"I've been in a similar position to you," she says cagily, not wanting to show her hand until all the cards are on the table. "And I *will* tell my story, but it's yours that will make people sit up and listen."

Sasha's jaw tightens as she puts her hands in the pockets of her cargo trousers.

"I promise you I will report it sympathetically and in your own words," says Stella, knowing she can't let this one get away.

"I . . . I don't know," replies Sasha, turning away as her eyes fill with tears.

"Please don't feel you have to disguise the hurt and pain," says Stella softly. "That's exactly what we need to show on the page."

"I can't bear to think about it," says Sasha, looking to Stella. "So to talk about it is going to be incredibly difficult."

"I know," continues Stella. "But we can't let this go on. You and I have the power to stop this—to stop it happening to any other women."

Sasha nods, sniffing as she wipes her nose with a tissue.

"Why don't you sit down and tell me what happened that night?" says Stella gently. "Take your time. We can stop whenever you want to and if, at the end, you've said anything you'd rather not be shared, we'll wipe it from the tape."

"And then you'll tell me what happened to you?" asks Sasha, her big brown eyes looking at Stella imploringly.

"That's the deal," says Stella, motioning to the sofa on the other side of the coffee table.

Sasha takes a seat and picks at the tissue in her hand.

"So, I'd been asked to perform at Mia Kingsley's sixteenth birthday party in Los Angeles," she starts. "But I was scheduled to do a show on the other side of the US that same night, so regrettably I had to turn the invitation down."

Stella nods, giving her all the time she needs.

"But Peter Kingsley's reps wouldn't take no for an answer and kept upping the appearance fee until it was getting ridiculous. They said Mia didn't want the party if I wasn't able to perform, so they would pay whatever it took to make sure that I could."

Sasha shakes her head ruefully. "In the end, they offered to send a private jet to get me from New York to LA, and half a million dollars to perform. I'm ashamed to say it was an offer I couldn't refuse—it was such a lot of money to sing four songs, but obviously I wasn't to know there was an unwritten clause in the contract."

She takes a deep breath. "Anyway, I did the show and was told that Peter Kingsley wanted to see me to thank me personally for going out of my way to make the occasion special for his daughter."

Stella resists the urge to grimace at the obviousness of his tactics—it's his classic modus operandi, but unless you know it, you'd be forgiven for feeling flattered by his attention. She wonders how many women had the foresight, or the chutzpah, to stop him at the pass. How many had been one step ahead of him, blessed with the pre-notion of where it was heading? But they would have had to make that call early; *before* they were alone with him, *before* he beguiled them with false promises, *before* he offered them a drink . . . otherwise it was already too late.

Sasha wipes away an errant tear as she goes on. "So I was taken to a bungalow on the estate and Peter was there, having a drink on his own—taking a moment away from all the madness, he said. I wasn't expecting anything more than a quick thank-you on the doorstep, but he said he had a surprise for me and invited me in."

Stella can see it all playing out so clearly in her mind's eye that she wants to call out: stop Sasha from going in; pull her back from the predator's clutches. She can see the look on Peter's face—the self-satisfied grin as she steps across the threshold—congratulating himself that he's enticed another victim into his lair.

"He gave me a glass of champagne and said he'd read in a recent magazine interview I'd given that my dream was to perform at Madison Square Garden and he could make that happen."

She bites down on her lip and shakes her head in despair, seemingly unable to believe her own naivety.

"It wasn't your fault," says Stella, reaching over to put a reassuring hand on her arm.

"He told me he needed to change his outfit and to follow him through to the bedroom while he discussed the details of how he was going to get me the gig. It's stupid, I know, and believe you me, I've beaten myself up every day since, but I really didn't see the signs. He was charming, interested in my career, telling me he could make all my dreams come true . . ." She snorts derisorily. "Maybe *that* was when I should have seen the red flags. When a man tells you he can make all your dreams come true, you can bet your bottom dollar that he's going to expect something in return."

"You were caught up in the moment," says Stella. "You would hope that in this day and age we wouldn't have to be on-guard, but although the #MeToo movement has made a great impact, there are still far too many men who think it doesn't apply to them." She looks at Sasha. "So, what happened next?"

Sasha pulls at the tissue coiled in her hands. "He started taking his clothes off while telling me that the promoter for Madison Square Garden was a good friend of his, who owed him a favor. He only had to put a call in to make it happen, he said, but the question was: how much did I want it?" She shudders and closes her eyes.

Stella's throat constricts.

"I froze, rooted to the spot in shock," cries Sasha. "But he seemed to take that as submission. So he pushed me onto the bed and . . ."

"I'm so sorry," Stella manages, swallowing the bitter taste in her mouth.

"I remember his weight on top of me—me shouting at him to stop, and then . . ."

"It all went black?" says Stella, finishing the sentence for her.

Sasha nods. "That's the worst part, for me. I guess other women might say they would rather be unaware of what was happening to them, but not knowing what he did to me is so much worse, it's what I struggle with the most."

"I get that," says Stella.

Sasha looks at her—like *really* looks at her, as if for the first time. "Were you . . . were you knocked out, too?"

Stella hesitates; she needs to choose her next words carefully if she's to convince Sasha that she's not a fraud and here under false pretenses.

"My story is a little different from yours," she says.

Sasha's eyes narrow, as if sensing that Stella's end of the bargain is about to be broken. "But I thought you said . . ."

"I . . . I was at a dinner party at Peter's house," falters Stella, conscious of keeping Sasha onside. "And I somehow allowed myself to be drawn away from the other guests." She tuts. "I make it sound as if it was against my will, but I gave my full consent to accompanying him to his bedroom. In fact, I actively encouraged it."

Sasha raises her eyebrows, not in a judgmental way, but more out of a morbid curiosity.

Stella takes a sip of her coffee before going on. "With hindsight, and much regret, I think I was trying to prove a point. To another woman, no less, who was doing her best to warn me off."

Sasha bites down on her lip. "But surely you, of all people, know what he's capable of. You've seemingly been protecting him for years."

Stella shakes her head. "I'd heard the odd whisper, been conscious of his wandering hands, but I never imagined he was . . . he was doing *this*." There's an uncharacteristic tug at the back of her throat.

"So what happened?" asks Sasha gently.

"He . . . he gave me a drink," says Stella, as she thinks back to the night before last, when her perception of the world that she occupied had forever changed. It seemed like a lifetime away; its edges were already blurred by the speed of events that had unfolded since then. Yet despite herself, and despite the pain and distress Peter Kingsley has inflicted on others, Stella can't help but feel selfishly grateful for this distraction. "The woman at the party had warned me not to accept any glass he offered me, but . . ."

"You *ignored* her?" gasps Sasha.

"I was arrogant. I didn't think it could happen to me."

There's that feeling again and she stops, waiting for the tightness to subside. Sasha reaches across and puts a comforting hand over Stella's, but it only serves to make her feel even more wretched.

"But then when I realized he would treat me the same as anyone else, I managed to swap our glasses at the last minute."

Sasha stares at her, wide-eyed. "So . . . you didn't actually drink it?" she asks.

Stella shakes her head, almost ashamed to have let her down. Sasha had thought they were kindred spirits.

"But wait," says Sasha. "Does that mean . . . *he* drank from the glass that was meant for you?"

Stella takes another sip of her coffee before placing the cup and saucer back on the table. "He knocked it back in one," she says. "All the while eagerly watching, waiting for me to do the same."

"Oh my god!" says Sasha, throwing a hand up to her mouth.

Stella can't help but picture Peter's lumbering frame as he launched himself at her, his beady eyes alight with the thought of what was to come. Except that, on this occasion, he couldn't possibly have imagined. "He came toward me," she says, "but I excused myself, telling him I needed to go to the bathroom to freshen up. I didn't know what was going to happen; how long it would take, whether it was even going to work . . ." She shakes her head. "But what terrified me the most was what if he *hadn't* put anything in the drink? Ironic really, when it was supposed to be meant for me."

"So . . . had he?" asks Sasha hesitantly.

Stella takes her phone out from her handbag and scrolls through, before turning it to show Sasha. "He was naked by the time I came back out," she says with a shudder. "Lying on the bed, wearing nothing but a grotesque smile."

She presses play on the video and they both watch in abject horror as the moving image takes a moment to focus on his exposed body.

"Hey, what you doing with that?" Peter's voice booms through the phone's speaker, making both women flinch involuntarily. The video zooms in on him raising his hand, in a futile attempt to block the camera's view.

"I want to be able to remember this," comes Stella's shaky voice. "To recall it whenever I need to."

"Turn it off," he mumbles, as the camera gets close enough to pick up the beads of sweat collecting on his bald head.

"Oh, OK," says Stella, feigning disappointment; but, listening back to it, she can hear the rising panic between the words. She still had the wherewithal to keep filming, although the camera angle has become a little skewed.

"Get on over here," says Peter, his words becoming elongated.

Tears well up in Stella's eyes as she hears her breath quicken down the phone, the memory of not knowing how this was going to play out still so raw.

"I've waited a long time for this," slurs Peter, his eyes becoming heavy-lidded. "So I expect great things."

There's a dull thud as the glass he is holding falls from his grasp onto the deep-pile carpet, and an audible gasp can be heard, but Stella can't be sure whether it's on camera or from Sasha, who's sitting transfixed beside her, with a hand over her mouth.

"This is why we have to do something," says Stella, clasping Sasha's hand and squeezing it tightly. "So that he never tries to do this ever again."

Sasha gets up and goes over to the window, wrapping her arms across her body as she looks out onto the hustle and bustle below.

"I . . . I don't know that I can," she cries. "It's already hard enough for me to live with, but if everyone out there knows about it, too, I don't know how that will make me feel."

Stella pulls herself up, unable to stop recalling the image of Yasmin Chopra's lifeless body hanging from the ceiling. That had been on *her* watch. Is she really prepared to be responsible for it happening again?

"I know this is going to be hard," says Stella, getting up and going toward Sasha. "But I'll be with you every step of the way. This is about retribution. This is about stopping Peter Kingsley, and other men like him, from doing this to anyone else. This is about taking back control." She turns Sasha to face her. "You will feel empowered by telling your story, not ashamed. This is your chance to take back what he took from you. To help other women feel less alone."

Sasha nods tearfully. "I want an eye for an eye. I want him to feel as violated as I feel. I want him to know what it's like to have your whole life turned upside down." She fixes Stella with a steely glare. "I want him to pay for what he's done to me, and every other woman he's preyed upon."

Stella's insides uncoil as Sasha's resolve strengthens and she raises her coffee cup in her direction. "May he rot in hell," she says.

37

Jess

My skin feels tainted by what I saw in Trevor Menzies's flat, my mind utterly devastated by what I heard. I'd never expected for a moment that what had happened to Tilly Ashcroft was merely the tip of the iceberg; that Trevor would have evidence of others having spent years languishing in prison for something they didn't do.

For the price of a month's rent, I'd negotiated the release of two tapes, banishing all thoughts of how I'd pay my landlord next week. Menzies had accompanied me to the cashpoint on Peckham High Street—my naivety urging me to believe it was because he was worried for my safety, but the realist in me knowing it was to protect his meal ticket from being robbed.

I felt sick as I listened to them, over and over again on the way back to the office, unable to accept the lies and corruption that had brought about the downfall of innocent people. But as shocking as it was, once I'd allowed the corrosive truth to work its way into my veins, the opportunities it afforded me were laid bare. Now I have the evidence to take to the highest in command; to prove that *The Globe* isn't only unethical and immoral, but is also operating illegally and in contempt of court.

But *who* do I give it to?

"Could I have a word?" I ask, poking my head around the door of Max's office, where Stella has swiftly made herself at home. It's as if she knows he's not coming back—maybe she's made sure he won't.

She looks at me, unable to hide her irritation. "I've got a paper to put to bed, so unless you're going to tell me that a bomb has just fallen on a kindergarten, then it'll have to wait."

"I *know* what's going on here," I say. "I know that you're all working together."

Stella looks at me impatiently, waiting for me to get to the part that's relevant.

"You talked a good talk earlier, pretending you wanted to do the right thing, and I almost . . . *almost* started to believe you." I look at her through narrow eyes. "But that was before I went to see Trevor Menzies," I say, almost too quietly for her to hear.

She looks at me with raised eyebrows to imply that she hasn't heard, but the way she says "*Sorry?*" suggests that she has.

"You know Trevor," I say sarcastically. "The man you'd trust with your life."

"What did you do *that* for?" she asks, her brow furrowed.

"I wanted to make absolutely sure that what Tilly Ashcroft had told me was true, and now I have categorical proof that not only was her version of events correct, but Trevor Menzies admits to driving Tilly to meet *his* dealer, because she didn't have a clue what to do or where to go, because she'd never taken drugs in her life."

I watch Stella needlessly check the cuffs on her silk shirt and can almost hear her embattled brain screech as it goes into overdrive, wondering how best to deflect what she knows is coming over the hill at her.

She shrugs her shoulders. "If you want me to say that your little friend is innocent, then I'm sorry to disappoint you, but she's not. I may push the boundaries to get a story, but I make absolutely no apologies for it, if it uncovers the truth. While I may lead a horse to water, I don't ever force it to drink."

"Maybe we should ask Tilly that, because from where I'm standing, I'd say you not only led her to water, but pushed her head under until she couldn't breathe."

I look at Stella square on, refusing to be intimidated by her unrelenting stare.

"And all to avenge those who dared to threaten Peter Kingsley's carefully constructed public image and expose him for the man he truly is."

"I would *never* manipulate a story in order to protect him," says Stella, so adamantly that I almost believe her. "Nor would I implicate someone in something they haven't done, on his say-so."

"So Yasmin Chopra wasn't on his hit list then?" I ask, guessing that she must have been, though I can't work out why.

"Yasmin was her own worst enemy," she says, her voice a little softer, as if to remind me that we were both witness to that.

Despite myself, I can't stop a tear falling onto my cheek. "How can you sit there and say that, when you know what you did?"

Stella straightens up. "Excuse me?"

"I *saw* the pictures," I blurt out. "I know they were fake."

Her top lip quivers and she fixes me with a look that could turn water into stone.

"What threat did *she* pose?" I shriek, unable to control the volume of my voice. "That meant you had to make it look like she couldn't give two hoots about the husband she loved and the children she adored."

"I don't . . . I don't know," stutters Stella, seemingly out of her depth for the first time.

I clench and unclench my fists, in a desperate attempt to stop myself from launching across the desk and knocking ten bells out of her. "You took everything that was dear to her and made it look like she was a callous and heartless slut, out for a cheap thrill. You *know* that wasn't who she was . . ."

Stella sits there open-mouthed, mute.

"So why did you do it?" I'm shouting now, desperate for a reaction. "What did Yasmin have over Peter Kingsley that made you do it?"

The color drains from her face. "You . . . you think there was a connection between him and Yasmin?" she asks.

"Well, why else were photos of her doing something she'd never do fabricated by you and splashed all over the front page?"

Stella shakes her head. "I . . . I didn't have anything to do with the photos," she says, looking as if she's battling against the thoughts raging inside her head. "I didn't know they were fake—they were sent to me anonymously, and when you didn't get anything decent from the interview—"

"Oh, so it's my fault, is it?" I bark, cutting her off.

"I didn't say that," replies Stella, curtly. "I'm just saying that Yasmin didn't give you what we needed, so . . ."

"So that gave you free rein to run roughshod all over her life?"

Stella shrugs her shoulders, but nothing about her suggests she's feeling remotely carefree. Her brow is furrowed, her eyes are wide and her jaw is pulsing involuntarily.

"And for your information," I hiss, leaning across the desk, "Yasmin gave me everything, and more. She gave me enough for the next day's splash, and the one after that."

Stella raises her eyebrows in surprise. "So why didn't you file it?"

I wish I knew. We sit in silence for a moment, each of us considering our next move.

Stella clears her throat and I can tell, from the way she's psyching herself up, that what she says next is going to be a game changer. "Peter Kingsley would pay handsomely for what Yasmin revealed to you," she says.

My mouth drops open. Of all the scenarios crowding my head, *that* wasn't one of them.

"Why would he want that?" I ask, somewhat naively.

Stella walks over to the floor-to-ceiling window overlooking the newsroom floor and, with sleight of hand, drops the blinds to block both *our* view and that of the fifty or so staff who are no doubt wondering what the hell's going on in here.

"He wants to prove that *The Globe* wasn't a contributory factor in Yasmin taking her own life."

I can't help but laugh. "It wasn't merely a contributory factor; it was the sole reason."

"That may be so, but Peter wants to make it look like she had a myriad of problems beforehand, which she couldn't see her way past."

"There is *nothing* in this world that would make me do that," I say, unable to believe what Stella's asking of me. Just when you think the tabloid press can't stoop any lower, the bar is placed on the ground. "I didn't share what Yasmin said because she spoke to me in confidence, and I wasn't prepared to break her trust. I've beaten myself up ever since, knowing that if I had, then perhaps you wouldn't have felt the need to run the photos. But if you think I'm going to share it now . . ."

"Peter's assigned me with the task of making sure you do," says Stella.

For some illogical reason I expect her face to break into a grin, because otherwise her loaded words could be wholly misconstrued. When it doesn't, a chill runs through every nerve in my body.

"Are you . . . are you threatening me?" I manage, unable to stop myself from falling into the chair behind me.

"I'm just saying that's what he's asked me to do."

"And if I don't cooperate?"

Stella lets out a heavy sigh. "Then I'm to employ whatever tactics I need to ensure that you do."

I stare at her, trying to see past the perfectly made-up veneer through to the inner layers of her moral fiber as I desperately search for a semblance of conscience. But if Stella has one, it's impossible to see it.

"So even though you know what you know, you're *still* his bitch."

Her eyes narrow. "I didn't say I was prepared to do what he asked, did I?"

"Well, let me make it easy for you," I say, holding my hands up in surrender. "You may as well shoot me now, because if the likes of Ray McAllister can't take you on and win, then I'm sure as hell destined to fail."

Stella's eyes flicker involuntarily before she slumps into Max's chair, desperately trying to make it look like she's in control of her body. But for those few short seconds, she's anything but. Her limbs don't appear to belong to her, and her top lip is suddenly glistening with a sheen of sweat.

"Wh-what do you know about him?" she manages.

"Well, I understand McAllister's been residing at His Majesty's pleasure," I say, gleaning what I remember from the hasty Google search I ran, on the way back from Menzies's place. "Because of what *you* did to him."

Stella swallows and looks at me with a set jaw. "He got what he deserved."

"But you and I know that's not true, and so does he," I say, unable to stop myself smirking. "I wouldn't like to think what his intentions are, now that's he out."

I watch as every sinew and muscle in her long neck twitches, satisfied that I've finally found the chink in her armor.

"You surely can't be surprised," I say. "You completely fabricated the evidence against him. Swore under oath that he was the proven mastermind behind a plot to kidnap the prime minister, all the while *knowing* that you'd set up the whole thing to entrap him."

She laughs inanely. "Do you have any idea how insane you sound right now?"

I stare at her unflinchingly.

"So you think I needed a story so badly that I would manufacture an outlandish scenario between the incoming prime minister and one of London's most feared criminals?"

"You didn't just manufacture it, you manipulated it, moment by moment, to fit the grotesquely warped narrative that you wanted to portray."

Stella runs her tongue around her top teeth, her mouth clearly devoid of moisture, and I revel in her discomfort.

"I wonder what *The Post* would do if they knew that you'd sent someone in to infiltrate McAllister's gang, under the pretense of buying a stolen painting, only to implicate him in a kidnap plot he knew nothing about."

Her expression is one of utter bewilderment and confusion. If nothing else, she's a good actress, but she can't fool me.

"Akin Demir did you proud, didn't he?" I go on. "I hope you paid him well for putting his neck on the line, even more so when the police magically found the gun he'd planted in McAllister's van."

"Akin Demir was a small-town criminal who got in over his head," rasps Stella. "*That's* why he came to us with his story. McAllister's plan scared him and he was looking for a way out."

I smile, forcing away the tightening in my chest and the crushing realization that I might have got this all wrong.

"So you *didn't* pay Trevor Menzies to find him?" I chance. "To supply the gun? To field back to you all the relevant information? So that you could be poised and ready at the allotted time with a SWAT team and a photographer?"

"What are you talking about?" she asks. "Trevor Menzies is a chauffeur—nothing more and nothing less."

I nod. "True, he also drives hopeful actresses to their own funerals, but it's supplying ex-convicts to infiltrate gangs and entrap them in kidnapping plots that seems to be the real moneymaker for him."

"Good luck with proving *that* in a court of law," says Stella, her faculties seeming to be slowly returning.

It's the moment I've been waiting for, and I can't help but smile. "I don't think it will be too difficult," I say. "Thanks to Trevor Menzies getting it all on tape."

38

Stella

It's gone 11 p.m. by the time Stella's first issue as editor goes to press. It had been a cloak-and-dagger operation, with the news floor cleared of all but a skeleton staff, each personally selected for their discretion. It had been a nail-biting wait, not least because Stella needed to push it through without resistance, but also because she has somewhere she needs to be.

However, as she walks through the bowels of the Peckham estate, with gangs hooting and hollering at her, she's wondering if it might have been wise to leave this visit until tomorrow morning.

But the thought of being able to sleep, with Jess's words taunting and goading her, is about as likely as Jess sharing Yasmin Chopra's final words in order to assuage Peter Kingsley. The only chance Stella has—not only of being able to close her eyes, but of going on living her life—is to hear it from Menzies himself; and to realize that Jess's ludicrous allegations are born of nothing more than a desperate need to overturn everything Stella and Global International stand for.

Pulling up the collar of her trenchcoat, as if that will offer protection from the rowdy delinquents languishing in the stairwell of

Hogarth House, Stella endures their jeers as she pushes her way through the middle of them.

"That's a fancy bag," says one as her grip on it tightens. "My sister would love that."

"The lift's broken," another calls out, as she pushes the button once, twice, three times, willing it to hurry up.

"Thanks," she says, hoping that her politeness will make them think twice about mugging her. Funny how your mind works when it's under stress.

The crude fluorescent lights flicker ominously on and off as she climbs the concrete stairs, and every now and then she peers over the rails to check that no one is following her up.

She's ever so slightly out of breath by the time she reaches the third floor and takes a few seconds to pull herself together. Not that it matters whether a faint line of sweat tracks her spine and darkens the underarms of her blouse. By the time she's finished here, she's sure to be sweating a whole lot more than that, but for now she smooths down her hair and applies her signature lip color, because without it she feels vulnerable.

The door to flat 314 is ever so slightly ajar and she tentatively pushes on it, retching at the smell that comes from beyond.

"Hello?" she calls out, into the still darkness.

Stepping into the hallway, Stella trails her hand along the wall, searching for a light switch.

"Is anybody here?" she says, hating her voice for sounding so feeble.

A noxious blend of urine and body odor assaults her nostrils, but there's something else. Using the cuff of her coat as a futile barrier, she forces one foot in front of the other, her free hand flailing in the blackness for a sense of security.

Her foot comes up against something, stopping her from going any further. She can feel her hand trembling as she reaches out, not knowing what it will happen upon.

Just a ruler's length away, there's a closed door and as she instinctively searches for the handle, she wonders if this isn't the point where she turns and runs. But she wants answers; she *needs* answers, and the only way she's going to get those is by asking the questions.

Taking a deep breath, she pushes down hard on the handle, throwing the door open, and in that exact moment a rush of air comes toward her, the force of which she's never felt before. A breathless roar rises up from deep within her as she is pushed backward, the power of it snatching her breath away. Stella thrashes out with all her might, as the silent and invisible force grapples with her, throwing her to the floor and kicking at her body aimlessly.

Curling into a ball to protect herself as the thuds continue, her senses are on high alert, listening, feeling, desperately wanting to see what's going on. But then, as quickly as it started, it stops and her assailant moves wordlessly away, their heavy breaths fading into the distance.

Stella doesn't move. She stays in a fetal position with her nose pressed into the foul-smelling carpet, waiting for a sign that whoever was here has now gone. She lifts her head up, praying that it's only the drum of her own heartbeat that she hears.

With nothing but silence all around, she slowly and carefully pulls herself up against the wall. Is she still in the hallway or had she made it into the room with the closed door, before the blows rained down on her?

She winces as she sits up, instinctively holding a hand to the pain in her side. Her ribs scream as her fingers press against them and, for a second, she wonders if she's been stabbed. She hesitantly feels for the warm wetness of blood, although there's nothing but the pulsing agony of a beaten torso.

With a strength she hadn't expected, her legs power her body up the wall and her arms stretch out to either side of her, still looking for that elusive light switch. When her right hand feels the familiar plastic casing, her fingers falter as she asks herself whether she really wants to see what is hiding in the darkness.

Feeling as if she's about to pull the trigger on a gun, Stella silently counts to three and closes her eyes as the switch flicks on; she waits for a noise or movement to tell her what the threat level is, but the lack of either gives nothing away.

Squinting one eye open, Stella scans the debris that litters the room. The filthy green sofa has been slashed repeatedly, exposing the foam blocks that would once have made it comfortable; and the contents of the sideboard, which has been overturned, flutter in the brisk breeze that is snaking in through the broken windowpane.

She takes a deep breath, the bottom of which sends a searing pain through her rib cage, as she turns her head toward the darkest corner of the room, which is shrouded in shadows. She tiptoes over the drug paraphernalia that lies strewn across the floor and reaches out to turn the floor lamp on.

As the spotlight falls on the armchair, Stella stumbles backward, her legs turning to jelly as adrenaline floods her body. Bruised and bloodied, Trevor Menzies sits with his eyes half open and his head lolling.

"Fuck!" Stella rasps, pushing herself across the filthy floor.

With her breaths coming in short, sharp pants, she rummages in her bag and pulls out her mobile phone, jabbing at the screen with shaking fingers.

"Fuck, fuck, fuck," she says, her voice trembling, as the line rings. "Pick up, please pick up."

"Hello?" comes a voice.

"It's me," she says breathlessly. "We've got a problem."

39

Jess

I ignore the ping of the first text—it's still dark outside. But the second and third make me sit up against the headboard, squinting at the illuminated numbers on the screen.

"Five thirty?" I exclaim out loud, knowing that I won't be able to get back to sleep again now. Messages and calls from a number I don't recognize jolt me awake, filling me with a sense of impending doom.

I can't believe what you've done . . . one starts. Sasha has gone into hiding . . . begins another.

I don't need to read any more. I already know what's happened and I have only myself to blame.

Getting out of bed, I grab yesterday's clothes from where I left them over a chair and head into the kitchen, hopping into my knickers as I go. I click on *The Globe*'s app and the headline Singer cries rape fills the screen. Below is a picture of Sasha Peterson.

My ears are alight with the feeling they're on fire, and my vision blurs, my eyes no longer able to focus on the images that I know are there.

"Fuck!" I exclaim, though I can't pretend to be surprised.

There was a tiny part of me that thought—*hoped*—that the worm might be for turning. Stella had talked the good talk, and for a moment I felt she finally understood the threat that Peter Kingsley posed to women, but it was short-lived, any feelings of empathy and compassion quickly replaced by the all-encompassing need to protect him from the allegiance that she knew was forming. No wonder she demanded that I leave the office after our encounter: she needed me out of the way so that she could stonewall any attempt by Sasha to tell the truth.

I can't even remember my journey into the office, my mind obsessively imagining Tilly Ashcroft, Sasha Peterson and all of Peter Kingsley's other accusers waiting to greet me outside the Global International Tower. Tilly thought she could trust me. She told me her story because I gave her my word that I would treat it with sensitivity and work *with* her to bring down those who had done her wrong. But yet again, just like Yasmin, I have let her—and the others—down in the worst possible way.

Who am I to think I could take on an industry that's getting more and more corrupt by the day? Believing that I could help turn it around and release the hundreds of people caught up in its widely cast net? I almost laugh at my naivety, questioning what I'm even doing heading back into the office at this ungodly hour. What's the point?

As I emerge from the lift, the newsroom is cloaked in darkness, the dawn of a new week little more than an hour away.

I hear Peter before I see him, his voice carrying his anger from Max's office. I stop, stock-still, behind a pillar.

"How the fuck could this have happened?" he yells. "You've made some monumental fuckups, Max, but this one . . ."

I stay where I am, knowing that I'll be seen if I carry on walking toward my desk. I want to hear what they're saying without them knowing I'm here, though from the wrath of Peter's voice I doubt he's able to rein in his temper for *anybody's* benefit.

"Nobody will know who it's alluding to," says Max, sounding like he's grasping at straws. "It could be anyone."

"It's not going to take a fucking rocket scientist to work it out, though, is it?" spits Peter.

"I-I really don't think people will imagine it's you for a moment," falters Max. "Why would they?"

"Because apart from actually mentioning my name, you've printed every other known fact about me," yells Peter. "Media tycoon, film-company owner, married man, three children—I mean, what the fuck?"

I can't actually see him, but I can picture him pacing up and down Max's office, manically rubbing his balding head.

"I've been shafted by my own fucking paper."

"I'm sorry," says Max, sounding panicked. "I just can't understand how this has happened."

"It's personal and professional suicide. I'm done for."

"I can assure you I'll be looking into this," says Max.

"Looking *into* it?" rages Peter. "This is *your* ship. You're at the helm of this limping liner, but I swear to God, if either it or I go down, I'll be taking you with me."

"Oh, come on," says Max, with a little more strength to his voice. "You can't pin this on me. I wasn't even here."

"So where the hell were you?" demands Peter. "When my reputation was being fucked over."

"I had to . . ." starts Max. "I had to attend to some business."

"Some *business*?" repeats Peter disbelievingly. "What business could possibly be more important than making sure that I—the man who has the ability to make or break you—didn't get his balls caught in a vice?"

Max sighs, and I risk peering round the pillar. He looks deathly pale and is wiping his brow with a handkerchief. "I had a problem I needed to deal with."

Peter lets out a high-pitched fake laugh.

"I don't know what Stella was thinking," says Max. "I repeatedly told her to watch her step, to make absolutely sure her sources were watertight, but what with this, and the matter of that Yasmin woman, I think some serious decisions need to be made."

Just hearing them mention Yasmin's name makes me want to run in there and demand that they tell the world the truth, but then I remember the bounty that's on my head to do exactly the opposite, and I stay where I am.

"So how big a problem could you possibly have had to make it worth abandoning the paper?" asks Peter, ignoring the slight against Stella.

"Bigger than you or I would like," says Max.

There's a loaded silence and I imagine them looking at one another, each of them waiting to see who will break the deadlock first.

"McAllister is back," says Max eventually.

"What does *he* want?" asks Peter gravely, the hysteria of a few seconds ago having dissipated.

"A pound of flesh," says Max dourly.

"You need to deal with this," replies Peter, with a threatening tone to his voice. "I've got enough shit on my plate."

"I will," says Max. "It's all under control."

"I don't want him knocking on *my* door," Peter goes on.

"He won't," says Max, though the tremor in his voice instills little confidence. "I'll get to him before he gets to you."

"You better had, and I want you—and Stella—upstairs in my office at 9 a.m. sharp. Someone's head is going to roll for this."

"I think her time has come," says Max.

I press myself up against the pillar, holding my breath as Peter heads my way. A whoosh of air precedes him, but thankfully he's moving too fast to notice me.

As soon as he's in the lift, I duck down, crawling across the news floor to the subs' desk, where I know a bundle of today's issues will have been delivered in the middle of the night.

I reach up, scrabbling for a pair of scissors, and hack at the ties binding them all together, releasing the top copy and pulling it under the desk, desperate to read between the lines of the salacious headline. My eyes fervently scan the copy, as quote after damning quote is attributed to Sasha Peterson:

He's made my life a living hell.

He's destroyed my dreams.

No woman should ever be alone with him.

Words like "Predator," "Attack" and "Monster" pepper an already inflammatory article, penned by a woman called Melanie Tooley.

My heart's pounding as I read the gut-wrenching story of a woman who was subjected to a horrific sexual attack by a man who, for legal reasons, can't be named. But Peter's right: you don't need to be Einstein to work out who it is. Certainly anybody in the media industry will see through the smokescreen in seconds.

How the hell had Stella, as editor-in-charge, allowed this to be printed? Or was this always her intention? Maybe she *had* been telling the truth yesterday, and my deep-rooted cynicism hadn't allowed me to believe her. Though it seems that Sasha Peterson had; otherwise, why would she ever have trusted Stella to tell her story?

I pull my phone from my bag and click on the messages from Tilly, which I haven't yet been brave enough to open.

I can't believe what you've done . . . she says. Thank you SO much. Now everyone will know who Peter Kingsley really is.

The next reads, Sasha has gone into hiding, but she's so relieved that it's finally out there . . . thanks to you and Melanie Tooley.

My head falls back onto the edge of the desk and I want to cry with relief. They've got what they wanted—what they deserved and, absurdly, they have Stella Thorne to thank for it.

40

Stella

Curled up in her bed, Stella can't help but feel grateful that Harry stayed over. She watches his chest rise and fall, comforted by the weight of the gun in his inside jacket pocket. She no longer knows who might be coming for her, but with Harry by her side, she feels as protected as she's ever going to.

She can't even remember calling him last night, but all of a sudden he was there, picking her up from the filthy floor of Trevor Menzies's flat.

"OK, I've wiped everything," he'd said as he half carried her to his car. "But is there anything I might have missed?"

Stella had looked at him numbly. He might as well have been asking her to recite Einstein's equation of relativity.

"Stella!" he'd shouted. "Did you touch anything other than the doors and light switches?"

She'd shaken her head, but in all honestly she really couldn't recall. All she could remember was being pounced upon by an unknown figure, before, quite literally, stumbling across Trevor Menzies's corpse, staring up at her from the armchair.

"What are we going to do now?" she'd asked.

"I'm going to take you home and you're going to pretend you were never here," said Harry.

"But someone *killed* him," cried Stella. "And then tried to kill me."

"But you don't think they saw you? They wouldn't have been able to identify you?"

"I don't know," she said. "It was dark and . . ."

"But you didn't see them, more importantly?"

Stella had shaken her head. "No, I couldn't see a thing. I couldn't even tell you if it was a man or a woman."

"Good," said Harry. "Then hopefully they won't see you as a threat that they need to concern themselves with."

They'd driven to her flat in silence, but she could hear the questions whirring in Harry's brain.

"Hey," he says now, as his eyes blink open to find her watching him. "How are you feeling?"

She grimaces as she puts a hand to her ribs. "Sore."

"Here, let me see," he says, carefully pulling the quilt away from her to reveal a blue-black bruise staining her skin.

"Ouch! Do you think you need to go to hospital?"

She shakes her head. "I think the fewer questions asked, the better, don't you?"

He nods. "Do you want to talk to me about it, then?"

She honestly doesn't know. It's all such a mess that she wouldn't even know where to start. Knowing McAllister would be intent on revenge for shopping him to the police was one thing, but the thought of what he might be capable of, if he knew he'd also been set up by *The Globe*—albeit without her knowledge—was something else entirely.

And as much as she wants to deny it, it seems Trevor Menzies is testament to that. McAllister must have tracked him down, knowing that he had the evidence to put her and Max away for a very long time. Had McAllister got what he wanted? Had he found the tapes that Jess had spoken about? Maybe it's not an eye for an eye that he's after—maybe he simply wants to kill them all, one by one.

Stella shudders. "Can you give me some time?" she asks. "I promise I'll explain everything when I know exactly what's going on."

"Whenever you're ready," says Harry as he pushes himself off the bed and brushes down his crumpled suit. "I will do anything to help you, but I can only do half a job if you only give me half the story."

"I know. But I need to get my head around what's happening," says Stella.

"You do trust me, don't you?" he asks as if it's only just occurred to him that she might not.

"Of course."

"OK," he says, leaning down to kiss her on the head. "Will you be all right if I get going?"

She nods, knowing that she's got to get herself into the office to face the music, which must already be building to a crescendo by now.

"I'll speak to you later?" he says, posing it as a question.

Stella gives him her most assured smile, although she can't help but feel vulnerable when she hears the front door shut, and she rushes to the window overlooking the street below to check that as Harry lets himself out of the communal door, nobody else lets themselves in. As if sensing Stella there, he looks up as he puts his motorbike helmet on and gives her a cursory nod.

She still hasn't turned her mobile on by the time she walks into the lobby of the Global International Tower, and she half expects Peter and his cavalry of henchmen to be standing to attention, ready to take her down. But it's eerily normal as she makes her way across the polished marble floor toward the lift—visitors are waiting to be collected by one of the building's 2,000 members of staff, and calls are being redirected from the switchboard.

Stella offers one of the receptionists an uncharacteristic smile and she's pathetically grateful when she smiles back. But she knows the shallow gesture will mean nothing by the time she reaches the news-room, and she spends the time it takes for the lift to ascend the sixteen floors to prepare her defense.

A hush descends over the entire news floor as she makes her way to her desk, and she hasn't even put her handbag down before Max storms out of his office, his face gnarled with anger.

"About fucking time!" he roars, walking straight past her. "Peter's office. *Now!*"

If she hadn't been through what she experienced last night and didn't have a hardened criminal baying for her blood, then the mere thought of being fired would be the single most catastrophic thing that could ever happen to her. But as it is, and aware that she brought it all on herself, in full knowledge of the consequences, she's almost looking forward to incurring Max's and Peter's wrath.

"I don't even know what to say to you," spits Max as they enter the lift that will take them to Peter's private quarters on the top floor.

Stella had imagined making this inaugural pilgrimage when she was handed the editorship, not to have her employment—from a company that she's devoted her life to for fifteen years—terminated.

"I'm sorry," she offers. "What's the problem?"

Max can barely look at her, let alone respond, as the doors open onto a sea of marine-blue deep-pile carpet.

"He's waiting for you in his office," says a harassed-looking woman, who clearly lives on her nerves. She looks at Max. "He wants to see her alone."

"Stella!" says Peter, greeting her with splayed arms and a wide smile. For a second she thinks he might embrace her in a warm hug, but suddenly his lips draw back, revealing pale gums. "What the fuck have you done?" he hisses.

The double doors, which separate her from safety, close heavily behind her and she suddenly feels uncomfortable, the memories of the last time she was alone with Peter now playing on repeat.

"I-I'm sorry," she says. "I have no idea what's going on here."

Peter throws his head back and laughs, but it sounds hollow, and sinister.

"You know, I expected great things from you." He looks at Stella with those beady eyes and she doesn't know whether he's talking about when they were together or her progression to the mighty heights of Global International. Both leave her cold.

"I went out of my way to make it easy for you," he goes on. "I took you into my inner sanctum, showed you a side of me that few get to see, trusted you enough to . . ." He looks away and Stella can't help but wonder what he thinks happened the other night. Is he deluded enough to believe that she allowed him to do what he wanted, what he intended? Or had he eventually woken up alone, confused and assuming he couldn't perform?

He'll soon find out.

"You were going to be my next editor and I gave you all the rope you needed to make that happen." He snorts derisorily. "But you've chosen to hang yourself with it instead."

"I honestly don't know what the problem is," says Stella.

"The *problem*," he roars, picking up today's issue from his desk, "is that this nameless assailant has *my* name all over him!"

"*You?*" cries Stella, for effect. "Why on earth would you think it's about *you?*"

She narrows her eyes and dares him to elaborate, enjoying being the cat to his mouse.

"I'm alluded to between every line," he growls. "There aren't many of us who fit the criteria you've so carefully carved out."

"I didn't touch the copy," she lies. "The legal team said that in order to safeguard ourselves we should print Melanie Tooley's piece in its entirety, so that she was wholly liable."

Even as Stella is saying it, she knows it sounds preposterous, but she's guessing Peter is too incensed to deal with the minutiae of the law. After all, he's never abided by it before.

"And who the fuck is this journalist?" he spits.

"Melanie Tooley," says Stella, keen to reiterate her name.

If he thought about it, he'd know *exactly* who she is; she's every woman who has endured sexual harassment, has been the victim of violent assault, has supported those who have been affected, and has created conversations to empower women and let them know that they're not alone. *She* is Melanie Tooley. Known as *#MeToo* to her friends.

"She's one of my most trusted freelancers and says the story is watertight. If it's called into question, she has proof; and if Sasha Peterson makes a formal charge, which I'm led to believe she will, then Melanie will be able to give us his name."

Peter paces the length of his considerably long office on short legs, rubbing at his balding head.

"I can't believe you've been so fucking stupid," he yells, stopping and turning to face her. "Did you never stop to think how this would look? What people would think? They're going to put two and two together . . ."

Stella shakes her head, but she can't imagine that her faux remorse is fooling him. "I'm sorry—maybe I should have thought it through more, but I'd been thrown in at the deep end. Max called in sick, I was under pressure to deliver today's paper and, when this came in, I thought it had *The Globe* written all over it. In fact, I thought it was even better than that, because I assumed the man in question was Michael Leith, the owner of *The Post*. A married father of three, media tycoon . . ."

Peter looks at her as if she's stupid. "Who *doesn't* have a sixteen-year-old daughter, who doesn't own a house in Los Angeles, who didn't have a well-publicized birthday party."

"Oh," she says, making it look as if the penny has finally dropped.

"Yeah, *oh*," says Peter caustically.

"OK," says Stella, sounding as if she has a way out of this. "So we just need to prove that it *wasn't* you. That it wasn't Mia's birthday, that you weren't in LA on the day in question—that you simply wouldn't do these despicable things."

She can't help but throw Peter a sideways glance, revelling in his obvious discomfort.

"Would you?"

41

Jess

The brief from Max is simple: call Ray McAllister's wife, pretending that I'm from *The Post*, and tell her that we're campaigning for a press that reports the news, rather than makes it.

"This is your chance to really make a difference," he says. "Stella is done for—she's upstairs getting fired as we speak, so now's our opportunity to strike. Now's the time to turn *The Globe* into a paper we're proud of."

I jump at it. But not for the reasons he thinks.

Christina's Café is down a tiny side street in Islington and although its red signage is cheap and tacky, the smell of frying bacon and brewing coffee is reassuringly welcoming.

A woman looks up from behind the counter as I close the door behind me, and we both instantly know who the other is. She looks me up and down with abject suspicion, before untying her apron from around her back and saying something to her toast-buttering colleague.

She nods her head in the direction of the corner table and I weave through the red plastic chairs that are ominously welded to the floor.

"Christina?" I say, offering my hand. "Maddie Baker from *The Post*. Nice to meet you."

For a second it feels like she's about to call me out, but there's little to no chance she could know that I'm an imposter. The real Maddie Baker is an investigative reporter who never has a photo alongside her byline and has no traceable internet presence, for Christina to know that I'm not her. And as judgmental as it may sound, when I spoke to her on the phone this morning, Christina didn't come across as being sharp enough to double-check.

She shakes my hand, but eyes me with caution.

"So you want to stop people like my husband being framed by people like you?"

"Not by people like me," I say, surreptitiously putting a Dictaphone on the edge of the table. "That's not what I do."

"No taping," she says, throwing a derisory glance at the recorder.

"OK," I say, sweeping it back into my handbag. I don't need what she's got to say on record anyway. "What we're hoping to do at *The Post* is put the power back into the hands of the police rather than the media. For so long, journalists have been able to set up and investigate alleged crimes with none of the safeguards, standards or regulations that the police are subject to. And *your* family knows, better than most, the catastrophic chain of events this can lead to."

"It was a flawed investigation from start to finish," says Christina bitterly.

"I know, because the justice system acted on a case presented by journalists instead of a law-enforcement agency. And you and I both know that your husband was set up because those journalists were prepared to do anything to get the story."

She grimaces, looking as if she has a bad taste in her mouth. "Ray spent four years in a stinking prison because of Max Forsythe and Stella Thorne, but we could never prove it."

I can feel the man behind the counter looking at me as I lean in. "What would you say if I told you I could?" I half whisper.

A faint smile plays on her lips. "I'd say my husband would pay handsomely for whatever you have," she says.

I take a folded piece of A4 paper out of my bag, open it and slide it across the table toward her. Christina's eyes scan it fervently.

"Is this some kind of confession?" she asks.

I nod. "This is just a fragment of a conversation with a man called Trevor Menzies. He was the middleman that *The Globe* employed to set your husband up."

She reads on, devouring the words I'd transcribed from the tape, before slamming her open palm down on the table, making the man behind the counter and the couple at the table by the door jump.

"I fucking knew it!" she exclaims.

"Trevor Menzies found Akin Demir, and Akin was the one who testified against your husband by saying the kidnap was all his idea. He was also the one who planted a gun in Ray's van."

"Is this all on tape?" asks Christina disbelievingly.

"It is, and I'm happy to give it to you . . ." I leave the sentence hanging.

Christina's eyebrows shoot up. "In return for?"

"I wondered if your husband wouldn't mind paying a certain someone a visit."

Christina can't help but smile. "I'm sure he'd be delighted, if you tell me where he needs to go."

"With pleasure," I say as I scribble the address down.

I leave the café feeling better than I have in days. The tide is finally beginning to turn and I'm proud of the small part that I've played in making that happen. Kudos must also go to Stella, who has seemingly put her neck on the line to get Sasha's story out there, when she must surely have known the consequences. But I still don't understand why she's done it. It doesn't fall in line with the path her career was destined to go along. The day before yesterday she was going all out to convince Peter Kingsley that she should be the next editor of *The Globe* and today she's exposed him for the predator that he is, in the very same paper.

What could possibly have happened to bring about such a dramatic turnaround?

I've not even finished asking myself the question when the answer suddenly occurs to me. I stop dead in the middle of the street, as the harsh reality hits home. There could only be one reason, and the tentacles of horror reach deep into my chest as it becomes clearer and clearer.

I look around the railway arch that I'm standing in, its walls dimly lit by the orange glow of fluorescent tubes hanging from the high ceilings, and I'm overwhelmed by an innate need to speak to her.

Rummaging in my bag, I pull out my phone and scroll down to her number, hesitating for a split second before pressing it.

"I'm sorry," I say breathlessly when Stella picks up. They're not words I would ever have envisaged saying to her. "For what he did to you."

There's a loaded silence at the other end before she clears her throat. "I got off lightly," she says. "Compared to others."

"You were going to tell *your* story in the paper today, weren't you? That's why you wanted Max out of the way."

"I had to do something," she says. "If only to warn others that there are still men like Peter Kingsley out there. I thought I could write it anonymously and intimate exactly who it was, without naming him." Her voice breaks. "But then when you told me about Tilly, Sasha and the others, it became about so much more than that."

"I thought you'd stitched them up," I say.

"That's an easy assumption to have made, but I'm not quite the person you had me down for."

"That's becoming apparent."

"Well, I've done all that I can do," she says. "But unsurprisingly they've cut me off at the pass. So now it's down to you."

"We can do it together," I offer.

She snorts. "I'm just about to be escorted out of the building—I don't know how much more help I can be."

There's only so much I can do on my own and, despite everything I thought to be true about the indomitable Stella Thorne and her questionable methods, *no one* knows how the media works like she does. I swallow the last iota of doubt that I have about her and decide to take my chances.

"Listen," I start. "There's a brown envelope taped to the underside of my desk . . ."

A train thunders above me and I flinch as a motorbike races past; it's revved growl reverberates around the curved walls, making my ears hurt.

Quickening my step, wanting to reach the other side so that I can finish what needs to be said, I'm aware of an engine slowing beside me. I pick up my pace even more, but it matches my tempo, and I side-eye its dark shape. There's a shuttering noise, like a door being pulled back, and I instinctively cower as a rush of something comes at me, seemingly from all sides. The pressure is intense as I'm pulled this way and that and, for a fleeting second, I wonder if I've been hit by a car, or if a bomb has detonated in the station overhead and the tunnel is collapsing in on itself.

"Stella!" I scream, as the phone is lifted from my hands by an invisible force. Instinctively shielding my head with my arms, I'm lifted up off the ground and carried through the air, landing with a thud. I cry out as my hip makes contact with something unforgiving.

There's nothing but darkness all around me and I'm struggling to breathe as hot air fills my nostrils. Am I trapped under rubble? I will myself to stay perfectly still, even though every fiber of my being wants to lash out, to test what's working and assimilate where I am. I dare to stretch out a leg, just to check that I can, wiggling my toes and oddly cursing myself for wearing my favorite black boots, today of all days. I slowly reach out an arm and although it's a little tender, it meets no resistance. What the hell's happening?

The heat on my face is intensifying and I imagine it having taken the full brunt of what I'm now sure is a blast of some kind. I recoil, terrified by the thought that my flesh is no longer protecting my bones. Despite my head doing everything in its power to tell my hand to stay where it is, my fingers move, like a separate entity, toward my cheek, not knowing what they'll find there.

I tap gently, but instead of the softness of my skin, they're met with a coarse woven fabric. Panicked, I grapple with both hands, desperately trying to find my face, but it's trapped behind a wall of what feels like burlap. I pull at it, feeling it loosen, and then suddenly there's a chink of light. I fight my way toward it, tugging and tearing at the darkness cocooning my head, and suddenly I'm free, reveling in the fact that I can breathe.

But no sooner am I grateful for that than I'm flung backward at high speed, sliding across a cold, hard floor.

I scream as I scrabble to hold on to something—*anything*.

"Shut up!" booms a voice.

I freeze. I look around me and realize that the sliver of light I was so happy to see is in fact bleeding through the newspaper that is covering the rear windows of whatever vehicle I'm in. Because it *is* a vehicle as I roll like a marble every time it takes a bend.

"What's going on?" I call out.

"You're going to need to shut her up," says a male voice.

It's then that it hits me: McAllister.

He must have been lying in wait for me to come out of the café, knowing that I wasn't who I said I was.

"Please," I say as adrenaline takes over, banishing the pain of my bruised bones and going some way toward making me feel invincible. "I'm on *your* side. I can help you get justice."

A gruff voice says, "Put your foot down" and I fall into the back doors, my flailing hands clawing at the newspaper on the windows with every chance I get, hoping that I can alert somebody to my plight. But there's no opportunity to get to my feet as we swerve this way and that, going far faster than London's roads allow.

"Help!" I cry, banging the back of what I now know to be a van. "Somebody help me."

They turn up the radio, drowning me out, and I fall against the cold metal wall, forcing myself to focus. With two against one, physical strength isn't going to get me out of this, so the only chance I've got is to stay one step ahead of them mentally.

I suddenly remember talking to Stella on the phone, calling out her name in the fracas. Had she heard me? Would she have known I was in trouble? Where had my phone gone? I frantically run my hands across the floor, the unevenness scraping the skin on my fingers, in the unlikely event that it has found its way in here with me.

Suddenly, we stop and I kick against the metal of the sides. "Please," I yell. "Somebody help me."

The door rolls back, and my feet make contact with something else.

"Fuck!" says a male voice. I squint at him holding his jaw, and feel buoyed by the possibility that I could take him on; he's young and slightly built. But my naivety is quickly brought into sharp focus by the appearance of another man, bigger and with a balaclava covering his face. I can only assume it's McAllister himself.

"Put your fucking mask on," he commands the other.

"Keep away from me," I yell, refusing to keep my thrashing limbs still. But I'm no match for him, and within seconds he's hauled me out of the van and is pushing me through a door and up some stairs. I force myself to remember every detail, knowing that it will help track them down after they let me go. *If* they let me go.

Magnolia paint peels off the walls running up either side of the staircase I'm being forced up, and the threadbare carpet thins out to almost nothing before being replaced by floorboards at the top.

"In here," says the bigger man, shoving me into a musty-smelling room. A solitary light bulb hangs from the ceiling and damp patches creep up the bare brick walls.

"What are you doing?" I wail. "What do you want from me?"

He roughly grabs hold of my wrists and binds them tightly to the cast-iron radiator under the blacked-out window.

"Tell me what you want," I say, attempting to get my warbling voice back under control. "I can help you."

He grunts as if he finds that hard to believe.

"I've got everything you need to prove that *The Globe* set you up. It's all on tape."

He stops tying and turns to look at me. "Where is it?" he demands. "Where's the tape?"

"It's in my office," I say, sounding so much stronger than I feel. "But you're going to have to let me go if you want it. It's hidden and I'm the only one who knows where it is."

His eyes narrow as if contemplating his next move.

"You can't get it without me," I continue, sensing an out.

"Don't you worry," he says, before shutting the door and sending two bolts across. "We'll find it."

I slump against the wall, forcing the sense of foreboding away, and pray that Stella gets there first.

42

Stella

"Where's Jess?" barks Stella as she storms into Max's office.

He looks at her with complete disregard.

"I *said*, where's Jess?"

"Weren't you supposed to have gone by now?" he asks, turning back to his computer screen and tapping away on his keyboard.

"I think something's happened to her," says Stella in a rush. "I was just on the phone to her and she . . ."

"She what?" asks Max, suddenly giving her his undivided attention.

Stella shakes her head, trying to dislodge the uncomfortable sense that something's not right. "We were talking and there was a noise . . ." It all happened so fast that she's struggling to remember the sequence of events. "There was the roar of an engine, men shouting and Jess calling my name, before the line went dead."

She considers telling him about the tapes she'd found in the envelope stuck to the underside of Jess's desk, but until she knows exactly what's on them, she should probably keep that information close to her chest.

"Well, have you tried calling her back?" asks Max.

"Of course I have," snaps Stella. "But it goes straight to answer-phone."

"OK," says Max thoughtfully, as he gets up from his desk.

Stella watches him go to the floor-to-ceiling windows and look out of the office that she honestly believed would be hers one day.

"So where is she?" Stella asks again. "Have you sent her out on a story?"

He turns to face her with a painful grimace, and a slow panic creeps across Stella's chest.

"I think we may have a problem," he says.

"What do you mean?" asks Stella, the sense of dread growing.

"I, erm . . ." he starts, never normally one to falter on his words. "I, erm, sent Jess to meet Christina."

Every one of Stella's senses goes into overload as the words reverberate around her brain. Her vision blurs, her tongue sours, her nostrils flare and the very tips of her fingers tingle with fear. But it's the fierce heat in her ears that she's focusing on, hoping that it means she's misheard him. She must have done.

"I thought it would be a way of finding out what McAllister's planning . . ." Max continues as Stella struggles to form any words. "So I sent Jess to go and meet Christina to find out where he is and what he's up to."

"Are you . . . are you fucking kidding me?" she cries eventually, her voice lilting toward hysteria. "What part of you ever thought that was a good idea?"

He goes to the window again, his jaw clenching. "I thought if she went in as Maddie Baker from *The Post*, it would pose little threat."

"Fuck!" rasps Stella, throwing her hands on her head, unable to believe he could be so stupid. "I mean, what were you—"

The shrill tone of Max's phone penetrates the tense atmosphere and Stella doesn't know if she's grateful or not. It certainly gives her a moment to think.

"What is it?" barks Max, snatching it up from his desk.

The silence that follows causes Stella to stop pacing the floor, so unaccustomed is she to Max taking a breath to listen to anyone that it rings alarm bells in her head.

She turns to see his eyes wide and his mouth agape. "Where is she?" he asks after what feels like an eternity, although the words only serve to send a shock of electric volts through Stella. This isn't good.

"Now, you listen to me," he says, his nostrils flaring. "If she isn't back in this office in the next hour . . ." He takes the phone away from his ear and looks at it as if the inanimate object holds unspoken words.

"What is it?" asks Stella. "Who was that? Where's Jess? What . . . ?" The words tumble out faster than her lips can form them.

Ashen-faced, Max looks everywhere but at her.

"Max!" she exclaims.

"That . . . that was McAllister," he falters, seemingly having the same problem with his words that she is. "He's got Jess."

"Fuck!" shrieks Stella, turning in a circle, not knowing what to do with herself. The thoughts that railroad her brain are meeting themselves coming backward. "What are we going to do? What does he want from us?"

"He wants retribution," says Max solemnly. "He wants revenge for what we did."

Stella forces herself to stand still and fixes him with narrow eyes. "And what exactly *did* we do?" she asks.

"The right thing," says Max with a choked restraint.

"Do you know Jess went to see Trevor Menzies?" says Stella.

Max shrugs his shoulders and looks at her blankly. "What for?"

"She wanted to know what really happened with Tilly Ashcroft, but it seems she got a lot more than she bargained for."

"Meaning?" asks Max with a furrowed brow.

"Meaning that he told her we engineered the sting on McAllister."

Max looks at Stella as if she's stupid. "We did," he says bluntly.

"We set it up so that we could catch him in the act and have the police there on standby."

Stella shakes her head. "Menzies told her that Akin was a plant whom he was instructed to find, by us. Menzies got the gun and gave it to Akin, who planted it in McAllister's van—all at the perfect time and place for the SWAT team to swoop in."

"Well, that's the most ridiculous thing I've ever heard," says Max.

"Did Peter Kingsley have something to do with it?" asks Stella, with nothing left to lose.

"Like what?"

She shrugs her shoulders, but nothing about her feels nonchalant. There's a young girl somewhere out there at very real risk of harm, through absolutely no fault of her own. Stella fingers the raised scar through her blouse and shudders at the thought of what Jess might be going through.

"I don't know," says Stella. "Something about a stolen painting?"

Max screws his face up as if he's considering what she's saying, but Stella's already one step ahead of him as she casts her mind back to five or six years ago, when a priceless piece of art was stolen from the Kingsleys' chateau in the South of France. Had Ray McAllister had something to do with that? Had the dogs been set on him in retaliation? She shudders at the thought that she might unknowingly have been a hound in the baying pack.

"How could you have thought for a second that sending Jess, an innocent pawn, into the clutches of a man who we know is out to get us was a good idea?" She looks at him, seething at his incompetence and the selfish, unthinking risk he's taken.

"I didn't think for a second—"

"You rarely do," she snaps. "You've made a rash decision that could end up with very serious consequences."

Max puts his hands on his hips and looks at her intently. "If he touches one hair on Jess's head, I swear to God I'll kill the bastard."

"If he touches one hair on her head, I'll kill *you*," barks Stella.

43

Jess

I can't stop shaking, but I don't know if it's fear or the muscles in my arms spasming from being in the same position for such a long time.

It's getting dark and I'm wondering at what stage someone's going to notice I'm missing. Surely they must be asking the question in the office? Give it another hour or two and Flic will be wondering where I am.

The ties are cutting into my wrists, but there's no way I'm able to loosen them. At least if they were metal I could rattle them against the radiator, in the hope of attracting someone's attention. Or maybe the vibration would be felt or heard by a neighbor, assuming there is one. There must be, as we haven't traveled far enough to be out of London.

"Hello?" I call out. "Is anybody there? Can anyone hear me?"

Slow, heavy footsteps come up the stairs and I don't know whether to be frightened or relieved. Bolts slide across and the smaller man, having remembered his balaclava this time, stands there, his body language signaling that he's as confused as I am about what both of us are doing here.

"You need to help me," I say, hoping to appeal to his sense of compassion. "I need to use the bathroom."

His head twists this way and that as if expecting to see a plumbed toilet in the corner of the room.

"You can't," he says, his voice muffled behind the mask.

"But I *have* to," I implore. "Otherwise I'm going to have to go right here."

"OK, OK," he says, sounding panicked. "But if I release you, you've got to promise you'll not try anything." He's clearly not a seasoned kidnapper.

I nod, making ready.

He bends down to loosen my hand restraints, huffing with impatience at how tightly they've been tied. I force myself to bide my time, knowing that if he thinks I'm going to try anything, it'll be as soon as I'm unfettered.

I rub at my chafed wrists, hoping he'll be kind and leave me with free hands, but as soon as I'm detached from the radiator, he binds them together again.

"It's downstairs," he says, helping me up onto dead legs, numbed by trapped nerves.

We squeeze our way down the narrow staircase side by side, our shoulders chipping off the already-peeling paint.

I thought I was in a house, but as he guides me left at the bottom of the stairs, it seems that I'm in some kind of lockup. I hadn't registered it before, but the room I came into—presumably from a garage or carport—is set up with two desks and computer monitors. It reminds me of the secondhand car dealership that features in a sitcom Mum and Dad watch on Comedy Central, except that there's nothing remotely funny about this.

He pushes me through a rudimentary kitchen toward a door at the end of the galley. "In there," he says, sounding like a teenager attempting to be a man.

"I can't do it like this," I say, holding out my bound wrists.

He looks like he's considering my request, but then thinks better of it. "You'll have to manage," he says.

I'm immediately aware of the broken skylight window as I go in and close the door.

"Don't lock it," he orders.

I cough and silently slide the bolt across, before closing the lid of the soiled pan and standing on it to peer out. I'm definitely on some kind of industrial estate, but there's little activity in any of the few units that I can see. Maybe it's later than I thought.

Reaching for the filthy towel beside the corner basin, I wrap it around my hand and cough again as I take hold of a piece of glass. It comes away from its frame easily, snapping like a sugar shard. If I can remove all the glass, I reckon I could just about squeeze myself through, although with my hands tied together, it's not going to be easy.

I cough again and pull away another piece of glass.

"What's going on in there?" asks the man, through the door.

"I'm not feeling well," I say, feigning a retch as I remove the final two shards. "Give me a minute."

I launch the top half of my body at the ledge and stick my head through the window, using my elbows to edge me forward as my hands are rendered useless. Squeezing my shoulders, making them as narrow as possible, I inch my way through the metal frame.

There's at least a six-foot drop on the other side, which I'm going to have to throw myself at headfirst. There's no other way for it.

"What's going on?" booms a voice.

My heart stops and I freeze. I'm so close to getting out of here; a few more seconds is all I need.

"She's not feeling well."

I retch again to keep the wolf from the door, but I can hear the handle being turned.

"And you let her *lock* it?" asks an exasperated voice. "For fuck's sake."

The whole room shakes as he attempts to shoulder or kick his way in, injecting my body with the shot of adrenaline it needs to get this done. With snake-like hips, I wriggle the top half of my body through the gap, feeling no pain as the few remaining shards of glass pierce the skin on my stomach. One final push to release my hips and I'll be free-falling onto whatever awaits me below.

It's only a split second of doubt that holds me back. But that split second is long enough for the door to burst open and my legs to be grabbed.

"No," I scream as I'm hauled back through the window. "Please, somebody help me."

The man I assume to be McAllister doesn't say a word as he shoves me back through the kitchen and up the stairs, throwing me into the room as if I were a rag doll.

"Please," I beg. "People will be wondering where I am. They'll come looking for me."

"Well then, we need to make sure they won't find you," is all he says, before slamming the door shut and bolting it again.

44

Stella

There's an uncomfortable atmosphere hovering over the newsroom as Stella packs her meager belongings into a crate that Gail had unceremoniously dumped on her desk. It's as if her colleagues have much to say, but are all too frightened to cross the precipice into the world of ostracism. She can't say she blames them—it's a dog-eat-dog world.

Lottie is the only one brave enough to approach, but Stella almost wishes that she hadn't when she sees the tears in her eyes. The unexpected pull at the back of her throat threatens to undo the carefully constructed barrier she's spent years building around herself.

"For what it's worth, I'm really sorry to see you go," says Lottie.

Stella offers a tight smile as she starts the long walk of shame through the office, which so many others have been subjected to—often by her.

Passing Max's office on the way, she slows down as she goes by his open door. "You've got one hour to find that girl and tell me she's safe," she says. "Or else I'm calling the police."

She doesn't give him a chance to respond; she just keeps on walking toward the lift, hoping it doesn't keep her waiting too long. The seconds feel like minutes, but as soon as she's in and descending, she pulls out her Dictaphone and earphones from the box, slipping them into her coat pocket as the lift doors open onto the lobby. Walking with purpose, because that's what people would expect of her, she strides toward the ladies' toilets and locks herself into a cubicle.

Taking one of the tapes out of the brown envelope she'd found on the underside of Jess's desk, she slides it into the machine and listens as a man who sounds a lot like Trevor Menzies starts talking.

"What if she gets in the car and wants to go home?" he asks.

"You can't let her," comes an instantly recognizable voice. "Whatever stunt you have to pull to get her to the pick-up, do it, because we *have* to get that shot of Tilly Ashcroft with the drugs."

"You're assuming she's going to know what to do and where to go," says Trevor. "What if she doesn't?"

"Then *you* need to take control," says Max. "Arrange the pick-up with your dealer, drive her there and get her to do the transaction."

"And what if she doesn't want to?" asks Trevor.

"There's another five hundred in it for you if you can get her on tape, doing the deal."

Trevor sighs. "You really want this one, don't you?"

"She needs to be taught a lesson," says Max.

Stella pulls out her earphones, her breathing coming in short, sharp gasps, her addled brain trying to make sense of the contract that's being entered into.

She fast-forwards the tape, stopping as Max's voice penetrates her eardrums once again, his sharp tone taking no prisoners. "I told you, I wanted proof of her doing the deal," he barks.

"But there was nothing I could do," bleats Trevor. "She didn't want anything to do with it. She didn't know where to go, what to say . . . I had to do the whole damn lot. You should be thankful you got anything from her at all, because all she wanted me to do was take her home. I had to go some to convince her it was a small price to pay if it meant she'd get a part in the movie."

Max sighs. "Tilly Ashcroft sitting in front of a bag of coke is not the same as her making the deal."

"Well, it's all I've got," says Trevor. "I can't magic up something that doesn't exist. That's *your* job."

So Jess was right. Not only was Tilly enticed to the hotel under false pretenses—a charge for which Stella regrettably accepts responsibility—but she was *forced* into supplying the drugs.

Stella leans her head back against the cold tiled wall and lets out the breath she was holding in. She has always managed to convince herself that she's only ever reported on the real people hiding behind their perfect masks, but in Tilly's case and, she fears, so many others, she's been duped just as much as her victims have.

Changing the tapes over, her chest tightens as she presses play, not knowing who or what she's going to hear.

"So a couple of names have been circling in the underworld," says Max. "McAllister being our prime suspect, and I need you to send someone in—someone you can trust—to find out if it's anything more than a rumor."

"I've got the perfect guy for the job," says Trevor. "But what happens if he discovers he's onto something? That he's found the painting? How are you going to get it back?"

"We'll worry about that later," says Max. "First, we need to find out who stole it."

"And if it's who you think it is?" asks Trevor.

Max laughs throatily. "Then we'll fucking destroy him."

Stella throws the Dictaphone into the box, as if holding it for a moment longer will contaminate her with the same disease as Max. Fighting to get the air that her lungs so desperately need, she fingers the crosses on the inside of her arm. What had it been for? A personal vendetta, carried out by Max on Peter Kingsley's behalf? Is that what it had *all* been for?

Had Max taken it upon himself to avenge anyone who dared to cross Peter or threaten to expose him for the man he really is? Or had he acted on instructions?

Stella remembers the hotel room where Christina had thought nothing of cutting into her flesh to remind her of the fatal error she'd made in setting up Ray McAllister for something he hadn't done. Back then, Stella had felt aggrieved at the miscarriage of justice, so trusting of Max that she never contemplated the story being anything other than the one they had printed.

She thought they were the same, she and Max, always prepared to go the extra mile for a good story, but this . . . This is something else entirely. She may not always have stayed within the lines of what was deemed morally right, but as she told Jess, while she might lead the horse to water, she has never forced it to drink. She had always given the victim a choice; or a "trade-off," as Max liked to call it. But these tapes proved there was never really any such thing.

45

Jess

It's impossible to know exactly how much time has passed, but it's dark outside and my shoulders have frozen into position, the ties that are binding me to the radiator now cutting into my wrists, giving no room for movement. Pain sears through every muscle and fiber as I straighten my legs out from underneath me, and I yelp as I attempt to pull myself up by just an inch.

I really don't want to show any weakness, but I can't stop a single tear escaping as I battle with both the burning agony and the fear of what's going to happen to me.

How had I been so stupid as to believe that McAllister wasn't going to want revenge for what had happened to him? I'd been naive to think that the promise of the tape, in return for paying Max a visit, would be enough to assuage the anger he must have harbored all these years. Although it would certainly have gone some way toward paying Max back for what he'd put Tilly through—for me, at least.

Yet despite the many things I could blame Max for, the fact that I'm in this position isn't one of them. This is my fault—for trying to be too clever, for thinking the McAllisters wouldn't see straight through my fake credentials, for expecting them to need proof of the miscarriage of justice that Ray McAllister had suffered. They don't need it from *me*; they already *know* what the powers-that-be at *The Globe* did. And if I'd thought about it for a second, underworld mobsters don't want legal retribution; they don't go through the courts to get their day of reckoning. *This* is how they collect their dues and, like a lamb to the slaughter, I'd made it easy for them.

A bolt of panic shoots across my chest as the door is unlocked and slowly opens, the pace making it seem all the more ominous. A shadow is slowly revealed, though it's too dark on the landing to see anything other than an outline. But when the figure steps into the crude lighting of the room, I stop breathing, the air in my lungs stagnating in shock. And relief.

"Max!" I call out, so grateful to see him that tears immediately fall onto my cheeks.

"Oh, thank god," he says, rushing toward me. "What have they done to you? Have they hurt you?"

I shake my head. "McAllister snatched me off the street and . . . and brought me here and—"

"I know, he called and told me," says Max, as he sets about untying my wrists. "I'm so sorry . . . I should never have . . ."

"It's not your fault," I say, unable to face the guilt of knowing that I'd gone to see Christina McAllister with the sole intention of throwing Max to the lions. I feel oddly grateful that my kidnapping may have stalled the operation.

"He said something about a tape?" says Max, battling with the shackles that bind me to the radiator. "That if he got the tape he wanted, he'd let you go."

My remorse is threatening to drown me.

"Max . . . I . . ."

He looks at me with an expectant expression.

"I-I told him I had a tape . . ." I say, stuttering as I try to find words that will somehow make this sound better than it is. "A tape that proves that you and *The Globe* set him up."

Max stops what he's doing to look at me. "Why would you tell him that—when it isn't true?"

"Because when I went to see Trevor Menzies, he gave me a tape of you and him talking about it." I can't bring myself to meet his unrelenting glare. "I heard everything—about how you were going to get Akin Demir to infiltrate McAllister's gang, plant the incriminating evidence and alert the police."

The muscles in Max's face twitch involuntarily, and for a moment I wonder if I've said too much. But I'd rather take the worst Max is going to dish out than what McAllister might have in store for me.

Just as I prepare myself for the onslaught of his vitriol, Max sits back heavily against the wall and lets his head fall into his hands. "You need to know what McAllister's capable of," he says. "Of what he did that meant we had to take matters into our own hands."

"Has this got something to do with a painting?"

Max nods resignedly. "McAllister held Peter Kingsley's wife and staff at gunpoint at their house in the South of France. He bashed them up pretty bad—his wife was so traumatized that she's not set foot in the house since."

My stomach turns at the thought of what McAllister had done to her, my mind frantically pushing away the notion of him doing the same to me. Max goes on. "He put them through hell—all for the sake of a painting that he was intending to turn to the highest bidder."

It occurs to me that if he didn't deserve to go to prison for the attempted kidnap of the prime minister, McAllister certainly deserved to serve time for his assault on Peter's wife and staff.

"I'm sorry. I didn't know," I offer.

"Why would you?" he asks, looking at me for the first time. "What I did was wrong, but it was about settling a score and when Peter

Kingsley tells you to jump, you ask 'how high?' I was a fool, I see that now, but if McAllister gets hold of that tape . . ."

"I know—I wasn't thinking straight. If I'd known . . ." I stop myself from continuing, wondering if it would have made a difference.

"We can't let him have that tape," says Max, as my wrists are finally released. "It will only make matters worse."

My arms fall heavily to the floor. "It's OK, it's safe. He'll never find it."

Max allows himself a small smile. "You're a clever girl," he says. "Where have you hidden it?"

I go to tell him, but a sudden bang from downstairs stops me.

"What the . . ." I start.

Max looks at me wide-eyed and puts a finger to his lips.

"Please . . ." a man cries out, his voice sounding hoarse with fear. "Please, I'm begging you."

"Where is he?" growls a deep Scottish accent. The question demands an answer.

"Upstairs," sobs the man.

"Fuck!" roars Max as he rushes to the boarded-up window. "We need to get out of here—*now*!"

He *knows* who's coming up the stairs. I can only hazard a guess, and the thought of being caught in the crossfire between these two archenemies instills me with even more fear than if I were facing McAllister alone.

Unable to hold myself up, though I don't know whether it's through panic or lack of strength, I slump against the wall as heavy footsteps climb the treads, the sound pausing as they reach the top.

The door handle turns painfully slowly and I squeeze my eyes tightly shut in the misguided belief that if I can't see, I won't feel. It's all I've got right now.

With a sudden rush of air, the door is thrown open and a man is standing there, looming over me, his presence unlike anything I've ever felt before. Although he's thinner and a little grayer than he was in the pictures in the newspapers four years ago, there's no doubting who he is.

Terror catches my breath and, try as I might, I'm unable to release my inflated lungs. My mouth dries up, but although I'm desperate for saliva, I'm unable to swallow. It feels as if my entire nervous system is shutting down, deserting me when I need it most.

"Well, well, well," says McAllister, looking around the room, his lip curling in disdain. "What a pleasure to make your acquaintance again."

The scream that I had ready in my throat is silenced by the barrel of lead that's pointing at Max's head. His face freezes, paralyzed by the knowledge that there's no way out.

"It's been a while," continues McAllister, picking up a chair from the corner of the room and effortlessly swinging it through the air, slamming it down in front of me. I jump and press myself back into the wall, willing it to swallow me whole.

Max's eyes slide frenziedly from side to side as his brain fires up, preparing for fight or flight, and I wish I could read his mind, rather than second-guessing which way he's going to go. Although seeing as McAllister is the one with the gun, the chance of flight being the best option is probably ill-advised. But what other choice do we have?

"Why don't you take a seat?" says McAllister.

I wonder if Max will take this opportunity to fight back, and I ready myself for any part I may be able to play in assisting him, but he falls down resignedly into the chair, having seemingly given up without even trying.

"The police are on their way," says Max as authoritatively as he can.

Oh, thank God. The tension that had coiled itself around every muscle slowly begins to unravel in me as the knowledge that it will only be a few minutes before we're safe settles into my frayed nerve endings. But the relief is quickly snatched away again.

"To arrest *me* or *you*?" asks McAllister, laughing throatily.

Max's chin juts out—an act of defiance—but the sweat stains under his arms suggest he's not feeling quite as rebellious as his body language implies.

"You know, I honestly thought you would lie low when I got out," says McAllister. "That you might have even shown remorse for what you did to me, but you've gone to a whole new level this time." He shakes his head, as if in faux regret at what he's about to do. "I mean, this lovely young lady is thrown into the lion's den of the McAllister family, under the pretense that she's campaigning for a fairer press . . ." He bears down over Max. "Sent by you, I would presume . . . ?"

Max stays silent, his focus aimed on the door, no doubt wondering what's taking the police so long.

"After which, she mysteriously disappears," McAllister goes on, as he paces up and down like a thoughtful Columbo trying to solve a crime.

It seems a rather pointless exercise when we all know who the suspect is.

"Have I got it right so far?" he barks.

"Th-that's what seems to be going on here," says Max, suddenly seeming small and insignificant.

"And good old Ray McAllister is once again perfectly in the frame for it."

Max shrugs his shoulders. "So it would seem."

McAllister lets out a belly laugh. "And by pure fluke, Max Forsythe is there, on the ground, perfectly positioned to cover the unfolding story."

"If you do something newsworthy and illegal, then I'll report it," says Max. "It's what I've always done."

McAllister shakes his head "But that's not true, is it? *You* create the news, orchestrating and manipulating it, directing and controlling it, without any thought of the consequences to other people's lives—as long as you get what *you* want."

"I'm not directing and controlling *this*," says Max with a wry smile.

"Not anymore," says McAllister. "Not when I'm the one with the gun." He smiles. "But this isn't just about a story, is it?"

"I don't know what you mean," says Max nonchalantly.

"What were you planning on doing with her, Max?" asks McAllister, nodding toward me. "She claims to have some pretty damning evidence against you—tape recordings no less, which prove that you framed me for the attempted kidnap of the prime minister. That would get you in a whole heap of trouble, not only with me, but also with the law." He looks at Max with raised eyebrows. "What lengths would you go to, to keep her quiet, I wonder? How far would you go to silence her?"

Silence *me*?

I look at Max, open-mouthed, unable to comprehend what McAllister's saying. Is he suggesting this is some kind of double bluff? That Max has set this whole thing up, knowing that McAllister would do exactly what he's done? Max is a lot of things, but he would never use me as bait for a story. And he would never cause me harm to keep his secrets secret. I drown out the incessant voice in my head that's trying to tell me he's been known to do so much worse.

"This . . . this is absurd," I croak. "Your men snatched me from the street as soon as I left your wife's café, otherwise, why would you be here?"

McAllister smiles. "I'm here because I had you followed after your meeting with Christina, and they saw a van pull up beside you, and you being bundled into it, clearly against your will."

"No," I say adamantly, shaking my head. "No, you did this. You brought me here, tied me up, kept me prisoner . . ."

McAllister nods knowingly. "So tell me this," he says, leaning in close. " If *I* did this to you, how do you think *he* knew where to find you?"

46

Stella

When the intercom buzzes, Stella presses the door release without even asking who it is.

"I'm in here," she calls out from the living room, where she's pacing up and down with a large glass of white wine.

"I'm sorry it's taken me so long," says Harry. "I had some things I needed to check out."

"So what's going on?" she asks, going to sit down on the sofa. But, feeling like a coiled spring, she jumps straight back up again.

"We've got CCTV of Jess leaving Christina's Café in Islington and making her way toward the station."

Stella looks at him expectantly.

"We can see her going into the railway arches, but there's no CCTV to pick her up as she comes out the other side."

"What . . . there's no camera there, or there is and she's not on it?" Stella crosses everything in the hope it's the former.

"There's no coverage until the station platform, but we've got no sighting of her there."

"So it happened in the tunnel?" says Stella, stating the obvious.

"We don't know that for sure," replies Harry. "But McAllister isn't stupid. He'll know there's a blind spot in there, and we've got to assume he would have taken advantage of it."

"OK, so we need to run a check on all the vehicles that went in after Jess did. It's likely to be a van, or a car with blacked-out windows. His lot used to run around in blinged-up Range Rovers."

Harry grimaces. "We're on it, but it's going to take time."

"We haven't got *time*," cries Stella.

"I'm doing everything I can," he says.

"Well, it's not enough." She pulls herself up. None of this is his fault. The blame lies firmly at *her* door, for not seeing this before it happened. And at Max's door, for knowing it might.

Just the thought of Max and what he's done—the positions he's put her in over the years, all to appease his depraved boss and keep the wolves from his door—makes her mad and sad in equal measure. How has their once-close relationship come to this? Was he ever the mentor she thought he was, or was she only ever being trained to be the puppet he needed to do his dirty work?

Her phone rings and she jumps, her frayed nerves making her feel like a cat on a hot tin roof.

"It's Flic, Jess's flatmate—you left a message for me to call you."

It's evident, by her saying those few words, that Jess has shared her thoughts on her boss. "*Former boss*," Stella corrects herself, though whether that refers to the fact that she no longer works there or the insurmountable fear that Jess isn't coming home, she's not sure. She banishes the latter possibility from her mind.

"Hi, thanks for calling me back," says Stella. "I'm sorry to bother you, but I came to your flat earlier, looking for Jess, and your neighbor gave me your number."

A contemptuous grunt comes down the line. "What do you want?" asks Flic.

"I wondered if you'd heard from Jess," says Stella, choosing her words carefully, trying not to scare her. Though how she can avoid that, she's not sure. "Have you seen her? Is she home?"

There's a moment of silence, and Stella imagines Flic walking around, checking the rooms, *willing* her to find Jess tucked up, safe and sound, under her duvet.

"No, she's not here," says Flic eventually. "Why? What's wrong?"

It's the question Stella doesn't want to answer, and yet she has to. "We had an incident at work today," she says. "Jess got caught up in something, and I wanted to make sure she'd got home OK."

"Well, she's not here, so *no*, she hasn't got home OK." Flic's voice is terse, but it's more high-pitched than before, a sign of rising panic.

"OK, could you let me know if you hear anything from her?"

"Is she in danger?" asks Flic.

"I'm sure she's fine," says Stella as an uncomfortable heat spreads across her chest. "If you could just call me when she gets in . . ."

"Wait," says Flic. "I've got her on Find My Phone."

Stella's heart skips and a breath catches in her throat as she waits, but she can tell, by Flic's heavy sigh, that the moment of hope has already expired.

"It seems Jess's phone went off-grid around three thirty this afternoon," says Flic. "The last known location was East Street in Islington."

Stella swallows the bitter taste in her mouth. "Maybe the battery ran out around that time," she says, although there's nothing in her tone that sounds convincing.

"Or maybe it was turned off intentionally," says Flic.

"Or she's in a bar, drinking them dry, none the wiser," says Stella, laughing awkwardly.

"I swear to God, if anything happens to her . . ." Stella goes to end the call, but not before she hears Flic say, "I'll hold you personally responsible."

"So what do we do from here?" Stella asks Harry, desperate to lighten the load that's weighing on her shoulders.

"The best thing *you* can do is stay calm," says Harry. He means it kindly, but Stella doesn't hear it.

"*Calm?*" she shrieks. "McAllister's already killed Trevor Menzies, he's threatened to kill *me* and he's currently holding a *Globe* journalist hostage. How do you expect me to stay calm?"

Harry comes to her and wraps her convulsing body in his arms. "We're doing everything we can," he soothes. "We're running vehicle checks, the monitoring service is tracking McAllister's tag . . ." He lifts her tear-stained face up toward his. "We'll get a break."

His phone vibrates in his pocket and Stella watches his face change as he answers it.

"OK, keep the line open," he says to whoever's on the other end. Harry has already turned around and is heading back to the front door. "I'll be in the car in two minutes. Do *not* lose him."

"Where . . . where are you going?" asks Stella.

"We've got a trace on McAllister," he says. "He's in Finsbury Park."

"Jess?" she says, almost too afraid to say her name.

"It could be," says Harry. "I'll call you as soon as I know anything."

"You're not going without me," says Stella, grabbing her jacket from the back of the sofa.

"Stella, it's too—" starts Harry, before seeming to think better of it.

"I'm coming," she says, leaving no room for discussion.

The roads are, thankfully, deserted as Harry's Range Rover speeds along the Embankment, its tires splattering the rain on the glistening tarmac.

The Houses of Parliament are mirrored perfectly in the River Thames, but the warm yellow glow that Stella normally finds so beautiful is now sullied by the secrets held within its famous walls. Corruption has been imbued in the fabric of the building for centuries, no matter which party is holding court, but the clandestine collaboration with the media makes them all untouchable. Had the prime minister known that the kidnap plot against him was fake? Had he and Max conspired together to gain publicity and votes for the upcoming election? Had the man who stands in the House of Commons every week, proclaiming to want a fairer Britain, been instrumental in sending an innocent man to prison for four years?

One by one, the men she'd revered and respected were showing their true colors, or maybe they'd always been a dirty shade of gray and it had taken someone like Jess to show them for who they really were.

"She's going to be all right," says Harry, as if reading Stella's mind.

"But what if she's not? What if McAllister's going to make an example of her to show us all how reckless we've been?"

Stella had always considered herself fearless, brave even, but now she realizes that all she's ever done is what powerful men have wanted her to do. She's allowed herself to be molded into a monster, an unfeeling, malevolent bully, who's lost all sense of what's right and wrong.

She opens Twitter on her phone and immediately the screen is alight with opinions on who Sasha Peterson's unnamed assailant is. She allows herself a small smile when she sees that *#itsPeterKingsley* and *#PeterKingsleyisguilty* are both trending. Mission one accomplished.

"We're two minutes away," says Harry, sounding a ticking time bomb in Stella's head.

There's a split-second hesitation as her thumbs tremble over her phone screen, a moment's uncertainty that she's doing the right thing. But then she remembers Sasha Peterson's haunted expression.

Stella watches the video play silently on her phone one more time and she shivers, knowing how close she came to being another of Peter's sadistic statistics. Ignoring the sting of fresh tears, she quickly tweets, *What happens when you swap the glass he gives you . . . ? #PeterKingsleyisguilty.*

Tagging @TheGlobe @ThePost @TheOracle @TheDailyNews @NewsOnSunday @SundayChronicle and @BBC, she attaches the video and sends the tweet into the ether.

This is for you, she says silently to Sasha, Tilly and all his other victims.

47

Jess

"H-how *did* you know where I was?" I ask.

Max looks anywhere but at me.

"Go ahead," says McAllister, giving him an encouraging nudge of the shoulder with his gun. "Tell her."

Max looks like he's swallowing pins. "He called me," he says. "And told me he was holding you hostage."

McAllister laughs, as only he can, because he's the one with the gun. "Did I *really*?" he asks, clearly amused. "And I suppose I told you where to find us as well?"

"The clues you gave me made it easy to track you down," offers Max, his voice small.

McAllister pulls a cynical face, as if wondering why he would take the chance.

"I'm not scared of you," says Max, daring to stare McAllister out. "I knew you were coming for me—you implied as much at my party the other night, and I assumed this was merely a ploy to get me here."

"Phone calls, parties . . . You really are letting your imagination go to work on this one, aren't you?"

Max looks away, his momentary bravado fading, and I want to go to him, will him to fight back, because if I can't rely on *Max* getting us out of this, then who *can* I rely on?

"OK, let's try this *one* more time," says McAllister. "Why don't you tell us how you knew where your young colleague here was."

Max's jaw clenches, but he stays silent.

"Let's bring your friend up here, then," says McAllister, backing up to the door. "See if he can jog your memory—that's if he can manage the stairs, of course."

I turn to Max as McAllister disappears, desperate for reassurance, but he's already making his way to the window again. I get to my feet in an effort to help him.

"Where are the police?" I cry as my nails rip trying to get purchase on the nailed-down boarding. "What's taking them so long?"

"They're not coming," he says.

My heart stops and my chest feels as if it might cave in. "Wh-what do you mean, they're not coming? *Why* not?"

"Because I haven't called them," says Max brusquely.

"But you said . . ."

"I said whatever I thought would get us out of this, but McAllister doesn't care about the police. He's looking at the big picture. He wants to finish this here and now. That's why we have to get out of here."

I bite down on my lip in an effort to still the tremor that's enveloping my entire body.

"What's going on here, Max? What did McAllister mean when . . ."

"He's trying to make us turn on each other," puffs Max, putting all his effort into prising the board away. His exertions only serve to ping one nail from its place. I want to cry at the futility of it all.

"We have to stick together," he goes on. "The only way we're going to get out of this alive is if we tell him where the tapes are."

My brow furrows as he goes against his own advice.

"It's our best shot," he says as if sensing my reticence. "Our *only* shot. Tell me where they are and I'll get us out of here."

"They *were* in the office," I say.

"*Were?*" he repeats, his eyes narrowing.

I nod. "Taped to the underside of my desk. But I don't imagine they're there anymore."

A twitch pulses in his jaw and his nostrils flare. "Where might they be now?" he asks, his tone measured, his body language anything but.

"I don't know," I falter, unsure of how much I should say, because there's a tiny part of me that still doesn't trust him. I force the doubt away. "I told Stella where they were."

"*Stella?*" he hisses. "But you know you can't trust her. You know what she's capable of."

I shake my head. "But she's not the one on the tapes," I say, daring him to look at me. "You are."

He lets out a heavy sigh. "But she was as much a part of it as I was. I may have been the one to issue instructions to Trevor Menzies, but Stella knew what we were doing, what was expected of us. We were the Pied Piper's rats. Peter played the tune and we went running."

"Here we go!" bellows McAllister as he throws a bloodied figure into the center of the room. With his hands tied behind his back, he falls facedown onto the floor.

I cower back into the corner as if afraid that whatever has happened to him is contagious.

"So let's try again," says McAllister, kicking the person and telling him to turn over. He groans as he rolls onto his back.

The man's bleeding profusely from the side of his face; his earlobe looks to be missing, but he's definitely the younger of the two men who were holding me against my will.

"Is this the man who brought you here?" McAllister asks, looking to me.

I nod, not knowing whether my answer will help or hinder me.

The young man looks both terrified and resigned to his fate as McAllister hovers menacingly above him. I can't help but wonder why he would do this to one of his own.

"And whose instructions were you acting on?" asks McAllister, kicking him again.

"*His*," says the man, spitting blood as he glares at Max.

Max closes his eyes, and the breath I'd been holding in—hoping against hope that my niggling skepticism was nothing more than misplaced suspicion—rushes out of my body.

Suddenly, Max charges forward, lunging toward McAllister as if he stands a chance, though even I can see he's launching a helpless cause.

McAllister's arm moves through the air at the speed of light, and I blanch at the sound it makes as the handle of his gun slams into Max's jaw. Teeth are knocked out of his gums, sending blood splatters across his shirt. His eyes roll back as he falls, his head lolling to one side as he lands heavily on the floor. Dazed and confused, he looks around.

"Please tell me this wasn't you," I cry, crawling on my hands and knees toward him.

"He needed to keep you quiet," says McAllister. "And in getting rid of you, he was able to frame *me*. Two for the price of one."

"But he didn't even know I had the tapes," I reason, more to convince myself than anyone else. "Not until *you* told him on the phone."

McAllister smirks and shakes his head as if unable to understand why I'm still willing Max to be innocent of any wrongdoing. "There *was* no call," he says impatiently. "He must have already known you had the tapes and the damage they could do."

"But he couldn't have . . ." I cry, looking between them, no longer sure who's on my side. "*Unless* . . ."

The realization strikes me like a lightning bolt, winding me with its force, leaving my chest feeling hollow and constricted.

"Did Trevor Menzies tell you?" I rasp at Max, my voice not sounding like my own. I bang myself on the head, unable to believe I hadn't worked it out before now. "You knew I'd gone to see him and he told you he'd given them to me, didn't he?"

Is that a smirk that's pulling at the corners of Max's mouth?

"*Didn't he?*" I yell, holding myself back from thrashing out.

"Satisfied?" McAllister asks, turning to me smugly.

I swallow my indignation. "I'm still not going to tell you where the tapes are," I say, though who to, I'm not sure.

McAllister gives a knowing smile. "Who's to say I don't already have them?"

"I do," comes a voice from the doorway.

48

Stella

Max spins round on hearing Stella's voice, his mouth going slack with shock.

"What are *you* doing here?" she asks him, struggling to comprehend the turn of events. She'd gone some way to preparing herself for coming face-to-face with McAllister, but *Max*? That's a curveball she wasn't expecting.

"Well, if it isn't Miss Stella Thorne," smiles McAllister, seemingly enjoying himself. "It must be my lucky day."

An overwhelming panic takes hold of Stella's chest, her brain going into free fall at the thought that she's walked straight into a trap. Harry must feel it too, as he bristles beside her, his gun aimed directly at McAllister's head.

She looks at Max, his face ashen, and silently asks how they'd allowed this to happen. McAllister had used Jess as bait to ambush them, and they'd both fallen for it.

"Wh-what's going on?" asks Stella, her voice laced with fear. She looks between the two men, waiting for someone to say something, but not wanting to hear it.

"If you want the tapes, she's your woman," says Max, nodding toward her. "She's as complicit as I am."

"No," says Stella, shaking her head vehemently. "I'm not the same as you."

"Sure you are," says Max with a grin that unnerves her. "You knew exactly what you were doing."

McAllister looks at Stella with raised eyebrows as if waiting for her to state her case.

"I was reporting on what I thought was a very real threat to the prime minister's life, but *you*—you had engineered the whole thing. You employed the services of Trevor Menzies to find a mole to infiltrate McAllister's world. He was never going to kidnap anyone, he didn't even have a gun on him that night, but you set it up to make it look like he did."

McAllister rams the muzzle of his gun into the side of Max's head.

Harry's arms flex. "Put the gun down," he says, slowly and deliberately.

Stella can see the muscles in McAllister's arm contract as his head battles with his body to do the right thing. She's not sure her brain would win, if she were the one holding the gun.

"I trusted you," she says to Max, holding the tapes up. "But all this time you've been plotting behind my back, putting me and so many others in danger; and all to avenge anyone who dared to cross Peter Kingsley. You may think *you're* the puppet master, but he's still pulling your strings."

"He's been pulling yours as well, I understand," says Max with a smirk.

Stella feels like she might be sick at the thought of Peter giving him a fictional account of what had happened the other night. She imagines the lies Peter could have told, the scene he might have set. But she swallows the bitter indignation when she remembers what she's posted on social media. No one will be left in any doubt about what really happened.

"You can have the tapes, but you need to let Jess go," she says, looking directly at McAllister.

"It's not him who brought me here," says Jess, looking at her wide-eyed, like a rabbit caught in the headlights.

The blood coursing around Stella's body suddenly feels like hot pokers prickling at her very conscience. The hairs on the back of her neck stand to attention at Jess's words as what they mean hit home. Sure that she's misunderstood, Stella looks at Max, but he refuses to meet her gaze.

"Are you suggesting . . ." starts Stella, before trailing off, unable to finish the sentence.

McAllister coughs. "Do you honestly expect me to believe that you don't know the depths this sorry example of a human being will go to save his own skin?"

Stella is more than aware of what Max Forsythe is capable of, but he would *never* stoop this low. *Would he?*

"He was setting me up again," says McAllister. "And if I hadn't trusted my instincts, this girl would likely never be seen again, and I'd no doubt be sent straight back to prison."

"Max?" questions Stella, desperately looking for affirmation that what McAllister's suggesting is wide of the mark.

Max shows no emotion; he doesn't even try to deny it as he wipes his mouth with the cuff of his once-white shirt.

Anger and revulsion course through Stella's entire body, upending everything she thought she knew. She's sure that what McAllister is saying can't possibly be true, but yet at the same time it all makes perfect sense. Still, she searches for a fragment that might throw doubt on his version of events.

"But you called the office to say you had her," she says to McAllister. He shakes his head.

"I was there," she says, oddly relieved that she's remembered something that proves Max couldn't be behind this. He may be a lot of things, but he wouldn't snatch Jess off the street, even if he did think she posed a threat.

McAllister laughs throatily. "I'm not sure that amounts to much, coming from another corrupt journalist."

Stella wishes she could argue the point, but somewhere between desperately wanting to be the best junior reporter, the best journalist and the best deputy editor, she has lost all sense of how to bring in a good story without using the questionable methods she once found so abhorrent.

When had that happened? When had she descended the slippery slope to the Dark Arts? And how many other good journalists had she dragged with her along the way?

She looks at Jess, so innocent and eager to learn, and yet from the moment she arrived, all Stella had done was encourage her to cross the line. She swallows the bitter taste of regret.

"But why would he take her?" she asks, still searching for a justifiable reason to exonerate the person she'd once trusted with her life. She turns to Jess. "Did Max know you had the tapes?"

Jess nods. "I told him I'd gone to see Trevor Menzies."

"Fuck," rasps Stella as the chance of Max not having anything to do with this diminishes by the second. "Is that why he's dead?"

Jess looks at Stella, open-mouthed. "Trevor Menzies is *dead*?"

"Jesus, Max," chokes Stella, leaning against the wall to steady herself. "What have you done?"

"Were you going to hang that on McAllister, too?" Harry asks Max.

A satanic smile crosses his face. "Well, he had the motive . . ." he says, throwing a gloating sideways glance at McAllister. "It was clear he was coming for *all* of us."

There's a flash of light and Stella instinctively cowers, assuming it's the glint of a bullet. But it's the glare of McAllister's huge signet ring as his hand travels through the air at speed, grasping the barrel of his gun. She flinches as the handle is about to make contact with the side of Max's head, but instead of the sickening sound of unforgiving steel meeting bone, there's a roar and the gun stops in midair as if halted in slow motion by an invisible force.

Limbs entangle, blood and spittle project across the room as Max grapples with McAllister, the pair of them refusing to relinquish control.

Stella knows it's impossible for Harry to get a clean shot of the target. She doesn't even know who the target is anymore.

"Get back!" barks Max, grabbing the gun and waving it around indiscriminately. "Or I swear to God, I'll kill the lot of you."

Stella can't even *feel* her legs, let alone move them. "Max . . ." she gasps, though she has no idea what she's going to say.

"Move!" he says, pulling Jess roughly to her feet and holding on to her arm. She looks at Stella with abject terror as the barrel is pressed into the side of her head.

"Max, for God's sake," starts Stella. "Think about what you're doing."

"Give me the tapes," he shouts.

Stella looks at Harry, who gives an almost imperceptible nod of his head.

"Will you let her go, if I do?" she asks.

"Give me the fucking tapes!" Max's eyes are popping, and sweat is beading on his forehead.

Stella's hand trembles as she holds the miniature plastic cases out to him, searching the face of the man she's known for fifteen years, waiting for him to laugh and tell her this is all a sick joke. But there's a blankness in Max's eyes, unseeing and unfeeling.

Snatching the tapes from her grasp, he swings Jess round to cover him as he moves backward toward the door.

"You've got what you want," says Harry with his gun still trained on Max's head. "So leave Jess here and we'll let you go."

Max makes a grunting sound as he navigates his way down the stairs, punctuated by Jess's whimpers as she is forced to go with him.

"What are we going to do?" asks Stella, looking wide-eyed at Harry as soon as they're out of sight. She desperately needs him to say everything's going to be all right, but all he offers is a look that seems as troubled as her mind.

"Stay here," he commands as he bolts down the stairs after Max.

Stella looks behind her to see McAllister standing there, baring his teeth. "What the hell did you give him the tapes for?" he bellows as she vaults down the stairs after Harry. "Now we'll never be able to prove what he's done."

"I can't imagine that's going to stop you doing what needs to be done," she says breathlessly.

Neither of them needs to spell out what she means. However this turns out, Max is a dead man walking.

By the time Stella's down the stairs and out in the yard, Max is half dragging Jess toward his car, with his gun firmly pressed into her head and his eyes fixed firmly on them all.

"Max, let her go," says Harry one more time. "If you take Jess with you, this isn't going to end well."

Max doesn't say a word as he manhandles her into the driver's seat of his Jaguar and gets in the back behind her.

"Shoot him," cries Stella as the car jerks and starts to move forward.

"It's too dark," says Harry. "I can't take the chance."

As the Jaguar moves off into the night, Stella can't help but wonder if it'll be the only chance they get.

49

Jess

"Max, please," I sob, feeling the indentation of the gun in the back of my neck. "It doesn't have to be this way. You can stop this before it goes any further."

"Just drive," he spits, digging the weapon in even harder.

I know my way around East London pretty well, but panic has rendered my sense of direction worthless. Through my tears, I see a sign for Hackney and my chest convulses as I imagine Flic lying on the sofa in her pajamas, working her way through a box set. I look at the clock on the walnut-veneer dash; it's minutes before midnight, but the hours I've been working lately, she probably hasn't even realized I'm missing yet.

"Turn right," barks Max, forcing me to veer away from the arrow pointing toward home.

"Why are you doing this?" I cry. "I thought you were on my side. I thought we were working together—to make *The Globe* something you could be proud of."

He laughs sardonically. "Did you honestly believe I needed *you* for that?"

My head spins, not knowing why he needed me at all.

"You were meant to keep an eye on Stella," he says. "You were supposed to report back on what *she* was doing, who *she* was talking to, so that I could stay one step ahead of her. All you had to do was be there when she messed up so that I could prove to Peter that she wasn't fit to be editor, because that's what she was gunning for, and I've worked too damn hard to have Stella come and sweep it out from underneath me."

"I did exactly what you asked," I say.

"But you kept digging," he groans. "Like a dog with a bone, you wouldn't leave it alone." His head falls against my headrest. "Why couldn't you leave it alone?"

"And let women like Yasmin Chopra and Tilly Ashcroft be treated so cruelly, while you were arrogantly boasting that you were turning *The Globe* into a fairer newspaper?"

"You should have walked away," he says as if it's my fault for having a conscience.

"I saw Yasmin's lifeless body hanging from the ceiling," I cry. "From the noose *we* put around her neck. How could I have walked away from *that*?"

"She was weak," says Max. "Every coup sustains collateral damage—it's impossible to avoid, and that one was worth the risk because it was the perfect opportunity to take Stella down once and for all."

Hot bile forces its way up my throat as I look at him in the rear-view mirror. "You bastard," I seethe as the steering wheel turns away from me. I over-steer to get it back under control and clip the curb of the deathly quiet road. "You faked the photos and planted them on Stella's computer for me to find."

I'd played the events of that night over in my mind again and again, each time wondering what I could have done differently, blaming myself, blaming Stella . . . but the real culprit is right here, unremorseful and unashamed.

"The irony is, I didn't need to do it," says Max, as I dare to believe that somewhere deep down there's a conscience fighting to get through. "Because Stella shot herself in the foot in the end by running the Sasha Peterson piece. Peter might have thought she could be groomed to do what I do for him, but nobody can—he can see that now."

"So Tilly Ashcroft, Ray McAllister, Trevor Menzies were all about settling scores on his behalf." My voice doesn't sound like my own, bitterness seeping from every syllable.

"Trevor was regretful," he says. "He'd always been good to me, but his first priority was drugs. He was never going to be able to resist making a quick buck."

"But this is all going to come back on you," I say, laughing hysterically. "You're not going to get away with what you've done—the lives you and Peter have destroyed. People are going to know. McAllister and Stella will make sure of it."

He scoffs. "If they want to get to me, they're going to have to get past Peter first. He won't let anything happen to me; he owes me too much. I've kept them *all* off his back, one way or another. He could never repay me for what I've done for him."

"He's not going to be able to keep the wolves from his door forever," I say. "And don't think he won't take you down with him, when he goes."

"He's Peter-fucking-Kingsley," Max snorts condescendingly. "Who's going to take *him* on? He's untouchable."

I pray that Max has underestimated the wrath that's coming over the hill toward both him and Peter-*fucking*-Kingsley. Because God knows, I'm not the only one who's desperate to see them both rot in hell.

"Turn left," he barks, prodding the back of my neck with the gun again in case I'd forgotten its presence.

"Into the tunnel?" I ask, wondering why we're heading to the south side of the river. But then I remember that he has a weekend place down on the coast, and I can't stop myself imagining that's where he's going to kill me and dispose of my body. He'll know the lie of the land, and he'll be confident of putting me somewhere that no one will ever find me.

A dagger-like pain catches in my throat, sharpening its delicate tissues as I think of Mum and Dad making it their life's work to find out what happened to me; of going to their graves without knowing what had become of their daughter. Maybe it will be better that way. I'd rather they were left with the memory of how I was when I was alive than the prospect of being presented with my remains.

The Blackwall Tunnel looms ahead, and the last thing I see as the curved walls cocoon themselves around me is the Global International Tower, its thirty floors aglow with square windows of lights against the night sky. Is Peter Kingsley in there right now? In his penthouse apartment on the top floor, or creeping around the offices in the middle of the night as I've heard he likes to do, his ego seemingly never satiated by the scale of his empire. Or maybe it's insomnia that keeps him awake; the never-ending fear of wondering when he's going to get found out. I hope so.

As the overhead strip lighting flickers, shuttering in my eyes like the strobe of a camera flash, I am overcome with the need to take back control. Why should I let Max kill me? Drive myself somewhere I'll never be found? If he's going to put a bullet in my head, let it be here and now, where the emergency services will be on the scene within minutes—hopefully to save me and arrest him.

There are a single car's headlights a little way behind us, and I know there's just enough space between us not to impact on its passengers. At least not physically; the scene they're about to come across will no doubt leave mental scars forever, but no matter what happens to me, I'm a stranger to them. Isn't it kinder to do it this way than to leave my parents with the grief of the unknown?

I check the rearview mirror one more time. The car is advancing. There are only seconds between us. It's getting harder to breathe and, as I push the pedal to the floor, I almost hope that a bullet takes me out first.

"What are you doing?" bellows Max as the car speeds up, and everything about me must tell him that I'm relinquishing control. I take my hands off the steering wheel and hold them in the air, surrendering to whatever outcome awaits.

It's the tiniest clip of the tire, but the car is lifted up and flies through the air. As we roll, I'm reminded of when I was taken out by a massive wave at Southend beach when I was eleven. It knocked my legs out from underneath me, and I turned and turned in the swirling water, not knowing which way was up.

I'm sure I've stopped breathing as the walls come toward me, getting closer and then moving further away again. There doesn't seem to be any sound as we flip over and over, seemingly in slow motion. The world is on mute, but I can see glass shattering all around me, can feel the force of gravity pulling me this way and that. There's a jolt to my neck and I imagine the steel pellet from Max's gun penetrating my jugular vein as singular droplets of blood hover around me, suspended in midair.

I'm waiting to be dead, but it seems a long time coming. Then suddenly there's a flash of light and everything goes dark.

50

Stella

Stella screams as she is thrown forward by Harry hitting the brake, hard and fast. He thrusts a hand across her in the vain hope that it will do a better job than the seat belt she's thankfully wearing.

The stricken car in front of them has landed on its roof, with plumes of black smoke seeping out from the bonnet and sparks flying out from the underside.

"Jess!" Stella yells, jumping out of Harry's Range Rover and running toward the mangled ball of metal.

"Stella, no!" calls out Harry.

But Stella can see Jess's unmoving head, her brown hair hanging upside down, and despite her brain telling her to go no further, her feet are listening to something else: the small voice that's emerging for the first time in years. The one that knows the difference between right and wrong.

"Jess!" she yells again as she falls to her knees and looks in through the shattered driver's window. "Jess, can you hear me?"

"Stella, we've got to get out of here," shouts Harry, dragging her back as the smell of petrol rises up from the tarmac.

"No!" she screams. "I have to get her out."

Harry barks their location into his mobile phone, while simultaneously trying to pull her away from the car. "It could blow any minute," he says. "It's too dangerous."

"I'm not leaving her," shouts Stella, clawing her way back and reaching in to release Jess's seat belt, which is holding her in midair.

"Help!" comes a throaty rasp from somewhere in the back. "Help . . . help me."

Stella can see the bloodied face of Max, encased in twisted metal, his eyes closed and his mouth gaping open, barely able to form words.

"Help," he moans again.

She yanks on the twisted seat belt, knowing she's not got much time. "Fuck!" she hollers in frustration. "It won't . . . I can't . . ."

Harry's arms entwine themselves with hers, reaching in to grab at whatever he can in his efforts to free Jess. Suddenly, the buckle unclips and he throws himself in, using his own body to cushion her fall. The sudden movement causes Jess to make a grunting sound—it's not much, but Stella accepts it with every ounce of optimism she can muster. "I've got you," she says as she and Harry work together to gently pull Jess through the shattered window. "Everything's going to be all right."

There's a clicking sound, like the ignition of a gas burner, as the errant sparks finally make contact with something flammable. The heat is immediate as a whoosh of flames lick the framework of the car.

"Stella, *move*," yells Harry as he maneuvers himself under Jess's limp body and staggers to his feet.

"Please, Ella . . ." calls out Max, stopping her in her tracks. His eyes are now open, looking at her imploringly, aware of what's going on.

The heat is unbearable, intensifying with every passing second, as the ticking time bomb gets louder and louder.

"Run!" shouts Harry, his tone ever more urgent.

"I'm sorry," she says, looking at Max. And she is. Not because she's going to leave him there, but because of what his family is going to be put through. The grief, the pain, but mostly the disbelief that he wasn't the man they thought they knew.

There's a crackle as the glass buckles and bows in the raging inferno, and Stella watches, catatonic, as the flames creep onto the fuel slick that the stricken car had left on the road. She *has* to move, but her legs feel paralyzed, cemented to the melting tarmac.

She can see Harry's distorted outline in the heat haze and wills him to reach through and carry her away, but he already has Jess in his arms.

"Stella!" he calls out.

The warning penetrates her brain at last, but just as she puts one foot in front of the other, there's an ear-splitting explosion. A flash of light, an intense heat and a force she can't withstand.

The last thing she sees as she's lifted off her feet is Harry's contorted face, screaming.

EPILOGUE

Stella stands her ground, refusing to buckle under Yasmin's husband's unrelenting glare. He's right, of course—she shouldn't be here, but she's not going to hide away in shame.

"I can promise you I won't let Yasmin's death be in vain," she says as he goes to move away.

He turns to look at her, his lip curled in disdain. "So you want to play the hero now, do you?" he says bitterly.

"Not to appease my own guilty conscience," she replies. "But to get justice for what happened to your wife."

He scoffs. "And how do you propose to do that?"

"I'm going to make sure *The Globe* can *never* do anything like this ever again."

He shakes his head, almost in pity, as the woman holding on to his arm moves him forward.

"Hi, Stella," says Jess, her face tearstained as she turns from the pew in front of her.

"I wondered if you'd be here," responds Stella, looking her up and down with concern. "I didn't know if you'd be out of hospital in time."

"I discharged myself yesterday," says Jess. "I wasn't going to let a few broken bones stop me paying my respects." She puts on a brave face as she lifts her plastered arm aloft.

"I'm glad you're on the mend," says Stella.

"*I'm* glad you got me out," answers Jess with tears in her eyes.

"It was a joint effort," says Stella, immediately wishing she hadn't, because she knows what's coming next.

"How is he?" asks Jess, looking at her with the same sympathy the nurses do, every time she walks into the hospital.

Stella swallows away the tug at the back of her throat, knowing that if she lets it take hold, she'll cry.

"I went to see him, before I left," Jess goes on. "But they wouldn't let me into ICU."

Stella pictures the man who saved them both, lying immobile in his hospital bed, attached to wires and surrounded by machines that breathe for him. The doctors had told her this morning that they were going to start bringing Harry out of his induced coma later today.

"He's going to be fine," Stella says to Jess, her voice brimming with forced optimism.

Jess takes hold of her hand, and the show of support sends a tear rolling down Stella's cheek. Peter Kingsley had gone out of his way to make Stella public enemy number one in the past two weeks, naming and blaming her for Max's death, McAllister's wrongful conviction, Tilly's fall from grace and Yasmin's decision to end her life. To have anyone go out on a limb to stand side by side with her—especially here—means more than Jess could ever know.

"I heard Kingsley was arrested last night," Jess says.

Stella nods. "Women are coming forward all the time. The case against him is growing by the day, and I'll do everything in my power to make sure he gets what he deserves."

Jess looks around, as if checking they're not being overheard. "Is that what you meant when you said you were going to make sure *The Globe* would never be able to do anything like this again?"

Stella nods. "I'm going to put a bomb under everything Peter Kingsley holds dear."

"Do you need any help with that?"

"I'll take all the help I can get," says Stella with a smile. Just then, her phone rings and, embarrassed that it's on loud, she rushes to answer it.

"Stella, it's Michael Leith at *The Post*. I wondered if you'd had a chance to consider the offer of the editor's position."

Adrenaline floods Stella's veins, setting every nerve ending alight. She'd tried to convince herself that she was done with the newsroom; that she no longer had the energy or the appetite to put the world to rights. But deep down, she knows that the burning flame is never going to be extinguished. At least not until she's done what needs to be done.

"A lot has to change," she says.

"Agreed," says Michael. "And you're the best person to do that."

"I want to start with a lawsuit against *The Globe* for wrongful death on behalf of Yasmin Chopra's family."

"I'll give you all the resources you need to make that happen."

"I don't want to just make it *happen*," says Stella indignantly. "I want to *win*. I want to destroy Peter Kingsley and everything he represents."

"I won't stand in your way."

Stella looks up at Jess. "And one more thing. I have someone I want to bring over with me."

Jess looks at her curiously, her head tilted to one side.

"Are they any good?" asks Michael.

"The best," says Stella.

"Then I'm sure it can be arranged."

Stella allows herself a smile and looks at Jess. "Well then, I think we have a deal."

ACKNOWLEDGMENTS

This is a book I've wanted to write for a long time and I knew, as soon as I started, that its message was destined to be one of empowerment and resilience. Although the media landscape has changed in recent years, and will no doubt continue to do so, there still remains a culture of bullying and manipulation that greatly affects those in the public eye. Certain outlets still have the ability to make or break careers, destroy relationships, and create a catastrophic maelstrom that, for some, is impossible to escape from. The power of the media should never be underestimated and, although this is a work of fiction, there are parallels that cannot be separated from fact.

Having worked as a journalist, I am all too aware of the damage caused by the unscrupulous few who give the rest of us a bad name. I hope that there will come a time, in the not-too-distant future, when those responsible will be flushed out once and for all, and **#bekind** will mean more than just a hashtag. But until then, we'll have to rely on Jess and Stella to right the wrongs.

Thank you, as ever, to my fabulous agent, Tanera Simons, and everyone at Darley Anderson, who continue to support my dream. And to Catherine Richards at Minotaur and Vicki Mellor at Pan Macmillan for allowing me the freedom to write what's in my head, wherever that may take us! Thanks also to all those behind the scenes who have the unenviable task of making each book stand out more than any other. It takes an army to get a book edited, printed, designed, promoted, and on the shelves so that you lovely lot might want to buy it. And when there are, quite literally, millions of brilliant books to choose from, it is always such an honor and a privilege that you choose mine. Thank you.

And to my gorgeous family and friends who put up with me when I'm in "the hole," it's getting easier . . . *isn't it* . . . ?!?

Love to all,

Sandie x

ABOUT THE AUTHOR

Harriet Buckingham

Sandie Jones has worked as a freelance journalist for more than twenty years and has written for publications including *The Sunday Times, Woman's Weekly,* and *Hello!* magazine. She lives in London with her husband and three children. *The Other Woman* was her debut novel and a Reese's Book Club x Hello Sunshine pick.

Read more from the
New York Times bestselling author
SANDIE JONES!

I WOULD
DIE FOR
YOU

Coming 2025!

MINOTAUR BOOKS